Laked

by

J L Wilson

Laked

Cover Art by *RJ Morris*

The Wild Rose Press, Inc.
PO Box 708
Adams Basin, NY 14410-0708
Visit us at www.thewildrosepress.com

Publishing History
First Crimson Rose Edition, 2017
Print ISBN 978-1-5092-1374-0
Digital ISBN 978-1-5092-1375-7

Published in the United States of America

I turned and caught a glimpse

of Luther Leroy's face. He was so stunned his mouth gaped open. Then he saw me looking at him and he quickly smoothed out his expression, the sharp look in his eyes changing to one of mild curiosity.

"I've handled weapons before," I said, figuring he was anxious about me holding the sharp blade.

"That's obvious. It's just that I haven't seen anyone but Arthur wield the sword for a long time." He eyed me nervously, his dark eyes flickering from my wrists to the tip of the blade.

"I'm not really using it. I mean, it's not like I'm chopping up any enemies or anything." I glanced sideways at Dewin when I said it. He backed off a step in mock terror. Or at least, I think it was mock.

"It's been in our family for generations. I was heartsick when Faye gave it away." Luther stepped forward to stand next to the box, looking down at the scabbard. "It's a precious piece of our history."

"Maybe Faye had no idea how you valued it," Dewin said.

"Bullshit." I raised the sword but it was hard. My wrists were barely up to the task. "Of course she knew. She probably did it out of spite."

"You didn't know my stepdaughter, did you?" Luther asked with a small smile.

"Not really. But she talked about it last night. She knew how Able cared about the sword." I lowered it carefully. "From what I've heard, anybody who uses it is cursed."

Dedication

To my mother,
who introduced me to reading at a very young age
and from whom I learned
to allow my imagination to take flight

Chapter 1

The bell over the doorway of my shop rang, announcing a customer. "I'm in the back," I called out. "Behind the bear. If you need help, just let me know."

Silence greeted my words. My shop, *Curiosity's, Too*, is a twenty by forty space packed to the ten-foot tin ceiling with, well, curiosities. I often only glimpsed customers while they wove their way through the place and I sometimes didn't see them except on the closed-circuit TV if I was back in the office, as I was now.

I glanced at the screen and saw a man at the threshold, looking around. According to the height indicator tape in the doorway, he was about six feet tall and appeared to be around my age, in his fifties or thereabouts, with short dark hair edged with gray, a square sort of face and very dark eyes. His nose was slightly off-center and he frowned while his eyes darted from side to side. He appeared very preppy in his gray suit coat over a burgundy crew-neck sweater and his faded denims. I couldn't see his shoes, but if he wore loafers, the professorial outfit was complete.

"In the back," I called again. "I'm having some computer issues I'm trying to fix. If you need anything, just holler."

The man lifted a hand in acknowledgment. "I came about the picture." He peered around the display of superhero lunch boxes and the bookcase full of comic books. "The one you posted on Facebook."

I glared down at the Android tablet which refused to establish a connection to my store's WiFi network. "Damn piece of shit," I muttered, tossing it onto the desktop and closing the front of my ancient secretary desk. I emerged from my miniscule office behind the glass display case full of thumb puppets and edged around Theo, the six-foot Smokey Bear I bought the last time I was in Yosemite.

"Interesting store," a voice said behind me.

I whirled, tripping on Theo's outstretched leg. I was saved from crashing into a display case of baseballs by a man's arm grabbing me around the waist. He pulled me upright and I found myself nose to chin with the man from the front entrance, caught in his arms like some kind of tango dancer.

"You're quiet." I took a step back, treading on Theo again. This time I managed to stay on my feet without intervention.

"Do you need help with your computer? I'm good with that kind of stuff." His gaze went past me to the open office door.

I smiled. "I'm good with computers, too. It's just a crappy tablet. I should never have bought a dot-zero."

He nodded sympathetically. "Always wait for the dot-two, at least."

I was surprised. Most non-tech folks had no idea that 'dot-zero' meant the first release of a product. It was a common joke in Software Land that a dot-zero release was where customers found the bugs for you.

"Are you the owner? A.V. DuLac?" he asked.

"I am she. How can I help you?"

"Where do you find these things?" His gaze moved

over the baseballs, the rack of postcards from the 1930s, the collection of sock monkeys in their holiday finery propped in two wicker picnic baskets, Boy Scout manuals of various vintages and a seven-foot tall replica of Gort the robot from the movie *The Day The Earth Stood Still*. The original movie, not that travesty of a remake.

"I like to travel and I collect stuff. You said you saw a picture?" I dared a glance at his shoes. Yep. Loafers. He was probably an escapee from St. George, our local college, located four blocks north. My store was in downtown Linn, just south of the campus. I usually attracted the younger set, not the teachers, from the small Iowa college.

"It was a sword in a scabbard. The scabbard was leather and carved with symbols." His gaze continued to travel from display case to bookshelf to the antique baby bed tucked into the corner covered with stuffed animals of assorted vintage. "Is that a dinosaur?"

"Velociraptor," I said. "I'm sorry, but the sword was acquired for my other shop. The original *Curiosity's*, in Northern Minnesota."

He removed his gaze from the three-foot-tall plastic carnivore peeking over the side of the baby bed and returned his attention to me. "I don't understand. You advertised it on your Facebook page."

"We can't advertise on our Facebook page," I corrected. "At least, we can't without paying a hefty fee. Instead we show people what we are acquiring and if they're interested—as you are—they can contact us and we'll discuss a possible purchase."

"That's a nice cover version of the song," he said, head tilted to one side.

I gaped at him. "I beg your pardon?"

"The song." He gestured toward the office. "*Because the Night.* It's a nice cover version."

I belatedly realized he was talking about the XM radio playing overhead. "Oh. That song. I don't think it's a cover version, I think it's the original. That's Natalie Merchant." I nodded toward the speaker on the wall. "Yes. Natalie Merchant."

He shook his head. "Patti Smith did the original one. 1977 or 1978, I think."

Damn my stupid tablet that wouldn't work. I itched to research that factoid on the Internet. I made a mental note to do so later. "Maybe," I conceded.

"Where's the sword?" He turned slowly like he expected to see a three-foot long weapon hiding behind a wheel or under the child's school desk opposite the baby bed.

"As I said, I acquire items for my two stores. I got the sword for my Minnesota store." The Young Frankenstein cuckoo clock chose that moment to announce the hour, with Igor strolling out from the castle and saying "Six o'clock. What hump?" The ceiling lights, which were set on a timer, dimmed slightly.

"Are you closing?" He peered up at the ceiling and frowned. "Is that a—"

"Yes, it's a replica of *The Spirit of St. Louis.* And yes, I'm closing, but there's no rush." I had no plans for my rainy October Saturday evening except a book, a fire in my fireplace at home, leftover chili and a cold glass of beer. Starting tomorrow I was taking a brief vacation, so my assistant manager was in charge of opening the shop at noon. This was my night to kick back and relax.

"So you're saying you don't have the sword?" The man followed me to the front of the store and the checkout desk, where I began my nightly routine of closing out the register.

"The item is en route from the owner to Northern Minnesota."

"Why there? Why not here?" He cautiously extracted one of my business cards from the plastic Godzilla on the counter, who had the cards in his mouth.

"I have a larger pool of potential buyers there for an item like that." I started my inventory program on the checkout computer and tallied today's profits.

"In Northern Minnesota? Who could possibly want to buy an antique sword there?"

"There are many wealthy vacationers with homes on the lake near my store. Several of them collect weaponry." I frowned at my reflection in my computer screen. Speaking of Young Frankenstein... My thick, loose brown curls rivaled Gene Wilder's in his younger days. I kept my shoulder-length hair pulled back from my face with clips, but I was looking particularly unruly today. Probably the damp weather, I decided.

"Does that mean you already have a buyer?"

"No, I don't, Mr.—?" I waited expectantly.

"Leroy." He pronounced it *La-Roy*, not *Lee-roy*. He stuck out his hand.

I gave his hand a brisk shake. "I don't have a buyer but I know of two or three people who will probably be interested. I also have a storage facility there, so if I don't sell it immediately, I can store it." I turned off the XM Classic Vinyl channel in the middle of The Beatles and *Yellow Submarine*.

"How much are you asking for it?"

"I haven't had a chance to thoroughly evaluate it yet." Years of dealing with persistent customers had taught me patience, so I kept my voice casual and dismissive. "If you'd like, I can contact you after I examine it and we can make arrangements for you to see it."

"You mean you haven't even seen it yet?"

Okay. He was starting to try my patience. "That's really not your concern, is it?"

"Of course it is." He regarded me with a steady gaze. "It's unusual to buy an antique like that, sight unseen? That's—"

I decided to nip this in the bud. "I know the rep. I trust her."

"Rep?"

"I have people who know my tastes. They contact me when they find something that will interest me."

"But how do they know it's authentic? Maybe it's a fake," he persisted.

This was getting annoying. "I trust them. If you're concerned about a purchase, then you simply don't have to buy it." I glanced at the clock. Six-fifteen. Granted, I didn't have any big plans for the evening, but it would be nice to get going. The prospect of a warm fire was enticing. I mentally amended my beverage choice for the evening and changed it to whiskey.

"I'm curious about the picture. Where was it taken?" Leroy smiled again, very briefly. I suspected he was a man who wasn't given to smiles but he knew social rules dictated them. "I thought I recognized the location. It appeared to be outside a home, at a lake. It looked a lot like a place I know. If you could give me some information about who is selling it, perhaps I could contact them and find out if it's the same place."

I shut down my computer and eyed him reprovingly. "Really? What's to stop you from contacting them yourself and buying the item directly? Please, Mr. Leroy. Don't insult my intelligence."

He had the grace to appear chagrined. "I'm sorry. This is very important to me. You see, my father—" He swallowed hard, his Adam's apple bobbing convulsively. "My father is dying. I believe that sword was in our family, a family heirloom. Through stupid actions on my part, I lost it. If I could get it, it would mean so much to him and to my mother." His gaze swung back to me. I think I saw tears in his dark brown eyes then he blinked quickly and turned, staring intently at my Darth Vader helmet with working breathing apparatus which sat atop a real saddle on a toy rocking horse.

"That's a prop from the movie," I said inanely, unsure how to answer his unspoken but desperate plea.

Leroy nodded but I'm sure he didn't track what I was saying. "Can I give you my phone number? I'm going to Northern Minnesota on a fishing trip in a few days. Maybe I'll be somewhere near where you'll be and I can swing by and see it?" He regarded me hopefully. His eyes were the darkest brown and quite large, like puppy eyes.

Good sense warred with sympathy. "Where are you going?" I inched my way past him to the front door.

"Avalon Lake. I go there every fall to fish." He smiled wanly. "My dad and I used to go there all the time."

Crap. What were the odds? My other store was on the south shore of Avalon. "It's a big lake. Whereabouts?"

"You probably don't know the place. It's just an old cabin in the west past of the lake, in a cove off Gawain Bay."

Well, double crap. All the bays on Avalon were named for Knights of the Round Table and Gawain wasn't that far from where I was going. In fact, it was just three miles or so north of where I'd be. Of course, it was three miles as the crow flies. By lake, it might be a lot farther.

Leroy pulled a tiny notepad from his coat pocket and jotted something on it then tore it off and handed it to me. "Here's my number. Please call me. You have no idea how important this is to me."

I glanced at the phone number. It had a 515 area code. "You're not from the college in town here?"

"No. I'm from Des Moines. That's my mobile number."

"You drove here from Des Moines on the basis of a Facebook picture?" Granted, Des Moines was only a two-hour drive. I held open the front door.

"I told you. It's important." He hesitated in the doorway. "Are you parked in front or back? Would you like an escort to your car?"

I almost took him up on his offer. The last few nights I had the feeling someone watched me when I left the shop. "I park in back. Thanks for the offer, but I'm fine. I'm used to it."

"Are you sure?" He glanced at the other stores across the street, all of which were closed or closing. The two-block long Main Street in Linn rolled up at five-thirty. Our two bars, the Sportsman's and Joe's Grill, were a block north and a block south, respectively, and the two downtown cafes closed after lunch in mid-afternoon. In another fifteen minutes the only sign of life on the street would be the lights on the storefronts.

"Thanks, but I'm sure. My car's just out back. I'm going north to close my shop there for the winter and I plan to evaluate the sword while I'm there. I'll give you a call after I've examined it." I held up the scrap of paper he gave me then tucked it into my pocket.

He nodded once then stepped out of the shop. "Thank you." This time when he smiled it seemed genuine. "I look forward to it."

I closed the door behind him and locked it then I headed for my office. I had a file full of legal papers to review while I was on vacation so I stuffed those into my soft-sided leather messenger bag along with my new Android tablet and other business files for the northern store. As I did, I knocked over the picture of my cabin on the shores of Avalon Lake.

I picked up the framed photograph and studied it. The house was set on a thirty-foot bluff overlooking a cove in one of the big bays of the lake on the boundary waters between Canada and Minnesota. My grandmother and her mother before her owned the land. My great-great grandmother was full-blooded Ojibwa and the land and much of the lakeshore was in her family.

My great-grandmother built the original cabin and my grandmother and mother remodeled and added to it with only minimal help from the men in their lives. The cabin could only be reached by boat and was

surrounded by pines and birch trees. It had two
miniscule bedrooms, a tiny bathroom, a kitchen-living
room combination and a deck as big as the cabin itself,
cantilevered over the lake, the foundation of which
rested on an enormous boulder on the edge of the shore.

I inherited it when my mother died and since I had
no children, I was trying to decide what to do with the
cabin and the land as part of my legacy. My great-
grandfather used to have a similar piece of property a
few miles north on the shoreline around a curve of the
lake from the "Girly Getaway," as the men called it. His
cabin had been more of a fishing shack, with an
outhouse and a crude shower in the woods.

That ramshackle piece of real estate was torn down
long ago and the land sold by my no-account great-
uncle, who had a grudge against my mother. An
enormous McMansion of a house sat there now, used
only for occasional weekend getaways by the owner,
who flew in on his seaplane, usually and not
coincidentally when I was there.

I tucked the picture into a desk drawer and closed
it. Out of sight but definitely not out of mind. I had a lot
of decisions to make during my time away from the
store and the key one was whether or not I'd sell the
cabin. The legal papers in my bag contained the deed to
the cabin, the land and the lakeshore access. It also had
the legally threatening letters from Mr. McMansion,
who was investigating action against me for allegedly
causing environmental problems at the lake.

It was just the latest salvo in an ongoing battle
which had turned my cabin from a welcome retreat to a
pain in the butt. When I lived in Minnesota, it was an
easy three-hour drive for weekends and an occasional

summer break. But ten years ago I came to Iowa to help my brother when his beloved wife got breast cancer. When she died six years ago, I realized I loved it here in this quiet little college town where my two brothers lived so I decided to stay. I sold my house in Minneapolis, found someone to manage my shop in Northern Minnesota and I opened my second store here in Linn, where I attracted college students from St. George and the nearby University of Iowa.

Selling the cabin would be wrenching not only because it would sever my ties to my memories and to a part of the country I loved, but because of who wanted to buy it. I anticipated an extremely unpleasant confrontation in the near future.

I touched my pocket where Leroy's phone number rested. Despite what I told him, I was almost certain the sword would be authentic and in exceptional shape. It used to belong to my brother-in-law, Hector, and my sister, Lib, was the person selling the sword. I contacted my brother Ari when I learned of Hector's death. Lib and I weren't on speaking terms, but I figured she would be hurting for cash. It turns out I was right.

Ari confirmed what I knew. Hector was an asshole and a lazy drunkard but he knew antiques and he knew how to care for them. Lib did indeed have some items she wanted to sell, among them a medieval sword.

I looked around the office one last time then pulled on my flannel-lined denim jacket. My assistant was an old hand at running the store in my absence, so I had no qualms about leaving it for a week or two. I clicked off my desk lamp and slung my messenger bag over my right shoulder then left by the back door, jiggling the doorknob to make sure it was locked.

The businesses on this side of Main Street were all attached buildings with a shared alley behind the stores separating us from those on the next street east. Because the alley was a tight squeeze, most store people used the parking lot at the top of the hill, leaving the parking places in front on Main Street for our customers.

I went left in the alley and started uphill, keeping my hand inside my zip-top messenger bag while I walked. A chilly mist swirled around the security lights behind the old brick buildings, giving the scene the feeling of a London movie set. It was only mid-October, but it felt like winter was lurking around the corner. My breath puffed out small clouds when I hurried along the unevenly paved alley.

My store was in the middle of the block so I only had to pass behind three other stores, skirting dumpsters while I went. I made a wide swing past the dumpster behind the Skillet Cafe, knowing from past experience that small critters might be hanging around it. When I veered to the right to pass it, I sensed someone behind me.

I turned, letting my bag fall off my shoulder to the ground. That freed my pistol, which I was grasping, from the bag. I had it up and aimed in three seconds at the man in the black jacket who was just a few yards behind me.

He gaped at me. "Calm down, lady. No need to get excited."

"Turn around and walk away." I kept my gun aimed at his torso. He was a big guy, broad through the chest. It was a good target.

Footsteps behind me. I immediately stepped back,

pressing against the rear wall of John's Lock Shop, the business opposite the Skillet on the other side of the alley. I kept the gun on Black Jacket while I glanced to my right.

Mr. Leroy was running down the hill, aiming for my would-be attacker. The guy froze for a second then he turned and ran. Leroy pounded past me and after him.

I quickly lowered my gun, my hand trembling. Leroy ran about ten more yards but it was obvious the guy was gone for good. He stopped halfway down the alley and glanced back at me then at the man, who was fast disappearing out of sight.

"He's gone." My words came out more like a croak than a voice. My throat was so dry I was surprised I could talk at all.

Leroy cast one last look at the fleeing man then he walked back to stand next to me. His impromptu run didn't appear to wind him at all and the only sign he had just dashed down the hill was his thick dark hair, which now was tousled. "Are you okay?" he asked.

My heart rate was settling back to normal. I replaced my Glock in the interior holster in my messenger bag. "What do you think you're doing? I might have shot you."

Leroy nodded at my messenger bag. "Do you always go armed?"

"Iowa is a concealed-carry state."

"That's not what I asked."

"It's really no concern of yours if I'm armed." I resumed walking toward the parking lot. My knees were shaky, but otherwise I was fine. I hate confrontations of any kind, so I wasn't surprised at how discombobulated I felt.

Leroy fell into step beside me. "Here I thought I was rescuing you." He sounded peeved.

I suppose I did sound ungrateful. "Thanks for the help. If you hadn't shown up, who knows what would have happened."

"Yeah," he said. "Who knows?" Now he sounded grumpy.

I tried another tack. "I have brothers. They have this whole male macho protect thing. My oldest brother Leo gave me a gun permit for my sixteenth birthday. My other brother gave me a Smith & Wesson." I clicked my car keys in my coat pocket and my Mini Cooper chirped at me from the parking lot twenty yards away. "My mother gave me the Glock as a wedding gift." I patted my messenger bag. "It's a European model."

"Interesting family," Leroy said.

"Yeah. We are. Thanks for trying to help." We reached my car in the almost empty parking lot.

"Do you need me to go with you to the police station?" Leroy pointed to the City Hall-Police-City Information sign on the building across the street from the lot.

"Police? Why?" I hesitated, my hand on my car door. "Nothing happened."

"But you drew a gun and—"

"Between the two of us, I think we scared the guy away. I have security alarms set at the shop, so if anything happens, the police and I are both called." I tried to sound matter-of-fact about the whole thing but the truth is I was tired and didn't want to bother with it. We had a meager police force in town, just one full-time officer and two part-timers. There was little they could do about a would-be assailant. I would do my civic duty, however, and stop by on my way out of town tomorrow and mention the incident to Charlie Perkins, who would be on duty.

"Oh." Leroy hunched his shoulders against the cold mist. "Well, okay."

I nodded. "Okay. Thanks again." I opened my car door.

"Um, I was wondering."

I paused in the act of slipping my messenger bag off my shoulder. "Yeah?"

"Is there a good place to eat around here? I'm staying overnight at the motel outside of town." He peered up at the parking lot lights, hazy through the mist. "I figured the trip back might be tricky at night with all this fog and rain."

Well, he had a point there. I didn't blame him. I hated driving at night and if you factored in the rain, it would be a messy trip. "There're two bars in town that serve reasonable pub food and a very nice restaurant about two miles west of here." I pointed to Main Street. "Just stay on the main road there and you'll end up at the Island Inn Supper Club."

"Could I buy you a drink?" Leroy's gaze bounced from my car then to City Hall then to the streetlight—anywhere but at me. His shoulders were still hunched and for some reason, I felt sort of sorry for him. He was probably staying at the Sleep Inn, which was clean and inexpensive but not exactly a hotbed of social activity. Here it was, six-thirty at night and he had a long night ahead of him.

And he might be a potential buyer for a rather

expensive sword I would be selling soon. I already paid my sister for the sword, but if it brought a hefty sum, I'd split the profits with her. Visions of a cozy little dinner at my house evaporated. "I should buy you one," I said with what I hoped sounded like genuine gratefulness. "After all, you chased that guy away. Why don't you follow me? We can go to the Island and have a drink and dinner."

I was glad I offered when I saw his relieved expression. The poor guy was probably one of those people who hated to dine alone. I would see them now and then when I was out of town on business, sitting alone in a bar or a restaurant, looking lost. I didn't mind solo dining at all, but apparently other people did.

"Is it a dressy place?" He touched his chest and his burgundy sweater. "I don't need a tie, do I?"

I glanced down at my jeans and my gray sweater under my denim coat. "Don't worry, Mr. Leroy. We'll be fine. It's not fancy at all."

"Call me Abel." He smiled. "I'm glad to hear it's not too dressy. My car is just over there." He nodded toward a red Chevy Equinox sitting in the far corner of the parking lot.

I grinned. "Your car looks like the big brother to my car."

He compared my red Cooper Paceman to his red SUV. "You're right." Then his gaze settled back on my little sports car. "I'm not sure I'll be able to keep up with you."

I swung my bag into the Mini and started to slide inside. "I'll drive slowly."

"I wasn't talking about the car." He smiled then walked to his SUV, hands tucked into his jeans pockets

as he whistled.
Because The Night.

Chapter 2

Well, what did that mean?

I drove on autopilot out of the parking lot and made a right turn at the stop sign near City Hall. The road wound around the college campus, a charming little place that could have doubled for the set of a Bing Crosby movie or something equally old-fashioned. I meandered along Main Street, checking the rear view mirror to make sure he followed me.

If I wasn't mistaken, Abel Leroy just flirted with me. It was three or four years since I was involved with anyone, so I was out of practice with the whole dating-flirting-mating thing. There were few dating opportunities in Linn, Iowa, population four thousand, but it didn't bother me much. I had more than my share of loves in my fifty-two years of life. And I even married once, a disastrous relationship which still haunted me, mainly because I used to see my ex-husband at family events because he subsequently married one of my in-laws only to have a messy divorce with her later.

No, now that I was approaching my so-called Golden Years, I was content to settle down with my friends to keep me company and the on-again, off-again companionship of the stray cat who adopted me.

Well, let Leroy flirt. He was probably married with three kids and a wife back in Des Moines. We'd have dinner and I'd drive north tomorrow, deal with The Unpleasantness and still have a week or so to relax before coming back here. I was pretty sure there would be wounds from The Unpleasantness, so I could spend the winter licking them and recovering from my battles.

I drove for a quarter-mile or so, then the road widened and I was outside town, dark farm country on either side of the road. I slowed, knowing deer or raccoons were a possibility. Sure enough, I spied a buck when I rounded a turn in the road, my headlights showing him in the field on the right. I checked the mirror and saw Abel slowed, too. If you live in farm country long enough, you learn to be wary on back roads.

Five minutes later I pulled in to the Island's spacious parking lot. It was the only building for a half-mile in either direction. The low, white frame supper club sat in this same spot since before World War II and while the decor was updated several times, it still had the feeling of an old-time nightclub. The lot was almost full and I found a spot in the back. Abel pulled in three spaces away from me.

"Looks busy," he commented while we made our way past parked cars in a light mist.

"It's always busy." I walked through the door he held for me and entered the foyer. "But we can always take a table in the bar if we have to." I smiled at the white-haired hostess behind the podium just inside the threshold. "Hi, Mrs. Steward. Do you have a table for two coming available soon?"

She consulted the chart on the podium, frowning. "It might be a while."

"How's the bar? Is it full yet?"

"Nope, the band doesn't start for a couple of hours." She waved a hand to the right. "You know where it is."

"Okay, thanks." I went left, along the outer edge of the restaurant, talking to Abel while we walked. "They always have a jazz group on Saturday night, so the bar fills fast. Looks like we timed it right." I walked into the attached bar room which ran the length of the restaurant, facing the road.

As I expected, most of the four-seat tables in the bar were empty. Wayne the bartender was behind the big oak counter and he waved when he saw me. He was in his late forties, a burly linebacker of a guy with a shaved head, a fierce-looking scar on the side of his face and a heart of gold. "Hey, Sunshine!" he called out.

I waved. "Is it still Happy Hour?"

"For you, it is." He laughed and turned to a waitress who came in with an order.

Abel and I took a table away from the entrance by the glass-fronted fireplace where logs crackled. I dropped my coat and bag on the nearby hearth and sank into the comfy cushioned chair. "I haven't been here for a few months. I forgot how nice this bar is."

He took the seat across from me. "It looks like they haven't forgotten you." He pulled a menu from the holder on the table and studied it, his eyelashes dark and long on his down-tilted face.

"It's a small town. Mrs. Steward works during the day at the beauty salon I use and Wayne's son runs the cafe next to my store in town." I leaned back and relaxed. "You tend to get to know folks in a small town."

"This is surprisingly quiet, given how crowded the restaurant is." He eyed the wooden tables, upholstered chairs and the long expanse of polished bar. "So many bars nowadays are all chrome and mirrors. This is nice."

"Hi, Ms. DuLac. Haven't seen you in a while."

I regarded the waiter, a slender young man in dark pants and a white shirt. "Hi, Tom. How's your son doing?"

He beamed at me. "Mallory is doing really good. Thanks for the tip about the hearing test. Once we found out Mallory was having trouble hearing the teacher and we got him a hearing aid, his grades have bounced back."

"I'm glad we figured out what was wrong. What's the special tonight?"

He gave us the lowdown on the nightly special and on my recommendation, we ordered the appetizer platter. "It's enough food to feed an army," I assured Abel.

"That works for me," he said. "I don't like eating a big meal at night anyway."

We ordered drinks and Tom hustled away, stopping at the bar to give Wayne our order before vanishing toward the dining room. Within minutes Wayne was at our table, four drinks on his tray. "Happy hour," he said, setting two Cosmopolitans in front of me and two martinis in front of Leroy.

"You're a champ, Wayne," I said, taking a sip. I sighed happily. "You make the best Cosmopolitan for fifty miles, I swear."

"Thanks, Sunshine." He went back to his domain, grinning.

Abel and I sipped our drinks in silence for several minutes, the warmth of the alcohol and the fireplace so soothing. All thoughts of The Unpleasantness faded, replaced by a sense of cozy quietude. I finally roused myself to make some social conversation. "What do you do for a living, Abel?"

"I'm a computer consultant. I evaluate hardware and software for several government agencies."

He stared at his martini glass when he said it and I thought his mouth narrowed, like he swallowed something sour. I almost asked him if his drink was bad, then he raised his head and he smiled at me. It was one of those fake smiles, though.

"That sounds interesting," I said.

"It's challenging." He sipped his drink. "It's started to bother me lately."

"Bother you?"

He frowned again. "I'm the senior man in our office and it seems like I often have to make unpleasant recommendations."

There was that word again—unpleasant. I nodded sympathetically. "That can happen. I used to be in the software industry and I remember when we would wait to hear if we got government funding or not. A project can hinge on funding and if we didn't get it, some people would be out of work."

He looked puzzled for a minute then he nodded. "Yeah, it's something like that." His gaze flickered around the room like he was searching for a new topic. "So do you always carry a gun?"

"I've handled guns all my life. I'm trained to use it and I'm comfortable carrying one." I sipped my drink again. I adored Wayne's Cosmos, which were the perfect mix of Cointreau, vodka and cranberry juice with just a hint of fresh lemon on the rim of the glass.

"It seems extreme, though. I mean, well, would you have shot him?" Abel eyed me over the rim of his martini glass.

"I might have fired a warning shot. And as to it being extreme—you're not a woman. You don't know what it's like to be a target. I spent some time overseas where it's not very safe, so I'm accustomed to watching out for myself." I regarded him steadily, daring him to disagree.

He started to argue with me then he nodded. "I suppose you're right." He gazed into the fire for a long minute and I was content to let the silence stretch, allowing good vodka and coziness to take charge once again. "Why are you going up north? You said something about closing your store. Are you selling it?"

"I close it for wintertime. There aren't many tourists in the winter. The ones who do go north are there for the ice fishing and the snowmobiling." I sipped again. Maybe it was the Cosmo. Maybe it was the fireplace. Maybe it was the desire to share my concern about the upcoming Unpleasantness. "I have a lake cabin there that's been in my family for a long time. I'm thinking about selling it."

"Really? Why?"

"The area is changing. People are building big lake houses now. My little cabin doesn't feel like it fits in anymore." It wasn't the whole truth, but it was truth enough.

"Yeah, I've noticed that." He sipped his martini. "Every year I go there, it seems like there's one more new house. There's even some guy who has a seaplane who lands in the bay. Can you imagine it? A private seaplane, just to run north to your cabin on the lake." He shook his head. "Some people have more money than brains, I guess."

Tom appeared with our appetizers, a lazy Susan which almost filled our table. He spun it gently while explaining our choices. "Chicken wings, celery and radishes, onion rings, potato cakes, parmesan cheese sticks, corned beef bites and bruschetta. And here're your dips." He set another mini-Susan next to the big one. "Ranch, Jalapeno, Blue Cheese and balsamic vinegar, plus your basic ketchup, mustard and sour cream. You guys need anything else?"

"Lord, no," Abel murmured, looking at the feast. "You weren't kidding when you said it could feed an army."

"I hope you brought your appetite. I'll check back on you in a few minutes." Tom went to the bar to pick up an order and chat with Wayne, with many glances our way. I'm sure my 'date' would be a hot topic of conversation for the next few days. Of course, I wouldn't be there to hear it because I'd be on my way to Northern Minnesota.

"Dig in." I loaded my plate with samples and we munched contently for a few minutes, taking sips of our drinks in between bites. Three of the other five tables in the bar filled and soon a hum of conversation added to the background noise of the restaurant.

"How's the drink, Sunshine?" Wayne asked, walking by our table.

"Perfect, as usual." I smiled up at him. "And the food is fabulous, too."

"Great. I'm glad your good opinion of us hasn't

24

changed even though we haven't seen much of you lately." He wandered to the next table to chat with the customers there.

"That's your nickname?" Abel asked. "Sunshine?"

"Yeah. My family gave it to me and it kinda stuck."

"Family? You're related to him?" Abel looked from Wayne to me.

"His wife is sister to my late sister-in-law, so I guess we are related. Usually I don't use my first name, I just go by Vivian." I contemplated the parmesan cheese sticks. Oh, what the heck. I was on vacation, right? Calories don't count when you're on vacation.

I glimpsed an expression of wide-eyed shock on Abel's face. I hastily glanced around us, wondering what stunned him. Everything appeared ordinary. "Are you okay?"

He blinked slowly. "Your name is Vivian? That's an unusual name."

"Not compared to my first name, it isn't." I munched on the cheese stick. "My mother was rather eccentric when it came to naming her children."

Abel tilted his head to one side. "What is your first name?"

I sighed. "My mom believed in the zodiac. We were all named according to our birth months. Mine was January."

He frowned. "You're named Capricorn?"

I laughed. "No. I'm Aquarius. My brothers are Leo for the lion, Archer for Sagittarius and Ari for Aries. My sister is Lib."

"Lib? What zodiac sign is that?"

"It's short for Libra," I explained. "She could at

least shorten her name to something normal. Unlike me."

"You have a big family," Abel said. "I was an only child. No siblings."

"My sister, Lib, and I aren't on the best of terms, but otherwise we all get along pretty good. I'm the youngest." I spun the appetizer tray and selected an onion ring, which was enormous, crispy and only slightly greasy. "Archer and Leo live here. Ari and Lib are out East." I focused on demolishing the onion ring while I considered tossing out the other juicy little tidbit about my family. Then I gave a mental shrug. What did it matter? He was just a potential buyer. "It's complicated because one of my brothers introduced me to my ex-husband, who later married my brother's sister-in-law. They're divorced and for a while it was tense."

"That's messy," he muttered.

"Yeah, isn't it? After I got divorced, my ex married somebody else. Then he got divorced from her and he married my brother's sister-in-law. Who divorced him." Abel had rearranged his expression to polite interest, which was nice of him, I thought. "She's sort of a serial wedder, if you know what I mean. Funny, it was her longest marriage. It lasted almost ten years. I'm sure Dewin is stunned she walked out on him."

"Dewin?" Abel drained his martini, his Adam's apple bouncing.

"That's the other thing that's sort of complicated."

"How much more complicated can it get?"

I sipped my Cosmo. "Ever hear of Dewin Software?"

He frowned, eyebrows drawn together. "I thought

it was pronounced De-win."

"No, it's Dewin. It rhymes with 'twin'. It's Welsh. Ever hear of it?"

"Of course I've heard of it. That's like asking if I've heard of Google or Microsoft or—" His eyes narrowed. "Wait a minute. There was a big stink about the CEO recently. He and his wife got divorced and she said the reason the marriage failed was because he still loved a former—" His eyes widened. "You?"

I sighed. "His ex-wife is such a bitch. She's the sister-in-law I told you about." I sipped my second Cosmo.

"What about you?" He tilted his head to one side. "Did you remarry?"

I shook my head, my curls bouncing. "Nope. What about you?"

"The same. Divorced, with two grown kids who live in California. Was your divorce okay or was it a fight?" His head was still tilted and I realized he appeared slightly bleary-eyed.

"It was okay," I said cautiously. I checked our demolished appetizer tray. "Looks like we were hungrier than we thought."

He nodded, head bobbing and still tilted. "Mine was a knockdown, drag-out fight. She took me for everything she could get. The house, the car, the kids, the house."

"Two houses?" I joked. "Really?"

He squinted at me. "Huh?"

"Are you okay?" I asked, keeping my voice low and glancing around at the other patrons. No one seemed to notice Abel was leaning to one side.

"It's the gin." He sighed loudly and straightened in

his chair. "I really shouldn't have gin. Really. Shouldn't."

Oh, shit. Just my luck I get a guy who can't handle martinis and we go to the one place in town that makes the strongest martinis on the planet. "Hold on a sec." I reached into my messenger bag and grabbed my wallet then got to my feet.

"Where are you going?" He peered blearily at me.

"To see about our bill. You just sit tight." I eyed him suspiciously, expecting him to try to stand. To my relief, he only nodded.

"Okay. You do that." He smiled beatifically at me, looking so happy I automatically smiled in return.

I went to the bar. "Hey, Wayne," I said. "I have a problem."

"What's up?" Wayne meandered to my end of the bar counter, busily wiping a glass as he walked.

"I think he's sloshed." I jerked my head in the general direction of my table.

"What? Two martinis? What the hell?" Wayne peered past me. "Yeah, you might be right. Looks like you'll have to drive tonight."

"That's the problem. We brought two cars. He's in town on a buying trip at my store. He's staying at the motel. Should I call a cab or what?"

Wayne frowned. "I don't know. Any drunks we get are locals. I suppose I can call the cops and they can take him to Cedar Rapids and throw him in the Drunk Tank."

"Oh, for cryin' out loud," I muttered. I turned to peer at Leroy. He sat bolt upright in his chair, his big brown eyes wide open and a crazy smile on his face. When he caught me looking at him, he wiggled his fingers in a small wave.

What the hell was I going to do with him? He wasn't drunk-tank drunk, just over his limit. "I'll handle it," I told Wayne. "I'll get him to his hotel, but we'll have to leave his car here. Tell the owner it'll be here overnight. Abel can come back tomorrow and get it."

"Are you sure? I know Earl won't mind if the car stays, but maybe we should just call a cab." Wayne's gaze went from me to Abel then back to me.

"A cabbie won't want to take a drunk," I said. "I think I can handle him."

"I don't know." Wayne leaned closer to me. "This might be some trick to get you alone with him up in his hotel room. Call one of your brothers, get them to help."

I almost laughed out loud. "I think I'm past the age where men would do that anymore, but thanks for the vote of confidence. I can deal with it without bothering Leo or Archer."

Wayne touched my hand, resting on the bar top. "You call me when you're done with him. If I don't hear from you in a half-hour, I'm calling your brother." He pulled over a cocktail napkin and scribbled a phone number on it. "Call me. Promise?"

I squeezed his hand. "I promise." I pulled three twenties out of my wallet. "Will it cover the tab?"

"More than." He scooped up the bills and turned toward the cash register at the end of the bar counter.

"Keep it. Split it with Tom." I tucked the napkin into my jeans pocket and made my way back to the table, weaving through the now-crowded bar. I was thankful it was filling with patrons. Maybe it meant people would be distracted and we could get out without attracting too much attention.

I pulled out the chair next to Abel and sat down, leaning close to him. "Mr. Leroy."

He peered blearily at me. "Able. I mean, my name is Arthur, but they call me Able because of my initials. A.B.L." Once again, he gave me that angelic smile.

I mentally adjusted the spelling of his name. "Okay. Able. You need to go to your hotel. I'll help you but you have to help me." I had my lips close to his ear, talking loud enough for him to hear me over the buzz of conversation around us.

He turned and for an instant our faces were inches away from each other. Then he pulled his head back and regarded me for a long minute. "Okay. I'm just the tiniest bit ineliabrated. Inelibrated. Incapacerated." He sighed. "You know what I mean."

"I do." I considered the long walk through the restaurant, back to the front door. "I'm going to bring the car to the side door, there." I pointed to my right, where the bar's exterior street door opened into the side parking lot. "Why don't you just wait right here until I bring the car around, then I'll help you outside."

"I think I should go with you." He put his hands on the table, narrowing missing his plate which held the remains of his meal.

Wayne appeared at my side. "Why don't I give you a hand?" he said, his voice just loud enough to be heard. "I know your back is hurting you today."

Able peered up at him, his mouth agape. Then he ponderously turned his head from side to side, seeing the looks from the other patrons. "Why, yes it is," he managed to say. "Thank you, sir. You are a gentleman."

I got out of the way, grabbing my coat and bag.

"I'm going to bring the car around," I told Wayne. "I'll meet you at the side door." I dragged on my coat then leaned over Able. "You go with Wayne, okay?"

He managed a feeble nod. "Will do." He smiled again, his happy, dazzling smile. "Thank you."

It was hard to stay mad at him when he smiled like that. I hurried through the restaurant and ran out the front door, car keys in hand. The earlier drizzle had stopped and a full moon shone brightly overhead. Within minutes I drove through the crowded parking lot and parked in the middle of the side lot.

Wayne and Able were waiting for me at the door, Wayne talking to Able and Able nodding, his eyes wide. When Wayne saw me, he put a hand under Able's arm and steered the amiable drunk among the parked cars. I got out and between the two of us we maneuvered Able into the front seat of my small two-seater sports car.

Wayne regarded me above the top of the car and shook a finger as I prepared to step into the driver's side. "You call me. My brother-in-law would kill me if anything happened to you."

I peeked through the sun roof. Able smiled up at me. "I think I'm safe."

Wayne just tapped the top of my car. "Call me. Drive carefully." He walked back through the lot to the bar.

I slid into the driver's seat. "Do you have your hotel key?" I asked. "Do you know where your room is?" I drove out of the crowded parking lot and onto the main road.

"Sure do." Able leaned precariously to his left and dug into his coat pocket, pulling out a set of car keys and a room swipe-card. "Here it is. It's gin. I just can't drink gin." He stared out his window for a long minute while I drove. Then he turned to me, swaying in his seat. "I've always done the right thing, you know? I went to school, I got a job, I got married, I had kids, I got divorced. I'm just a fucking statistic."

Rather than drive back through town, I took the highway that bypassed the town. There was more traffic, but it would get us to the hotel faster. "I'm sure you're more than that, Able," I said while I merged onto the highway which, thankfully, had little traffic.

"I hate my fucking job," he muttered. "I investigate people who—"

"Investigate?" I got into the right lane, knowing my exit would be within a mile or less. "I thought you said you evaluate software."

His head whipped around so fast I swear I heard something pop. "Evaluate. Yes." He once again stared out his window, humming softly.

It took a second for me to recognize the song, another Natalie Merchant tune. *Cowboy Romance*, a song about two drunks who have a casual afternoon hook-up after they met in a bar. I sincerely hoped his mind wasn't heading in that direction.

A few minutes later we reached the hotel, a three-story structure next to the grocery store on the outskirts of town. "You can park around back," Able said. "My room is right there."

I breathed a sigh of relief. I didn't want to navigate him through the lobby if I could help it. I drove past the three-story building and parked near the center exterior door. "Do you know how to get to your room?" I asked hopefully.

"Sure. I'm good. Sure." Able leaned forward to stare through the windshield at the hotel building. "I think it's there." He fumbled for the door handle.

I got out and came around the back of the car, reaching him just as he almost fell out. I got a hand under his arm and helped him upright. "Right there," he said, slinging an arm around my shoulders. "Right there."

I took the car keys and the hotel key-card out of his hand and helped him stagger to the door. I swiped the card and we entered, Able tugging me to the left. I glanced at the key-card but it didn't have a number on it. I prayed he would remember where his room was.

My prayers were answered. He pulled me to stop outside a room two doors from the exit. "Right here," he said.

I tried the key in the lock and, thank you God, it worked. I opened the door and Able stumbled inside. "Okay," I said, "here you are. All safe and sound." I paused inside the threshold, flipping on the light switch near the door.

Able grabbed hold of the bathroom doorway to steady himself. "Sorry. It's the gin. I can't drink gin." He took a faltering step forward, into the room.

"We all have a weak spot." I jiggled his car keys, debating where to set them.

"What's yours?" He tugged at his sweater collar.

I steadied him while he swayed. With my luck he'd crash into the dresser and kill himself. "White wine."

"Hunh?" He gaped at me like a turtle, his head stuck forward and his eyes in little slits. "'Scuse me?"

"White wine. A good Riesling will knock me on my butt."

"Well, that's—" He blinked and fell backward onto the bed.

I approached him cautiously. "Able?" I leaned over. He was sound asleep, snoring softly.

I jotted a note on the hotel notepad, telling him where his car was located. I put the note and his keys on the dresser. I paused before I left the room then went back and slipped off his shoes, setting them under the desk. Then I took an edge of the king-bed coverlet, draping it over him.

He opened his eyes. "You're very beautiful, Sunshine," he whispered.

I smiled. "You're very drunk."

"I am. And you are." He closed his eyes and was asleep again in seconds.

I turned off the light when I left.

Chapter 3

I called Wayne from my car and reassured him I was fine then I drove to my home, a Craftsman-style house on the northeast side of town. It was part of a cul-de-sac neighborhood of older homes with small back yards abutting a county park. The house had two bedrooms on the main floor which I used as a den and a craft-sewing room. The one large attic room I used as my master bedroom. I bought the house from a now-deceased college professor who built it when he first started teaching at the school and it still had a vintage, 1920s feel to it.

Curio, the stray cat who dropped by occasionally, wasn't in evidence. He usually showed up at noon near my detached garage when I came home for lunch, looking for the kibble I put on the back porch for him. I had already told my next door neighbor I would be out of town and she would handle kibble duty in my absence.

I poured myself a glass of red wine and took my beverage and a magazine to bed. I fell asleep an hour or so later and dreamed about trying to help Able Leroy into his room while the doors in the hotel kept changing in front of us.

The next morning I considered stopping at the police station on my way out of town to discuss last night's accoster, but common sense prevailed. There was nothing to investigate and no real harm had been done. I would mention the incident at our business owners' meeting in two weeks, though. We needed better lighting in the areas behind our buildings.

Satisfied with my logic, I was on the road by eight in the morning, taking the Interstate north. We weren't quite at peak leaf season here in Iowa, which meant it would be perfect in Minnesota. I had a long drive ahead of me, but it was one I made many times, so I had my favorite stopping places along the route. I cranked up my XM radio channel and set the cruise control.

I wondered how Able was feeling this morning. I had his phone number and I was tempted to call him, but in the end I decided there wasn't any reason to. I would evaluate the sword and scabbard. If they were as good as I hoped, I would call Able and maybe he could take a look at it before I offered it to my other potential buyers.

The Minnesota border had just zipped past my window when my radio quieted and my phone rang, linked to my car via sync technology.

"Hey, Sunshine, I heard you had a hot date last night." My brother, Archer's, teasing voice made me visualize his face, oval like mine and with the same head of thick dark brown curly hair, now liberally sprinkled with gray. Archer was five years older than me. He and our older brother Leo were my mainstays while growing up after my father died and later when my mother developed dementia. She died a few years ago and that was one of the causes of the feud with my sister, who objected to my mother's hospitalization in her later years.

"I suppose Wayne called you," I said. "He's such a

busybody."

"Once a brother-in-law, always a brother-in-law. He said the guy was drunk. What's going on?"

I related the story of Able Leroy, potential buyer, while driving along the Interstate. I was far enough from any metro area and traffic was still light, so I felt comfortable splitting my concentration between the road and my story about escort duties.

"Well, I can sympathize with the guy," Archer said when I finally wrapped up the telling. "Wayne's martinis knock me on my ass, too. I'm glad you were able to get him to his room without any problems."

"I didn't know what else to do. Wayne suggested I call the cops and let them handle him, but that seemed extreme to me."

"You probably shouldn't have gone alone with him to the hotel." Archer sounded like a chiding parent reminding a recalcitrant daughter about the rules.

"Wayne knew where I was. I knew he'd call out the troops if I needed it. Besides, you guys trained me well. I was pretty sure I could deal with him if he got out of hand." I thought of Able Leroy and I smiled. "He was a happy drunk. He kept apologizing."

Archer voice resumed its bantering quality. "Well, that just means you can guilt him into paying a good price for the sword. I can't believe you bought it."

"I knew Lib would be hurting for money and I can afford it, so I figured why not."

Archer laughed. "It must have galled her to ask for help."

"She didn't exactly ask. I heard about it from Ari. I told Ari to tell Lib I'd buy it. You know how Lib holds a grudge."

"You have to learn to be less honest when someone asks your opinion about the man she's going to marry."

"Hector was an asshole. She asked what I thought and I told her. Add it to her ongoing bitch about how I handled Mom and no wonder she won't talk to me."

"Always the diplomat. It seems like you're always bailing out Lib. You helped her when she got divorced and you lent her money to get her business going. How much did it cost you?"

"Just call me the Bank of DuLac," I said lightly. "I made a killing when I cashed out my stock options and I know some investment counselors. I can afford it."

"Do you think the guy will buy Hector's sword? Is Lib really hurting for cash?"

"Of course she is. You know what a dickhead Hector was. I'm not sure if Leroy will buy the thing or not. If he doesn't buy it, I know a couple of people from the Cities who have vacation houses on the lake. They might buy it. I'll store it at the lake if I have to."

"Are you going to sell the cabin?" Archer's question seemed to hang in the air in front of me, wavering above the road signs while they whizzed past. "If you sell the cabin, will you sell the shop, too?"

"I don't know. For now, I'll be happy if I can make a decision about the cabin. I don't have to worry about the shop until later, since we're closing it up for the winter anyway. I'm hoping I'll have a chance to spend some time there and think about it without any distractions."

"What are the odds it will happen? Every time you show up, Dewin shows up, usually with a girlfriend or a wife in tow."

I sighed. My ex-husband, Dewin Mervyn, had

bought my grandfather's cabin on Avalon Lake, promptly torn it down and built a three-million dollar McMansion in its place. I could see the reflection of his lights from my humble little cabin and I often heard the music from his parties. "Maybe this time he won't. His divorce was just finalized. Maybe they'll be in court or something."

"You can hope. I hate to see Dewin drive you away from the lake. I think if you sell the cabin, you'll regret it someday."

"I'm sure I might but I'm getting tired of fighting him. He's determined to make my life miserable and the cabin is the one place he can do it easily."

"He's still pissed off that you get residuals for the software code you wrote for his company."

"Twenty years ago and still going strong. I was quite the programmer in my day and it's paid off."

"Between that and the stock options when you left, you've made a good living off of Dewin Software. I'm sure it still sticks in Mervyn's craw."

"I certainly hope so." I checked the upcoming road sign. "Listen, I'm getting close to the Cities. I'm going to need all my wits about me to negotiate traffic."

"Okay. Drive carefully and say hello to the lake for me."

"Will do. Thanks for calling." I ended the call and the music resumed, a medley of Beatles songs which kept me alert through the treacherous traffic around Minneapolis.

I stopped north of the metro for a late lunch then continued on my way, getting off the Interstate south of Duluth and heading northwest on two-lane county blacktop roads. The foliage change was so gradual I didn't notice it at first, but finally I realized I was surrounded by brilliant fall colors, startling yellows of birches and the dark red and oranges of the maples. The effect against the pale blue sky was breathtaking. I've always thought autumn was a Midwesterner's reward for enduring the brutally hot summers and the frigid winters. It appeared as though this leaf season would be stellar.

I stopped once for a cup of coffee and a break but kept pressing on, anxious to reach the lake before dark. By four in the afternoon I pulled in to Avalon, Minnesota, a miniscule town on the southwest edge of Avalon Lake whose town sign read *Welcome to the Land of Camelot*.

The place did have the feeling of unreality, so far removed from the world. During the summer season it was a bustling little city, but once tourists left, it reverted back to its normal population of one thousand hardy souls who lived on the edge of the Boundary Waters Canoe Area Wilderness. The BWCAW was one of the last truly last wild places in America and the people who lived here learned to respect its ways or else they regretted it.

Curiosity's was located on Main Street, between the Camelot Cafe and the Queens' Coffee Shop and down the street from the Keep-It-Clean Laundromat. The store was closed by this time of day, keeping off-season hours of ten to four. I drove through town and headed northeast on the county road leading to the lake.

Twenty minutes later, I pulled in to the gravel lane meandering through the woods to Sydney "Sy" Eckert's house. Sy was my store manager and also my go-to guy when it came to anything I needed for the cabin. His house was situated on a peninsula on the mainland, a mile of open lake across Cador Bay from my cabin. Sy had lived there all his life, serving as a guide for summer tourists and winter caretaker for a couple of the smaller resorts nearby.

I tucked my Mini Cooper in the cleared area near the woodpile under the stand of birches where it would be out of way of Sy's ancient but pristine green pickup truck. His house was slightly uphill, perched on an outcropping of land. The single-story log house was angled east-west, so most of it faced the lake with a big open porch that jutted out, protecting the dock underneath.

I grabbed my messenger bag from the passenger seat of my Cooper and my soft-sided duffel from the trunk then walked the twenty feet down the gravel path framed by flowers to the door. An old wooden wheelbarrow planted with herbs was near the west-facing door, angled so it caught the last of the sun. Just inside was the kitchen, where I thought I smelled potatoes cooking.

"Hey, boss, how's it going?" Sy came out of the house to meet me. His thick white hair was cut close to his head in a Marine buzz cut and his broad shoulders strained his denim shirt. Sy was pushing seventy but he could still out-fish and out-trap most men half his age. He credited his Ojibwa grandmother for his sturdiness and his German grandfather for his stubbornness.

I credited his hardiness to his wife, Kay, who came behind him, wiping her hands on a kitchen towel. "I figured you'd get here before dark," she said, smiling at me through the screen door when I set my bags near the wheelbarrow. She was a petite, wiry woman with iron gray hair almost as curly as mine. Unlike me, she kept hers cut short so it formed loose ringlets on her head.

I glanced to my left, where the shimmering expanse of lake stretched into the distance, the setting sun silhouetting the forested far shore. "Yeah, I hate boating in the dark. I'm always afraid I'll miss my marker and end up cruising around all night. It's a damn big lake." My skin crawled at the thought.

"How was the drive?" Sy asked while I stretched, easing tense muscles that could finally move.

"No problems. Some construction north of the Cities, but otherwise not bad. Of course, there was a bunch of traffic going south, but I was going north, so I didn't care."

Sy snorted. "Leaf peepers. Tourists taking pictures of the leaves. Like our leaves are any better than theirs."

"You have a lot more leaves than they have in the city," I commented. "And yours are a few weeks earlier than theirs. Let's face it. I'd rather see a forest of trees with beautiful leaves than one or two here and there in a suburb."

"May not be that way for too much longer," he grumbled.

"What?" I eyed the canopy of trees shading the east and south side of his house. Here on the west side it was clear and the north side facing lake was clear, of course. Otherwise all that could be seen was forest and the sparkling waters of the lake. "They're not logging around here, are they?"

"If those L.D.C. people have anything to say about it, they'll clear cut the shoreline and toss up more of those big houses," Sy said with a grim frown.

"L.D.C.?" I turned to Kay, who was shaking her head at her husband. "What's that?"

"Lakefront Development Corporation," she said, stepping out of the house onto the path.

"Or Loud Dumb Cocksuckers, depending on who you talk to," Sy muttered, shooting a dark look in the direction of the big house out of sight around the bend of the lake.

"Wait a minute." I looked from Kay to Sy. "You mean some corporation is trying to buy up land? They can't do that, can they? I thought the state mandated that large developments couldn't be done on the shore."

"That's farther east of here," Kay said. "They're creating a state park and the mandate is for the land around the park, not the whole lake. I'm sure the state will have a say in how developments are done, but you know as well as I do that money talks."

It was probably my imagination, but I thought I heard an accusation in her voice. I didn't blame her. I blamed myself. My marriage to Dewin Mervyn made him aware of my little piece of paradise. And it was his vendetta against me that made him determined to ruin it for me and by association for everyone else on the lake.

"Yeah, they're offering some folks a nice chunk of change for their land." Sy picked up my duffel. "I'm not planning on selling. I always hoped one of the kids might want to come here and live, but they're too happy in the city, I guess." His disgusted tone of voice clearly said what he thought of that.

Kay shook a finger at him. "Let's not go down that road again, Sy. We've had fifty good years together out here. There's no reason our kids would want to follow in our footsteps."

Sy started to argue then he realized it would get him nowhere. "Some of us old-timers are getting together and we thought we might hire a lawyer, just to see if there's anything we can do to stop it."

"Are their plans in the public record?" I asked, my mind racing.

"What do you mean?" Kay asked.

"Have they come up with some actual blueprints or do they have plans that show where they want to build and what they want to sell or build?"

"I think so," she said. "Why?"

"If it's in the public record, then it's available for scrutiny by legal parties." I pulled out my iPhone and accessed my contact list for my phone. "Damn. I forget I can't get much of a signal here." I tapped a note into my To-Do list app. "I have a brother who's an attorney," I said while I saved the note. "I'll give him a call when I'm in town tomorrow and see if he can give me some pointers."

"Does that mean you're not in favor of them selling off the shoreline?" Sy asked. "Last time you were here you weren't sure if you wanted to keep the cabin or not."

I stared at the lake, the undulating swells of the waves so hypnotic and peaceful looking. "I'm not sure what I want to do, but I'm pretty damn sure I don't want to sell my peninsula to somebody so they can put up some big houses."

"I was hoping you'd say that." Sy's relief was evident in his wide smile. "That chunk of land of yours is worth a lot of money."

"Not to mention the fact it's right across the bay from us." Kay shot Sy an admonishing look. "There goes the neighborhood."

"Don't worry." I tucked my iPhone back into my jacket pocket. "You guys will be the first to know if I decide to sell it."

Kay laughed. "They'll have to dynamite us off this land. Well, there's nothing we can do about it tonight. You're welcome to stay for supper if you'd like. Sy can motor you to your place when we're done."

"Oh, I don't think so," I said reluctantly. "It's tempting, though."

"Your boat is gassed up and ready to go if you want to go by yourself," Sy assured me. "I went out yesterday to the cabin and made sure everything was okay. Plumbing's working and the electric is fine." He winked at me. "I set the ice maker on so you'll have some ice for your drink once you get there."

"I put in a few groceries, just enough to get you through the week. And I made some of those cookie dough bites you like so much. They're in the fridge, too." Kay tucked her towel into the waistband of her jeans. "Sure you don't want to stay for supper?"

If I stayed, it would be too dark for me to go alone to my cabin so Sy would have to take me and my boat across the bay. "Thanks, but I think I'll get to the cabin before it gets dark. I'll come in tomorrow, Sy, and we can talk about the inventory. I'm expecting a package to arrive sometime soon and we'll need to evaluate it."

"Already here," Sy said. "Came this morning. I stored it out at the Shack."

The Shack was our metal pole barn on the outskirts of Avalon where I housed my boat in the wintertime, Sy's snowmobile in the summertime and large items I acquired for sale, like furniture, yard ornaments, windows, doors and other oddities of architectural interest.

"Good. We'll look at it tomorrow." I picked up my messenger bag. "Is the radio charged?"

"Of course." Kay reached into the kitchen and pulled the two-way radio transceiver from its cradle on the wall. It was the mate to the one sitting in my cabin's bedroom. "We tested it yesterday."

"Good." I gave a rueful grin. "I'm so used to being always in touch, either by computer or by phone. It makes me nervous when it's gone."

"Not to worry. You need us, you call us." She set the phone back inside.

"Well, let's get you loaded up." Sy squinted at the western horizon. "You've got another couple hours or so of daylight, but I know how you are about night boating."

I slung my bag over my shoulder and waved to Kay, following Sy down the path to the dock under the porch. We stowed my gear in the utility boat I used, an inelegant but serviceable fifteen-foot aluminum craft with a twenty-five mph outboard. It had a two-foot side depth and could seat eight in a pinch, but really only four comfortably. I used it to motor back and forth from the cabin to the shore.

"You remember how to drive this thing?" Sy asked while I settled myself in the rear of the boat and pulled my life vest and my red linen scarf from the big red cooler bolted to the inside of the boat.

He asked the same thing every time I came to the lake and got into the boat and every time I answered the same. "It's like riding a bike, Sy. You never forget." I tied the scarf around my head to keep my curly hair from getting tangled in transit then buckled on the life vest, making sure it was securely fastened.

"Yeah, but if you forget and fall off this bike, you'll get damn wet." He cast off my lines and gave me a gentle push away from the dock. "I'll meet you in town in the morning. I have to take the truck in early to have it serviced, so I'll see you at the store."

I waved a hand in acknowledgement then focused on navigating the boat away from the shore and the boulders jutting out of the water to the left. I knew these waters well and I was a reasonably good boater, but I also knew the lake could be unforgiving if I got cocky.

It was a relatively smooth crossing tonight. The mail boat had already passed and there weren't any late afternoon fishermen. They would probably be returning in the next hour or so, using every minute of daylight they could. The wind was cold in my face and I kept my head tipped down and my eyes locked on the opposite bay, which was surrounded by land like a mother with arms embracing a child.

No matter how many times I made this crossing, I was still terrified, my hands wet with sweat on the tiller while the cold air made them clammy. These excursions to the cabin were a test for me to face my biggest fear in life. It didn't matter that I had an excellent reason for being terrified because I came near to drowning when I was younger. It didn't matter that I took swimming lessons, Red Cross lifesaving lessons and I was a certified Red Cross lifeguard and had CPR and rescue experience.

I was still deathly afraid of the water. I could manage swimming pools, but put me in a boat on a big lake and it was all I could do to keep my lunch down and my bowels solid. I managed on sheer willpower alone. I loved being *at* the lake. I just hated being *on* it.

So I treated it like any unpleasant task. Knuckle down and get it done and don't think too much about it. Don't think about the unknowable depths of the water under the boat. Go slightly right here to avoid that small island. Go left now because of the rocks near the shore. Stay in the channel so you're out of the worst of the wake zone when that boat goes by. Go slowly and steadily. Don't rush, don't hurry.

I puttered across the lake, terrified of going too fast and hating that I had to go slow because I wanted it over with, I wanted to be on land, I wanted to be safe and unmoving and nowhere near the water.

Fifteen minutes later I eased the boat against my dock on the opposite shore. The hilly land surrounding the bay cut off sunlight so I was now in twilight. I tied up at the side of the dock and shucked off my life vest, tucking it and my scarf back into the cooler. I tossed my bags onto the planking then pulled myself up onto the wooden dock. Twenty feet away was the rocky shoreline, with trees and shrubs overhanging the dock and the stairs leading to my cabin.

I slung my bags over my shoulder, checked my boat moorings then strode onto land, breathing an enormous sigh of relief when I put the lake behind me. I walked up the six wooden steps to the landing, pausing to grab a couple of logs from the stack under the deck. Then I continued up the next five steps, made a right turn and went three more steps until I stood on the deck overlooking the lake.

The sun was sinking down, sending fiery fingers of light across the water's surface, rippling when a boat motored past, out of sight. I tapped in the security code on the French doors then I was in my living room, a space barely big enough for the two armchairs and the love seat on my left.

I put the wood near the fireplace on the right, noting that Sy laid in a good supply of logs for me already. I dropped my bags on the couch and went into the kitchen, separated from the living room by the tiny two-person wooden table and the counter. I flicked on lights while I went through my cabin-arrival routine, running the water and checking the gas range. I went into the back bedroom behind the kitchen and flicked on the lights. I kept one twin bed here and my desk against the window overlooking a tiny and shallow cove where muskrat and mink could be seen now and again.

I went back to the front of the cabin and made a left into the main bedroom, taking my duffel bag with me. The bed was set to the left of the door, angled back against the wall with a sliding glass door on the far side of the bed leading to the wraparound deck. Unpacking didn't take long, just a matter of adding what I brought to what was in the closet. I put my Glock on the bedside table farthest away from the sliding door, checked the charge on the two-way radio, then went into the attached bathroom, flushing the toilet and running some bath water to make sure everything worked.

By the time I was done, darkness was settling over the lake. I considered taking my camera and going down to the dock to snap some pictures, but inertia got the better of me. Instead I checked the kitchen, discovering snack-sized bags of potato chips in one cupboard and some cheese and salami in the fridge. I greedily devoured two of the cookie dough bites, my favorite dessert of all time. Then I made up a small snack plate, munching while I poured a glass of red wine from the box I kept under the counter.

I walked out onto the front deck and sat in one of the three dark blue Adirondack chairs, savoring the quiet around me. I heard a boat in the distance, the motor a whiny whir noise but otherwise there was nothing except the faint calls of birds and the splash of something swimming in the cove. The air had that dusty, leafy smell with just a faint tinge of wood smoke. Somebody probably had a fire going in a fireplace.

The cabin faced southwest and because of the surrounding terrain, it was protected from the main body of the lake, although the bay where it sat was almost half-a-mile wide and nearly that size in length, like a small lake in the lake. Behind me to the north was Canada, about twenty miles through hilly forests and untouched wilderness. The border undulated south here. Campers and fishermen often found themselves on one side or the other of The Line when they portaged and camped in the Boundary Waters.

I owned the two rocky peninsulas surrounding this small bay. Ahead of me to the west was a larger peninsula and around that peninsula was where my grandfather used to have his cabin. Now a huge six-bedroom mansion sat on that rocky outcropping, its windows facing the lake like some unblinking monster. It was three stories tall with decks and porches and two docks down by the lakeshore. If the wind blew right—or maybe I should say, blew wrong—I could hear the music from their parties.

Tension, stress and worry seeped out of me while I

munched on my salami and chips and sipped wine. There is a certain freedom in having no communication with the outside world. I had no obligation to check my email, answer a phone, or watch the latest television show or movie. It's odd how those supposedly enjoyable tasks can become chores when they're always pressing on you, always clamoring for attention.

I rested my head against the back of the chair and turned it slightly to look at the sunlight on the lake. That's when I heard the faint scrape of a footstep to my right on the rocky slope above the cabin.

Someone or something was moving almost silently through the trees surrounding my cabin. It could be an animal, but somehow I doubted it. It was too late in the day for daytime animals and too early for the nocturnal ones. Most critters avoided contact with humans and I'm sure any critters nearby knew I was around.

I edged forward in my chair and stood, setting my wine glass on the floor of the deck. I didn't give any indication that I heard anything. Instead, I went to the door, moving unhurriedly until I was inside. Then I raced into the dark bedroom, ducking around the door to the left and the night table. I grabbed the two-way radio. I kept it in my left hand and my Glock in my right. I turned to leave the bedroom.

And almost walked into a shotgun pointed at my stomach.

Chapter 4

Offense is the best defense.

My brothers drilled that into my brain time after time. Women were often afraid to be aggressive. *Don't be afraid. Be mad. Be bold. Be loud.*

I glared at the man in the doorway holding the shotgun. He was well lit by the lamp near the living room chair and so was his shotgun. He held it waist-high, not shoulder-high, so I had a view of the safety, which was on. "Who the hell are you and what are you doing in my house?" I demanded. I flicked on the two-way radio, which crackled to life.

The man's gaze went to the radio then to my gun. "Drop it," he said, gesturing with the shotgun.

I watched the move. He had his finger on the trigger guard, not the trigger. At least he knew how to handle it. "It's my house." I didn't move a muscle. "You drop it."

His dark eyes narrowed. He was young, with thinning blond hair under a dark blue billed hat, a pock-marked red complexion and a slender build. His black jacket and jeans let him blend in with the darkness in the doorway. "How do I know you're the owner?"

"Who are you and why do I have to prove it to you?" I kept my eyes on his face, using my peripheral vision to keep track of the shotgun, which had lowered slightly.

"Vivian? Everything okay there?" Kay's voice was loud in the silence of the cabin.

I lifted the radio to my lips. The guy tensed but he didn't raise the gun. I took that as a good sign. "No, it's not okay. Some guy just broke in to my cabin."

"I didn't break in," the guy said. "I'm guarding it."

"What the hell—Sy! Vivian has trouble. Get the boat out!" Kay's tone was brisk and had all the authority of a woman who raised three sons and didn't take crap from anybody.

"Wait a minute." The guy lowered the shotgun completely, letting it hang at his side. "Hold on, no need to get so upset here. I'm just guarding the cabin."

"Do you know anything about a guard here?" I said into the radio. I glared at the guy and he glared back at me, but I thought I saw worry or maybe uncertainty in his squinty eyes. I didn't raise my gun but he kept glancing at it. "Yes, I know how to use it," I said in answer to the unspoken question in his eyes. "And yes, I will."

Sy's voice crackled through the radio before the guy could answer. "Mr. Moneybags has somebody watching out for his place. Is that Bailey Court?"

The guy looked so relieved I almost laughed. "Yeah, it's me," he said. "Is that Sy Eckert?"

"He says he's Court," I spoke into the radio. "Young, blond, about six foot tall?"

"Yeah, that's him. Put him on the radio. I'll give him a piece of my mind." I could imagine Sy standing out on his deck, glaring across the lake at us through binoculars while he talked into the two-way radio.

"That's okay, Sy. It's a misunderstanding. I'll talk to Dewin about it when I see him." *Talk* wasn't what I would do. I would tear a strip of skin off my ex-husband when I set eyes on him.

"You want me to come over there and toss him off the deck?"

I smiled. "Thanks for the offer, but no. I'll send him packing."

"Okay. You need anything else, you call. We're right here."

I flicked the Off switch on the radio and tucked it into my back pocket. I kept my gun at my side. "You can leave now," I said. "And tell Dewin I don't need anybody keeping an eye on my house."

"Mr. Mervyn told me to watch out for this place special," Court said. "I was out in the boat, checking the shoreline and I saw the lights." He didn't look particularly worried that he had just trespassed into someone's house. In fact, he seemed pissed off that I was there. "I came around the land side, just in case somebody was here who shouldn't be."

"Somebody was here," I said. "Me. You're the one who shouldn't be here. I'll deal with Dewin. You leave." I nodded toward the door.

Court took my hint. "Yes, ma'am. Sorry for the interruption." He hurried through the room, moving so fast he almost tripped on the braided rug.

I followed him to the door, flipping on the outside light so I could watch him wend his way down the path above my steps leading to the cove. The motion light at the dock came on and the last I saw of him, he was walking through the woods along the shoreline. A few minutes later I heard a motor start.

I went back to the bedroom and put my Glock on the nightstand then I stepped out onto the deck through the bedroom door. Court was moving out into the lake, his high intensity light bobbing. I went back to the living room and shut off the lights so I could walk out to the deck and follow his progress into the lake.

When I was satisfied he was gone, I picked up my wine glass and plate and went back inside. So much for a nice, quiet evening, I thought gloomily. I locked the door, put a couple of logs in the fireplace and settled down for another glass of wine in the dark with only the firelight to keep me company. It took a long time for my pulse to return to normal and I had nightmares that night when I finally slept.

Consequently I was in a piss-poor mood at nine-thirty in the morning when I walked onto the dock and saw the dark gray clouds in the east. The weather turned gloomy overnight with rain splattering my windows while I slept. It wasn't raining now, but from the looks of the clouds I might be between two rounds of showers. I wiped off the boat seat with the towels I brought and checked the bottom, breathing a sigh of relief when I saw I didn't need to bail it out.

I dropped into the boat and buckled my life vest over my messenger bag, which was draped across my front. I eyed the lake warily while I tied on my scarf then I set off. In the bay it wasn't too choppy but once I cleared the peninsula, I saw whitecaps. I gritted my teeth, goosed the motor and got across as quickly as I dared, my stomach a flip-flopping mess by the time I docked at Sy's.

Kay left a note for me on the kitchen door. *Gone to town. Hope Bailey didn't do anything stupid, although scaring you like that is stupid enough. Talk with you later.*

I backed my Cooper out of its spot and was on the road just as rain started drizzling down in earnest. The chill in the air reminded me that this was the North Country, where winter often set in fast and hard.

I made a mental note to start winter-proofing the cabin. I could put the wooden shutters on the small screened porch and replenish the mothballs I sprinkled under the cabin near the supports to keep the critters at a distance. The solar panels on the roof would ensure steady electricity, enough to keep the baseboard heat on and the pipes from freezing. I would try to get there once a month during the winter and Sy would visit every few days to make sure things were fine. It was a system we'd used for decades and hopefully, please God, it would continue that way.

While I drove I replayed last night's encounter in my mind. Dewin knew I would be coming to the cabin in the fall because I always spent time there when the leaves changed. And he knew that I was armed and I was competent.

The fact that Dewin knew those two things made me wonder. What if last night's confrontation had gone differently? What if one or the other of us had shot at the other one? It would be very convenient if I was embroiled in a legal battle with the authorities about my use of a firearm. And it would be doubly convenient if Bailey Court shot me, thus ridding Dewin of the main impediment to his purchase of my cabin.

"You're a suspicious and cynical woman," I muttered. With good cause, I had to admit. My ex-husband was probably capable of just about anything to get what he wanted. He wanted me and he couldn't have me. So he'd take the next best thing—something

56

dear to me. If he could get it by hook or by crook, he would. I added another checklist item to ask my brother the lawyer about.

Twenty minutes later I rounded the final curve into Avalon. There were about a dozen cars parked on the two-block main street. I parked at the Queen and went in for coffee, a donut and a good gossip with the owners, a lesbian couple who owned the place almost since I could remember. Fifteen minutes later I walked into *Curiosity's.*

Like my store in Iowa, this was a small space, about fifteen feet wide and thirty long with three center sections that had what Sy called The Tourist Crap. Sweatshirts, T-shirts, books about the lake, local jams and foodstuff and other knick-knacks, many made by local artisans and craftspeople.

The remainder of the store held assorted oddments I acquired in my travels or were sent to me for consignment sales. Framed paintings, door stops, sets of china, figurines, a box of tools, a ten-foot-tall carved Indian statue, a bookcase of Nancy Drew and Hardy Boys books, a picnic basket full of doilies and linens— that all occupied the first four feet of space when you walked into the shop.

The rest of the store was the same, small groupings of objects here and there with room to walk between them. Sy's desk/checkout area was at the front of the store, near the window where he could look out and wave at people when they walked by. He sat on an ancient wooden desk chair which wobbled precariously every time he shifted his weight.

"I called Bailey Court and I told him what I thought of that stunt he pulled last night," Sy said the minute I walked through the door. "You should go to the police and report him and that asshole who hired him."

"No harm done," I said. "Thank God he knew how to handle a shotgun, though."

Sy's feet landed on the floor with a thud when he straightened, the chair almost tipping him out. "What the hell? He had a gun?"

"Yeah. The jerk walked right into my house." I dug my fingers into my damp curly hair and shook off moisture. "He told me Dewin wanted him to keep an eye on the cabin especially."

"Well, that's stupid. Everybody knows I keep an eye on the place. Why is Moneybags paying somebody to creep around your place? No offense, but there's nothing there to steal. I can see having somebody watch that hotel he calls a house, but your place? That reminds me. Some folks at the garage were talking. They said folks were out at Dewin's private dock, going to the house with cleaning supplies. Is Moneybags coming to town?"

"Good question." I knew the answer, of course. Every time I came to the cabin, Dewin showed up, too. He was probably paying somebody in Linn to keep an eye on me. Of course, knowing him, he might have a wiretap on my phone. I wouldn't put anything past that son of a bitch. "I'm sure I'll see Dewin and when I do, I'll discuss his so-called guard with him."

"You need any backup, you let me know." Sy said it very seriously and I knew he meant it. There was no love lost between the Lord of the Manor and the people in town. Dewin made a lot of enemies when he designed a multi-million-dollar house and imported all of the workmen, the materials and the craftsmen to build it. Not a penny of local money was used in its construction and that still rankled with folks in town.

"Thanks, Sy. It's a relief to know you're so close." I noticed an unusual package sitting on his counter. "What's that?"

Sy handed me a rectangular box beautifully wrapped in black cloth adorned with bright red peace symbols, fluorescent flowers and other symbols of the so-called Hippy Movement. It was about a foot long and half that wide and somewhat heavy. "A guy dropped this off this morning." He smiled broadly. "Insisted I make sure you get it."

I hefted the package. "I wonder who would leave me something. It's not my birthday." I examined the object. A square knot of cloth sat on top of the box, tied in such a way that it formed a rosette. Other than that, I saw nothing holding the cloth in place.

"He was anxious that you get it." Sy nodded thoughtfully. "Yeah. Anxious. Go ahead. Open it." He leaned forward, his shrewd brown eyes looking from me to the package.

I tugged at a corner of the rosette. The fabric slid away from the balsawood box it covered.

"How's that done?" Sy tipped forward to examine the fabric, which lay now on his desktop. He touched some of the creases. "It's like that origami stuff but with cloth."

I set the box down and flicked the tiny bronze clasp on the side, lifting the lid. Nestled on top of shredded red paper inside dark gold foil wrapping was a bottle of Hugel Riesling Jubilee 1998. "This is a really good wine," I said, touching the dark brown bottle. "I've had it before. It's very nice."

Sy peered into the box. "I like a red wine myself."

"This is sipping wine." I pulled out the small white pasteboard card tucked next to the bottle.

I owe you dinner, an abject apology and a chance to reciprocate. Able.

P.S. I figured out "Sunshine." It took some thought.

I smiled while I replaced the card and closed the box. I tried to refold the fabric so I could see how it was done, but somehow it didn't come out right.

"Seemed like a nice guy," Sy commented, once again resuming his devil-may-care posture and tipping back his chair. "He was here a few minutes ago."

"Really?" I glanced at the Betty Boop clock on the wall. It was ten-thirty. "When?"

"When I opened he came in. I mentioned that the Castle has a good breakfast."

The Castle was local-talk for the Camelot Café, which had a medieval motif. "Really?"

"Yep." Sy nodded toward the window in the general direction of the small restaurant next door. "He's probably still there."

"I should probably go over and say thank you." I smoothed back my hair, scowling when I felt how bouncy it was. The mist on the lake crossing had reinvigorated my curls. I glanced down at my outfit. I wasn't exactly styling today, with my faded jeans and dark blue flannel shirt and denim jacket. "I'll just drop in and say thanks. I'll be back in a minute."

"I'll be here," Sy said with a smile. "Not going anywhere. You take your time."

I started to leave then I remembered why Able

Leroy was in town, besides apologizing to me, that is. "You said that package is out at the Shack?"

Sy nodded. "Yep. You want to go check it out later?"

"Yeah, let's do. I want to get it priced and cleaned if needed. We've only got a few good weekends before the snow flies. If I'm going to sell it to somebody who vacations here, I want it ready to go as soon as I get an offer."

"Probably wouldn't hurt to get it checked before Moneybags gets here, too," Sy noted. "I saw on the shipping papers who owned it. Moneybags might make a stink about you buying something from somebody in the family."

"You know my family history too well, Sy." I'm sure he remembered the time a few years back when Dewin got in a snit because I bought some jewelry from his sister-in-law. It wasn't family heirlooms or anything. He just felt like making a fuss.

Story of my life, I thought as I left the shop and made a right turn. Ever since Dewin Mervyn came into my life thirty years ago, I was plagued by him like that damn white whale was plagued by Ahab.

I ducked under the awning to avoid the rain and walked into the Castle shaking droplets off my denim jacket. Most of the ten booths were occupied, but the three tables were empty. Able sat facing the front door at the second booth on the right. He wore a gray-black-and-red flannel plaid shirt, jeans and a heavy denim coat, fitting right in with the woodsy decor of the place. His dark hair was tousled, probably due to the baseball cap lying on the table next to his plate.

He smiled when he saw me, standing and sliding

out of the booth. "I'm happy to see you. Does this mean you accept my apology?"

My piss-poor mood evaporated. "Of course I do," I said.

"Join me for some coffee?" He gestured to the other side of the booth.

"I've had my quota for the day, but I'll take a glass of orange juice." I smiled at the waitress. "Just O.J. for me, Barb. A tall one."

"You got it. Good to see you back. Staying a while?" Barb's benevolent gaze went from me to Able then back to me and I could see the questions in her eyes. Barb's mother and my mother were old friends. My mother left town as soon as she possibly could but Barb's mother stayed, marrying her high school sweetheart. Barb did the same, but that marriage ended in divorce a few years back, leaving Barb with four children and a job as a waitress in the summer and on welfare in the winter.

There but for the grace of God go I, I thought. "Just here for a week or so," I said. "We're closing the store for the winter."

"I heard your ex is coming to town soon." She filled Able's coffee mug from the pot she held. "Funny how he always gets here about the same time you do."

"Yeah, how 'bout that." I shrugged. "I just can't get rid of him, I guess."

"Uh-huh," she said dubiously. I'm sure she wondered why any woman in her right mind would divorce a man who was handsome, wealthy and crazy in love.

"I do want to apologize," Able said, sipping his coffee.

Barb took the hint and walked away, coffee pot poised to fill mugs at the other booths on her way to the kitchen at the back of the cafe.

"I'm not in the habit of passing out with someone I've just met," Able said. "I can't handle gin. I'm fine with one martini, but two just knocks me for a loop." He smiled apologetically. "I think I was just having such a good time, relaxing with you and talking. Then, before I knew it, the second martini was gone and I was acting like an ass."

"It's okay," I assured him. "Wayne's martinis will knock anybody out."

"I didn't do anything stupid, did I?" Able asked, pushing his plate to one side and leaning forward, hands clasped around his coffee mug.

"Don't you remember?" I said it teasingly.

His eyes widened. "I didn't sing, did I?" He shook his head in despair.

"No, you didn't sing. You did talk about your job a bit."

His hands tightened on his mug. "Really? What did I say?"

"Oh, just that you hated it and you felt like a statistic." I tilted my head to one side, trying to remember his words. "Something about evaluating people or something and sometimes hurting people. We talked about how government funding can really mess with companies."

Able stared at me, his eyes puzzled. "I said that?"

"No, I did. You said something about how your decisions could affect people and I told you about software companies and how we used to have to wait for government funding." Now it was my turn to frown in puzzlement. "At least, I think we talked about that. Anyway, you weren't unpleasant at all, so don't worry about it."

"Well, I don't remember much, but I remember the bartender telling me about your brother." Able smiled ruefully. "He told me if I hurt you in any way both he and your brother would come after me and tear my arms off and beat me to a pulp with them."

I laughed out loud. "Wayne said that?"

Able nodded solemnly. "I believed him, too."

I smiled at Barb when she set my orange juice down in front of me. "Archer doesn't have a mean bone in his body," I told Able.

Barb grinned. "That's the truth. You look out for Leo, though. He's a rascal." She walked away, shaking her head and smiling.

"I take it your family is well known in these parts." He glanced around the small cafe.

"Yeah, we've spent a lot of time here over the years. When we were growing up, this was our summer place." I sipped my juice. "Thanks for the bottle of wine."

"I meant what I said." Able toyed with his coffee spoon, his dark eyes flickering to me and away. "I'll be happy to take care of you if you ever want to tie one on. It's the least I can do."

"I'll keep that in mind. How did you do that gift wrap?"

"It's Furoshiki. It's a Japanese folding technique. I had a close friend who was Japanese and he showed me how to do it." Able stared intently at the tabletop, his mouth narrowed.

"Not a pleasant memory?" I asked softly.

He frowned. "He was a very good friend. We worked together a long time. But he died. It was hard for his family. Hard for all of us, really, who worked with him. He was so young and his death was—well, it seemed so unfair."

"I'm sorry." It was obvious this friend's death still shook Able.

"No, I'm sorry. It seems like whenever we're together, I end up spilling my troubles to you. First my job, now my friends." He regarded me thoughtfully. "You have a way of pulling out my secrets, I think."

My phone pinged me from my purse. "Sorry." I pulled it out and checked the screen. "It's my To Do list. I need to call my brother on a landline while I'm here in town. I can never get a signal from my cabin."

"Do you want to use my phone?" Able reached in his shirt pocket and held out a smartphone. "I can get a signal just fine."

"Really?" I took it. Sure enough, he had five bars, where I only had one on my phone. "No, that's okay. I can use the phone in the store."

"Go ahead." He took the phone from me, tapped a few icons on the screen then handed it back. "I'll go pay the bill. Go ahead. It's the least I can do to repay you for all your help." He slid out of the booth and stood. "Take your time. I'm on vacation." He winked and headed for Barb, who watched us from behind the lunch counter.

"Thanks." I checked Ari's phone number in my contact list and tapped it in on Able's smartphone keypad. Ari's secretary answered. I identified myself and within seconds was talking to my older brother.

"Hey, bro, I need some help," I said.

"That's a first," he said. I could imagine him in his glass-walled office, looking out on the Manhattan streets. "Did you get that thing from Lib to sell? Where are you calling from?"

"I got it but I haven't sold it yet. I'm at the cabin. Listen, Sy told me about a consortium that's trying to buy out the landowners here." I gave him a quick lowdown on what Sy told me. "Can you look into it for me? Isn't there some environmental loophole we can use to stop wholesale development?"

"I'm sure there is," he said. I heard clicks on his keyboard in the background while he typed, probably taking notes. "We went through this when Dewin bought Grandfather's cabin. He had to adhere to environmental laws at the time. Speaking of which— did you know he's under investigation?"

"What?" I watched Able chat with Barb, laughing at something she said. Able was such an easy-going guy, so laid-back. And very sweet about the whole drunk incident.

"I heard from a friend, who heard from a guy, who heard from someone in Justice that there's an ongoing investigation about Dewin Software."

My attention snapped back to the phone. "What? Why?"

"I couldn't get details, but I have an idea about it based on some rumors I've heard floating around. Any company that writes code used by the U.S. government has to comply with U.S. copyright law. What if somebody at the company is selling the code on the black market?"

"That's ridiculous," I said automatically. "Every bit of code has to be verified and submitted through the legal department before it can be released. I remember what a pain in the ass it was."

"What do you mean, it's submitted?"

"Before a product is released, the project managers have to fill out all these evaluation forms to make sure the code complies with corporate and government regulations."

"So who verifies that what they say is right?"

I opened my mouth to reply then closed it. "I don't know," I admitted.

"You know as well as I do that Dewin's company is developing some cutting-edge stuff. That might be worth some real money. That place of his on the lake isn't far from Canada. What if he is doing something illegal? You know there's no way to track people going through the border there."

"Dewin doesn't need the money," I said, my thoughts tumbling over each other. How could someone steal a big piece of software code? Could someone do it?

Of course they could. Even as I questioned it, I could envision several ways to do it.

"Yes, he does need the money. He's in trouble financially." Ari spoke with all the assurance of someone in the know.

"Not."

"Yep. Dewin's in trouble or so I heard. The British economy and the Euro are in the toilet and his company is having trouble."

"That's impossible," I said. "Dewin is too savvy for that."

"Not savvy enough or so I hear. Hold on."

I stared at the scuffed laminate tabletop. I hadn't

been in close contact with Dewin for years, so I suppose anything was possible, but Dewin had a very astute financial mind. It was hard to believe he was in trouble.

Ari came back on the line. "I have to go to a meeting. I'll get back to you about the legality of this consortium thing. Is this the number I can reach you at?"

"Try my regular cell phone number or the store. I'm just borrowing someone's phone right now."

"Okay. Good to talk to you. Have a shore lunch for me, okay?"

"Will do." I tapped the End icon and set the phone down, frowning.

"Problems?" Able asked. I hadn't heard him, but now he stood next to the booth.

I handed him his phone. "I'm not sure."

"Well, if I can help, let me know." He smiled and moved to one side when I stood. "Any word on that sword and scabbard I'm interested in?"

"As a matter of fact, my store manager told me it arrived yesterday." I headed for the cafe's exit, pausing to wave good-bye to Barb. "I was hoping to go out to my storage site today and look it over."

"Mind if I tag along?" He held the door for me and I stepped out onto the sidewalk. The rain had stopped although the dark clouds overhead told me it would probably resume soon. I hunched my shoulders when a brisk wind whipped past us.

"I should probably look it over first," I told Able. Movement out of the corner of my eye caught my attention. A dark gray Porsche Cayenne SUV had just parked across the street. I stared, my stomach once again flip-flopping.

My ex-husband got out of the Porsche. He walked around the SUV and opened the passenger door. A stylish, slender woman stepped out, her tailored dark pants and chic fitted jacket like something out of a Woolrich catalog.

Dewin saw us and raised a hand in greeting.

"Speak of the devil," I muttered.

Chapter 5

Able followed my gaze. "Wow. I didn't realize we were doing a photo shoot for *Vanity Fair*. Had I known, I would have dressed appropriately."

I smiled at his wry comment, which was right on target. Dewin was, as always, elegantly handsome with his curly salt-and-pepper hair, neatly trimmed dark gray goatee and mustache and his aristocratic oval face. His gray tweed suit coat was perfectly tailored and his black jeans, dark gray shirt and black boots appeared fitted as well.

I eyed the woman, who matched Dewin in looks and style. Her black leather high-heeled boots made her his height, almost six-foot and she had long, shapely legs, amply displayed in her tight pants. Or maybe they were leggings or those "jeggings" that I'd seen advertised. They were so tight it was hard to tell. Her short dark jacket covered a loose lightweight green sweater and her blonde hair was upswept into an elegant chignon. A Coach bag, large enough to be a briefcase, dangled from one shoulder. It was hard to judge her age, although I guessed she was in her thirties.

They both moved with sinuous grace when they crossed the street, like movie stars on a red carpet or royalty approaching a palace. The effect was diminished when a disreputable looking mini-van puttered toward them. Dewin shot the driver a disgusted glare when he jumped out of the way.

"Brooks Brother," Able muttered. "Or maybe Ralph Lauren."

"Her, maybe," I conceded. "But Dewin always bought Gucci or Armani." I dug my hands into my Wrangler jacket pockets. "The closet in his Paris apartment is bigger than my living room in Linn."

Able shot me a quick, quizzical look. "His apartment? It wasn't yours, too?"

I shook my head. "When we were married, we lived in London and Chicago. He keeps apartments in Paris and Rome and he has a house in Athens. As well as the monstrosity out on the lake." I scowled at Dewin, who came to a stop in front of me. "You want to tell me why you hired some guy to patrol my bay?" I demanded.

"So pleasant to see you, Vivian." He had a rich, deep voice that carefully enunciated each word. He pronounced my name in the French style, *Vivi-anne.* "You're looking beautiful, as always."

"Cut the bullshit, Dewin. It's bad enough you're stalking me but now you're sending some poor townie to stalk me, too. The shotgun was over the top, even for you." I glanced at the woman but she didn't appear fazed by this accusation of stalking. If she was one of Dewin's new women, she either didn't care or she already knew about his penchant for tracking my every move.

In fact, she wasn't even paying attention. She eyed Able with a speculative gaze and he watched her warily, like a dog checking a stray cat he didn't know. When he heard the word *shotgun*, though, Able straightened, moving slightly ahead of me, turning so he blocked Dewin. "What? Someone tried to shoot you?"

For some reason, I found his defensive move cute. It was a long time since anyone tried to defend me. First the alley behind the shop and now this. Able was shaping up to be a knight in shining armor.

"I'm sure it wasn't that dramatic," Dewin said, his voice chilly and his eyes on Able, who now blocked any access to me.

"No, he just broke into my cabin, scared the crap out of me and claimed he was there to protect me." I glared at Dewin. "On your orders."

"A misunderstanding. I'm sure he just took his duties too seriously." Dewin turned to the woman who stood next to him, obviously dismissing my concerns about the intruder. "This is Faye Morgan, CEO of Scabbard Software Securities. Faye, this is—"

"Vivian DuLac," I interrupted. "And Able Leroy." I nodded toward Able, who regarded both Dewin and the woman with equal amounts of distrust and amusement.

"It's a pleasure to meet you," the woman said, extending a hand. "You have quite a reputation in Dewin's company."

"All positive, I'm sure." I shook her hand, my red knit gloves looking very bright against her chic black leather ones.

She turned to Able. "What are you doing here, Arthur?"

I blinked widely. "You know each other?" I asked Able.

"You're not the only one with a complicated

family tree," he said, his eyes locked on the woman. "Faye is my stepsister. How's Margo doing? And Morris?"

"Funny you should ask. Margo retired and Morris is CIO of Scabbard. He's flying in today."

Able laughed, a short, bitter sound. "Seriously?"

"You didn't answer my question. What are you doing here?" Faye Morgan's gaze went to me and I smiled innocently.

"I'm on vacation." Able finally turned to me. "It was such a surprise to find out that Sunshine and I have cabins just a mile or so from each other." He smiled when he saw Dewin's frown at the use of my family nickname.

I smiled, too. It was fun to see Dewin look peeved. It didn't happen often. "It was a pleasant surprise." I moved so I was closer to Able, nudging him with my elbow. "I'll show you mine if you'll show me yours."

"Deal. In fact, I was just going to ask you to visit later today and I'll cook dinner for you. It's the least I can do." He winked at me, making sure Dewin saw it. "Maybe I can soften her up for negotiations."

"Negotiations?" My ex-husband straightened, his dark eyes narrowing. "What are you negotiating?"

"Sunshine has something I want to buy. And I'm afraid she'll make me pay an arm and a leg for it." Able checked his watch. "In fact, we were just on our way to look at it."

I silently blessed him for his ploy. "Yes, we were." I waved to Sy, who watched us out of the *Curiosity's* window. "I'll let Sy know we're heading out there. Do you want to drive, or should I?" I glanced down Main Street. "Where's your car?"

Able jerked a thumb over his shoulder. "In the back parking lot. I'll drive. I owe you."

Dewin smiled. "Maybe we can tag along."

I shook my head. "No way. I haven't even had a chance to examine the item thoroughly. I don't want a bunch of people crowding me."

"We're hardly a bunch of people." His smile started to look forced.

"No," I said firmly. "We don't need the company." Sometimes rudeness was the only thing he understood.

Dewin ignored my attempt at a brush-off. "It's good we ran into you. We need to discuss a few business matters." He glanced at the dark clouds overhead. "Perhaps we can get together at my house this evening to go over things."

Dewin's McMansion was only a half-mile from my cabin, as the crow flies. It was more like a mile or more along the lake, which was the only way to get there at night because the overland route through the trees along the marked trail was barely visible even in daylight.

"I don't like boating at night," I said. "As you well know."

"I'll send a boat for you," Dewin said. "What time, Faye? Six? Six-thirty?"

"Arthur and Miss DuLac are dining together," Morgan said smoothly. "We don't want to interrupt their evening plans." She turned to me. "We're considering merging our companies. We're having an Executive Summit at Dewin's house. A few people are flying in from my Chicago office tomorrow. We kick off our planning meetings tomorrow night and continue them on Wednesday and Thursday." She tilted her head to one side as though considering an idea. A tendril of blonde hair wisped around her ear. "Maybe you should sit in. After all, you know the product almost as good as anyone." Then she turned to Able. "Your input might be valuable as well."

"I'm sure it's changed since I worked there," I said. "It's been fifteen years."

"Some of your ideas and concepts were truly innovative. We're always looking for the next great idea." Morgan smiled, revealing perfect white teeth. "I'm sure we can benefit from your presence around the conference table." She looked at Able when she said it.

I ignored her pretty smile. "The fishermen aren't going to be too happy about a seaplane landing and taking off on the lake."

"Seaplane? Really?" Able said. "We're in bass and walleye season, you know. Where do they land?" he asked me.

"Arthur, perhaps you can bring Vivian to my house for dinner this evening," Dewin said. "That way you can inspect where my plane will be landing to make sure it won't disturb your fishing plans." He and Morgan exchanged looks and she nodded thoughtfully. "We can discuss our ideas with both Arthur and Vivian and get their input before our meetings start."

"I don't think that's such a good—"

"Come for cocktails at six." Morgan glanced warily at the sky when light rain began to fall. "We need to get to the house, Dewin, and see if the plane arrived with our supplies. Morris should be there by now, getting things organized, but I want to make sure we're all set for our meetings tomorrow night." She took a step away, back toward their car.

"We'll see you tonight," Dewin said. "I can't wait

to get caught up on what's happening with your brothers." He turned to follow Morgan.

"We're not coming," I said flatly.

"I don't mind," Able said. "I can boat you over there. No problem."

"There, you see? No problem." Dewin kissed me quickly on the cheek. "So good to see you again. Isn't it amazing how we always run into each other like this?" His dark blue eyes fixed on mine with flinty determination. "Amazing." He turned and put a hand under Morgan's elbow, steering her across the street.

"I don't really want to spend the evening with my ex-husband," I snapped.

"Well, it was either have me take you or they would send somebody. Then you'd be trapped there for hours. This way I can say I'm not comfortable being out on the lake too late and we can leave early." Able frowned, peering past me and ignoring my frosty expression. "I think the gentleman would like to chat with you."

I turned. Sy was in the store window, gesturing me inside. "You didn't need to volunteer to take me," I said over my shoulder to Able. "If you hadn't I could just ignore his request."

"Excuse me, but I don't think that's true." Able followed me into the shop. "Your ex-husband doesn't look like a person who can take no for an answer."

"Trust me. He's had to take a no answer from me more times than I can count."

"Really?"

I turned so fast Able walked right into me. "Don't get snide with me," I warned.

He held up his hands. "Sorry, but, well, you have

to admit, it sounded funny." His mouth quirked in a half-smile.

I tried to frown at him, but I was having a hard time repressing a smile. I went to Sy where he stood behind his desk. "I suppose you saw that the asshole is in town."

"Yep. Kay called. Said the plane landed about an hour ago. I gave her the package, like you asked." Sy spoke to Able, nodding toward the desk, where the box still sat.

"Thanks. I appreciate that." Able touched my arm. "I'm sorry, but I did what I thought was best. If you want, I'll call him and cancel."

"Cancel what?" Sy asked.

I looked past him to the street where Dewin was backing the Porsche out of his parking space. "I got the royal summons to the palace tonight. I refused, but then Able volunteered to drive me, so now I'm stuck."

Able held out his hand. "I'm Able Leroy, by the way."

"Sy Eckert." Sy shook Able's hand then regarded me. "Good idea to go over there and schmooze. Maybe you can get a handle on what Moneybags is up to. You know—be a spy in the enemy camp. And at least this way you don't have to be out on the lake after dark alone." Sy nodded to Able. "Thanks. I'd worry like hell if she was out there."

"Will you cut out the poor little me talk?" I snapped. "It's not like I'm incompetent or something. I just don't like boating at night."

"Uh-huh," Sy said, his tone clearly showing he was simply humoring me.

"That's not unusual," I insisted.

"Living on a lake and being afraid of the water is a tad unusual," Sy pointed out.

"You're afraid of the water?" Able asked.

I threw up my hands. "Do you want to look at that sword now?"

"Seriously? You have a lakeside cabin and you don't like to—"

"Fine. I'll go out and look at it without you." I made for the door.

"Don't you want to take your wine with you?" Sy asked.

"I'll get it later," I fumed. I grabbed the door and emerged into a downpour. "Damn it." I huddled under the awning while I fumbled in my bag for my car keys.

"I'm sorry. I seem to keep pissing you off." Able emerged from the store behind me. "I can drive. My car's just out back."

I spied my car, halfway down the street in the rain, which was coming down in sheets. "Okay." I pushed past him back into the store. "We're going to the Shack. I'll be back in an hour or so and we can do inventory then."

"Whatever works for you is fine." Sy resumed his seat behind the desk and pulled out a thick book. "I'll get caught up on my reading."

"He's been reading *War and Peace* since I've known him," I commented, weaving my way through the crowded aisles, pausing once to straighten a display of T-shirts.

"It's probably not real busy now at the shop."

"Mondays are always slow because most tourists go back home on Sunday nights. We'll get a few leaf peepers, but that's almost done. In another week it'll be a ghost town until snowmobile season." I turned to rearrange some postcards on a rack.

Able peeked into the Sauna Selection, a closet that contained all sorts of items useful in a sauna. "I wish I knew this place was here when I had my sauna."

"A sauna? At your cabin?" I stopped at the back door.

"My ex-wife and I had a place on Pelican Lake. She got it in the divorce. We had a nice sauna and a hot tub right off the lake." He shrugged. "Somebody else owns it now. She sold it and moved to California."

"Well, that's probably a blessing. At least she doesn't appear on your doorstep every time you turn around," I said sourly.

"Yeah, but she took the kids with her. And my ex-best friend." Able moved past me. "Come on. I'm parked just a few feet away." He went out into the rain, his shoulders hunched.

"Open mouth, insert foot," I muttered. It sounded like Able still had a few wounds left over from his divorce. Once again, I thanked God I didn't let Dewin talk me into having kids. What a disaster that would have been.

I followed Able, almost running him down when he paused by the passenger door of his SUV. He opened it for me and I jumped inside, pulling the door closed behind me. Able raced around the car and got into the driver's side, his denim jacket dark with dampness. "Damn, it's getting cold," he said, touching the keyless ignition. "We might get snow tonight."

"Not the sort of night we should be out boating," I said. "I'll call Dewin and cancel."

"I have a covered boat." Able turned in his seat to

look over his shoulder and saw my peeved expression. "I do. It's a launch. We'll be fine."

"No, we won't be fine. You might be fine, but I won't be. I'll be stuck talking to my ex-husband for hours." I regarded him thoughtfully. "And you'll be chatting with your stepsister. Did you know she was here?"

"Of course not." He said it a little too quickly to be believable. "This is the first I've heard about the merger."

"Merger? Oh, the two companies. Do you know anything about the company she works for? What kind of software do they do?"

"I know a lot about it. I built the company from the ground up before I was ousted." Able's voice was distinctly bitter now. "Where am I going?" He backed out of his parking space.

"Go right here then left at the stop sign." I ran my hand through my damp hair, shaking my curls out of my eyes. "What do you mean you were ousted?"

"My ex-wife, Gwynne, got a big chunk of company shares in our divorce. She and my ex-best friend collaborated with my stepsisters, Margo and Faye. They arranged for me to be removed as CEO." Able's hands opened and closed on the steering wheel.

I wondered if he imagined throttling someone. "When did this happen?"

"The divorce? We split up almost fourteen years ago, but it took a while for Gwynne to file for divorce." His lips thinned into a tight line. "It was a big flipping mess. She ran away with Lenny, but he got her best friend pregnant. So he was going to do the right thing and marry Elaine, but in the end, Elaine told him to take a hike. So he went back to Gwynne, then she filed for divorce and I contested it and—" Able shook his head. "A mess."

"Wow. I'm sorry. Compared to that, mine was easy." I stared at the rain-soaked landscape, the gloomy weather a match for my memories. "I married Dewin for all the wrong reasons and as soon as I realized it, I tried to end the marriage. But he just wouldn't take no for an answer."

"I told you so," Able said with a grin, making the turn at the stop sign. "What did your manager mean about being a spy in the enemy camp?"

"Sy said some corporation is trying to buy out homeowners on the lake front. He thinks Dewin is behind it."

"Is he? Why would he want to buy land here?"

"Maybe he's going to put in a fancy resort or something." I dug into my bag, finally finding my key ring. "Go straight for two blocks then make a right."

"That could be useful. A resort would bring in some good money, wouldn't it?"

"Not if he does it the way he handles his house. He didn't use a single local person to build it and he doesn't do any of his shopping here. What if he builds some kind of destination resort and they fly people in?" That was exactly the kind of thing Dewin would do I could imagine my little peninsula being the last green place on the entire shoreline, surrounded by a grotesque Disneyland theme park touting the Great Outdoors.

Able was silent, mulling that over while he drove. "Then maybe Sy was right. Maybe you do need to find out what he's up to. And I want to find out what my stepsister is planning for my company."

"It's not yours anymore."

He shot me an angry glare. "I still care what happens to it."

I avoided his eyes by staring ahead. "There. On the right."

"Wow. Can't miss it, can you?" Able pulled off the road onto the gravel lane between tall pines. Straight ahead was The Shack, a bright red metal building like the kind you see in the country all the time. Instead of machinery, mine housed, well, stuff. It had a double-wide white front door and two white shuttered windows above, giving the building the appearance of a wide-eyed face.

Able pulled into the front gravel parking area near the double doors. I started to hop out but he put a hand on my arm. "I have an umbrella. Hang on."

"The rain's letting up."

"Just wait. No reason to get wet if you don't have to." He reached behind me into the back seat then got out of the car, jogging around to hold the umbrella above me when I opened the car door on my side.

He kept it over me while we splashed through puddles to the front of the building. I had my key ready and got the lock and padlock undone in record time. "Aren't you worried about break-ins?" Able asked while I slid the door open.

We ducked into the building and I flipped on the lights before pulling the door closed behind us and entering my code into the security panel. The rain made a steady patter on the metal roof, loud enough to be noticed but not enough to be intrusive.

"I have motion lights and door sensors hooked to the police in town. And when we built it, my brother gave me some specs on what to do. We added wire mesh at ground level and heavy-duty plywood."

Able bent down to examine the boards and mesh on the lower half of the interior walls. "That should stop anybody from cutting through the metal walls," he admitted, leaning the umbrella against the wall so it could drip on the concrete floor.

"I'm not too worried." I blew on my hands. "I'm not going to turn on the heat. It takes a while to warm up. I'll get here early tomorrow and get it started then we can look at the sword in better light and in warmth, if you're still interested."

"Oh, I'm interested," Able murmured behind me.

"You haven't even seen it." I maneuvered my way through the maze of furniture, toys and bedframes. I turned when Able didn't answer. He was watching me, a thoughtful expression on his face. "What?"

He shook his head. "Nothing. This place looks like something out of that *American Pickers* show." Able stooped to examine a claw-foot bathtub. "How do you keep track of it?"

"I have an inventory. Plus photos." I pointed to the floor. About a foot from where he stood was a red painted X. "I stand in each spot and take a slow video with my camera, panning three hundred and sixty degrees. There's a spot every ten feet."

Able peered ahead. "There's a method to your madness," he murmured. "Where do you get it all?"

"Whenever somebody is tearing down an old house, I get in first and see what I can salvage. And sometimes people call me and ask me to sell stuff for them. I have several items on consignment." I edged around a stack of fence posts, my gaze fixed on the big workbench at the back of the building and the long, rectangular wooden crate sitting there. "That must be it."

"Are those authentic or reproductions?"

I turned. Able stared at the dozen or so framed travel posters hung on the walls. They were all two-by-three feet rectangles, all in the Art Nouveau style. "They're originals," I said. "My mother collected them."

"It's quite a collection." He peered at the *Normandie* poster depicting the massive ocean liner full-front. "It must be worth a lot."

"Yes and no. I can get buyers for individual ones, but I won't break up the collection. Of course, they're not for sale, so it doesn't matter." I reached the workbench. The pine box was about five feet long and three feet wide and two deep. I lifted one corner. It was heavy, too.

This part of the Shack had several large workbenches where I could set out items to examine under the higher-wattage lights above. I started to clear newspapers off the table to give me an uncluttered surface to work on.

"Why aren't they for sale?"

"Sentimental value," I said, moving a box of doorknobs to one side. "Mom grew up in Duluth and she hated it. She told me once that she saw those posters in a magazine when she was a teenager and she swore she'd visit each place on the posters. And I think she did."

"Good to have a goal," Able commented.

"It was motivation for her, that's for sure." I went to the crate and lifted one end. "Help me with this, okay?"

He stepped forward and took the other end. Between the two of us we got it moved to the empty wooden workbench. I grabbed a crowbar and began prying off the lid, carefully working my way around the perimeter, Able watching me.

"You know, your ex-husband and Faye remind me of that Eagles song. *Life in the Fast Lane.*" He hummed a few bars of the song.

I removed the last nail. "What?"

"He was brutally handsome and she was terminally pretty."

I laughed out loud. "Yeah, I think you're right. She's a good match for him, although she's probably too young." Then I snorted. "Like that's ever stopped him."

"She's forty-five. I don't think that's too young, but it's a moot point. She has a lover."

Lover? An old-fashioned term and one I hadn't heard used very often. "She looks like she can handle herself. A lot of people find Dewin intimidating."

"You mean a lot of men?" He moved closer to me, his eyes on the box.

I shrugged. "Well, yeah."

"So he's rich, handsome and polished. Can he gut a deer in the woods? Does he know how to make the perfect boilermaker? Can he catch his limit fishing for bass on the lake?" Able grinned. "Those are important things. Suits and cars—" He snapped his fingers. "So what?"

"I like the way you think."

Able carefully edged his way around a stack of hubcaps to stand next to me. "And, of course, the most important thing. You know—the woman thing." He looked at me sideways, his eyes snapping with laughter.

"No, I don't. What is that?"

He put his lips against my ear and whispered, "How to keep her happy in bed."

I drew back. "Really? And you think you know how to do that?"

He nodded solemnly then crooked his finger, drawing me closer. I felt his breath on my ear when he whispered, "Don't steal the covers."

I laughed again. "You have the right priorities. And speaking of covers—let's see what we have here." I lifted the lid off the box and set it to one side then took some pictures with my phone. A manila envelope was immediately inside. I pulled it out and checked the contents. "The paperwork," I said, skimming through the dozen or so pages of text and photographs detailing the provenance of the sword. It appeared to be complete, but I'd have to go through it in detail later. I tucked it into my messenger bag that I dropped on the floor.

Able leaned forward when I pulled off the fitted foam casing to reveal a sword in a leather scabbard nestled into a customized velvet surround. The grip of the sword was black and worn-looking in contrast to the cross-guard and pommel, which were silver and incised with intricate lacework, entwined with flowers and symbols of some kind.

The scabbard was about six inches wide and tooled with an elaborate floral design etched into the sturdy leather. I touched it, running a finger along the flowers. It felt as solid as wood and was burnished a deep mahogany color. "Beautiful craftsmanship. I don't even see a seam." I snapped some more pictures.

"It's more than three hundred years old," Able said softly. "Maybe older."

"That's impossible. A scabbard couldn't remain in such good shape for that long." I reached into the box to pull out the scabbard and sword.

"Let me. Please." Able stepped in front of me and before I could stop him, he pulled scabbard and sword out of the box. He leaned back, grasped the scabbard in his right hand and drew out the sword with his left hand, all in one fluid motion. The blade shone brightly, looking as if it was made yesterday and not centuries earlier.

Able lifted it easily, apparently unsurprised by its weight and heft. I've handled enough swords in my day to know that each one is individual, with unique balance. Able brought the sword up flawlessly in a classic salute, the blade vertical in front of his face. He smiled at my startled expression. "I've missed handling it," he said.

Once again I realized that I was all alone with Able Leroy. First his hotel room, now here, miles from anyone and him with a weapon in his hand. Either I was losing my sense of safety or I trusted him. It was years since I trusted anyone, so that must mean I was losing my sense of safety.

Able laughed. "I practiced for hours with this blade. Other kids learn to play football. I learned fencing and swordplay. Maybe that's why I never got a date in high school."

I grinned at his self-deprecating comment. Okay. Maybe I was starting to trust him.

His cell phone rang. "Sorry. I'm expecting a call."

He carefully sheathed the sword and set it back in the box then he pulled his phone from his pocket and wandered to the back door, standing there to talk. I resumed my examination of the sword, pulling it partway out of the scabbard to look the blade and taking more pictures, some close-up. I couldn't see any nicks or chips in the metal, which was amazing given its age. I had an appraiser I worked with in Duluth, so now that I knew it was a viable piece of inventory, I'd call him and ask him to examine it.

I eyed Able while he talked on his phone. He wasn't handsome, but he was attractive in a boy-next-door, plain sort of way. Able reminded me of Michael J. Fox or that other actor, what's-his-name, who always played the sidekick to a big star. You didn't really notice him until you got to know him and then you realized that he really was, well, a nice guy.

Able turned and caught me eyeing him. I pretended to stare into the box but I was really just thinking about Able and how he had appeared in my life. When he finally rejoined me, he seemed worried.

"Problems?" I asked, putting the lid back on the box and tapping in four nails to hold it loosely in place.

"Nothing big. I have to take care of a couple of things this afternoon. Can I come back to your store and get you later on?"

"I should get my boat back to my cabin," I said. "I'll need it tomorrow."

"We'll tie it to mine and I'll tow it. Tell you what. I'll do my errands then run back to my place and change. Do you want to meet at your store?"

"Why don't you meet me at Sy's house? That's where I dock." I went to a map of the lake posted on the back door. "Sy's right here on Cador Bay. His dock is under his upper porch. I'll tell him to run up the Iowa Hawkeye flag so you know where to go."

"Perfect. I'll meet you there at five, okay? We can drop your boat at your cabin then we'll go deal with Moneybags and the Witch."

I grinned at his apt nicknames. "That should be fine. We'll examine the sword more closely tomorrow, if that works for you." I took my messenger bag with the documentation for the sword and started for the door.

"Sounds good." Able followed me to the front of the building. "I'm sorry if I jammed you up by volunteering to drive you to his place. I promise we can leave early. I don't have any problem pretending to be scared of the lake at night." He grabbed his umbrella. "Don't think we'll need this."

"It's not so much that I'm scared." I gestured him ahead of me through the front door. "It's just that the lake is so deep and when it's dark—"

"You don't have explain," he interrupted. "I know what you mean. I just try not to think about it. I suppose that's one way to handle fear. Just don't think about it." He waited for me to lock up then we walked to his SUV. "I'm curious to see your cabin. Maybe tomorrow you can come on out to mine and I'll cook dinner."

Good heavens. Once again I was going to be alone with Able Leroy in the middle of nowhere with no one else around. I took a deep breath as I considered it.

Well, life is risk, right? I turned and smiled at him. "That sounds like a plan."

I sure hoped I wouldn't regret it.

Chapter 6

Able met me as promised at Sy's house a little after five in the afternoon. The rain, thank God, quit and I caught a glimpse of blue sky through the clouds on the horizon. Able and Sy tied my boat to the back of Able's twenty-five-foot fishing boat, which had a windshield and a heavy tarp-and-plastic roof that kept the front half of the boat dry.

Kay and I watched their activities from the dock. "He seems like a nice enough man, but I still worry," she said.

"Dewin has a landline so once we get there I'll call and let you know we arrived fine."

"It's not that so much. It's afterward, when he drives you back to the cabin."

I already gave that concern some thought. "Tell you what. I'll call you when we leave Dewin's place. And I'll use the signal once I get to the cabin."

Kay nodded so vigorously her curls bobbed in the breeze. "Good. On-off two, on-off two, on, is that right?"

"Yep." I put an arm around her shoulders and gave her a quick squeeze. "Thanks for worrying."

"Once a mom, always a mom. You have a good time."

"Yeah, right. A night with Dewin."

"And him." Kay nodded to where Sy and Able

were talking next to his boat, Sy gesturing toward my peninsula and probably giving Able the best directions for getting there. "Like I said. He seems like a nice man."

I walked out on the dock to join the two men. Able had changed into black jeans and a brown sweater under a heavyweight windbreaker. He jumped down into his boat and went forward to the wheel. I wrapped my scarf around my head and Sy handed me my life preserver from my boat. I slipped it on then Sy helped me down into Able's boat, keeping a tight grip on my hand until I was steady.

"You kids have a good time," he said, tapping the roof of the boat lightly. "There might be rain later, so take it slow."

"I will," Able said, holding out his hand. I clasped it and he pulled me to the swivel seat positioned next to his in the stern. "Ready?"

I tucked my messenger bag on the floor at my feet. "Yep. I'll talk to you later, Sy."

He waved while we pulled away from the dock. I turned back and saw Kay put her left hand with crooked fingers to her head in the universal symbol for *call me*. I waved an acknowledgement.

Able piloted us out into the lake. "You're calling her later?"

"Yep. I promised I'd check in."

He nodded, eyes going right and left to look for boat traffic. "Makes sense. You're out here with a strange man."

"Yep." I figured I didn't need to elaborate. He understood.

I realized that was odd. I was accustomed to my

brothers talking about safety and common sense. But Able was a stranger. Most men just didn't know or didn't think about the fact that a woman had to consider things like where to walk at night, how to handle being alone with a stranger, or something as simple as walking to her car after hours from a job.

"I want that sword," he said. "Name your price."

"I don't negotiate on open water," I said with an attempt at a laugh. "I'm at a big disadvantage."

Able shot me a quick glance. "Okay. Just promise me I have right of first refusal."

"I can do that," I conceded. I turned to our right where a fishing boat loomed on the horizon. "They're going pretty fast."

"Yep." He slowed, letting the faster boat zip by in front of us. "How long have you been divorced?"

I clung to my seat while his boat bobbed in the waves. "Twenty years. We got married when I was twenty and we were married for about ten years. We set up his company together."

Able glanced at me with a wry smile. "Young, struggling couple working together for a common dream?"

I shook my head, the wind grabbing the ends of my scarf and making them flap. I tucked them back into my jacket. "Dewin always had backing from his father, so we weren't exactly struggling. But it was a struggle to develop software twenty years ago. Think about it."

Able was quiet for a few minutes then he got the boat going forward again when the waves subsided. I silently blessed him for that. I knew his boat could handle the bouncing, but I knew that I couldn't. "Yeah, programming back then was a lot different than now.

Did you work on the search engine project when you were there?"

"That's about all I worked on. Back then we didn't have a lot of other irons in the fire." I would never forget those eighty hour weeks, sleeping in the office and hacking code at all hours of the day and night. It was the best of times and the worst of times, I guess.

"That search engine was the basis for all the ones that followed," Able said.

I grinned. "Yeah. My royalty checks still prove that."

"Lucky you."

"I earned it," I said with some pride. I focused on the lake in front of us, watching Able in my peripheral vision while he steered. Unlike my little utility boat that had to be controlled from the back by maneuvering the motor, Able's boat had front steering and an actual dashboard. It seemed steadier than my boat, but of course it was a lot bigger, too. The boat was dinged up and well used. "Do you fish a lot?"

"As much as I can. There's some fishing around Des Moines, but nothing as good as here." He drove with confidence, eyes constantly scanning the lake.

"How long have you had a place on Gawain Bay?" I swiveled the chair to the right. Gawain started about a half-mile in that direction, to the north of an outcropping of land.

"Almost fifteen years. I got it after my divorce. I used to bring my kids here for summers when they were little. I got them at Christmas and for a month in the summertime. The rest of the time they were in California with their mom."

He spoke about it easily but I thought I detected an

undercurrent of nostalgia, or maybe longing. "How old were they when you got divorced?"

"My son was nine and my daughter was only six. Gwynne's husband was as much a father to them as I was, I guess. They knew him, of course, because he used to be a friend of mine."

I considered how to answer that and decided honesty was the best policy. "Well, that means they were lucky. They had two fathers who cared about them."

Able laughed. "Now I know why they call you Sunshine. You find a ray of light even in the darkest thing. It's not just the song, I guess."

"You figured that out, hmm?"

He hummed a few bars of *Age of Aquarius.* "Yep. Took me a minute. But it's not just the song. You have that philosophy, don't you?"

"No use crying about the rain," I said.

He sang softly, "Always look on the bright side of life."

I laughed. "Are you a *Spamalot* fan, too?"

"Absolutely." He slowed the boat. "Where should I dock? Anything to look out for?"

I straightened in surprise. We had somehow gotten three-quarters across the lake and were approaching my cabin. How did he do it? I was totally distracted and unaware of my fear while he drove. "I usually tie my boat on the left side of the dock. There are some submerged rocks, but they're right against the shore."

"Okay. I'll pull up on the right side and I'll move your boat to the left once we've docked." He made a small adjustment when another boat crossed behind us, causing a wake. I barely felt it in his larger boat. In my utility craft I'd be swaying and clinging to the sides.

Able approached the dock, cutting power at exactly the right moment. We bumped against the planking and he had us moored and steady before I was barely turned around. He helped me out then he unhooked my boat and pulled it around to the other side of the dock and secured it. I handed him my life jacket and scarf and he tucked them into their compartment on my boat.

"Do you have a life jacket I can use when we go to Dewin's place?" I asked, leading the way up the steps to my cabin.

"Sure. I should probably wear one, too. Seeing you put one on reminded me. I guess I take it for granted that everything will be okay when I'm on the lake."

I grabbed a couple of logs from the stack and continued upward. "I never take anything for granted on the lake." I tapped in the security code for the door and we entered the living room. I dropped the logs near the fireplace and put my bag on the coffee table. "I'm going to change clothes then we can go to the palace."

"Okay." Able wandered toward the kitchen. "Nice place."

I headed for the bedroom. "Have a seat. It'll only take me a minute." Then I remembered my manners. "Do you want a drink?"

He shot me a reproving look. "I'm driving. No booze for me."

I blew out an exaggerated sigh of relief. "Glad to hear it." I closed the door and quickly changed out of my jeans and flannel shirt into nicer jeans and a sweater. I examined my face in the bathroom mirror and dabbed on some powder and mascara then rejoined Able in the living room. He held one of my family pictures that usually sat on the end table.

"That was fast," he said, setting the picture back in its spot.

"I'm low maintenance. I would usually take a gift for the host, but since I was coerced into going, I'm not going to." I flicked on the light over the stove and the one near my armchair then went to the door, grabbing a windbreaker from the hook nearby.

"That's okay. I've got it covered." Able left first, waiting for me on the deck.

"Really? You brought a gift for Dewin?"

"And one for you. Seemed the least I could do since I sort of blundered you into going."

I smiled at that so-true description. "You brought me a gift? Where is it?"

"You'll see." Able followed me down the steps to the dock and helped me into his boat then cast off the lines. "Here's your life jacket." He handed me a battered old jacket, which I dutifully buckled on. Then he pulled one on too, but didn't buckle it. "Which way?" he asked, backing away from my dock.

I gestured toward the way we'd come. "We have to go around the peninsula there and then through another bay and around another peninsula. So go south then north then eventually we'll go east again. You can stick pretty close to the coastline. The lake depth drops off."

Able steered where I pointed and I took advantage of his distraction to shoot covert looks around the interior of his boat. I didn't see anything like a gift, though. I turned again to face the front and caught him watching me.

"You won't find it," he said with a grin. "I have a couple of hiding places on this boat."

I pretended nonchalance. "I was just curious, that's all."

"Is that why you named your store *Curiosity*?" He kept the boat well clear of the shoreline, which was reassuring but also nerve wracking. On the one hand, I knew we wouldn't hit any rocks, but on the other hand, it meant we were over deeper water.

"I named it for a dog I had who used to come to the store with me. His name was Curiosity. He died after I moved to Iowa and it seemed like a fitting tribute to name my second store after him, too." I smiled at the memory. "He was a good dog, really. He did kill a cat once, but the cat was feral and meaner than a snake. I didn't blame Curiosity for doing it."

I eased my hands down to grip the sides of my seat. This part of the peninsula was very hilly, with steep, rocky bluffs overlooking the lake. "Go straight north now, around the point and across the small bay there. I always imagine I'm going around Italy right about here. My peninsula is a little heel and we're going to the other peninsula, the toe of the boot."

Able made the turn smoothly, leaving the protection of my small cove to motor into the larger lake. We were silent for several minutes while he negotiated the choppier waters. "This is a good fishing spot. I hope your ex isn't landing a plane around here."

"Sorry to disappoint you, but he is. You'll see once we get around the point." I stared up at the rocky land on my right. "I always worry a boulder or two might fall down."

Able glanced at the shore. "They've been there for thousands of years. I think they'll probably stay there. How much of this do you own?"

"From the shoreline to the interior, a mile or so. My property line ends right about…" I leaned forward again. "Right about here." We rounded the point of the 'toe.' "My grandfather owned this peninsula and my grandmother owned the other one. I bought some of the land from my mother's brother, but he sold off the shoreline to Dewin."

"Awkward." Able piloted us into the next cove.

"Awkward doesn't cover it," I said grimly. "There it is."

Able peered up through the windshield. "Whoa."

"Yeah." I tugged my life jacket tighter. "How 'bout that."

Dewin's mansion sat on a rocky bluff about thirty feet above the shoreline. It was set back from the steep drop-off, making it look like it was on the verge of falling. Take any log cabin, add about three-thousand square feet and make most of it windows and that's what Dewin's home was. It was a log cabin only in the sense it was made of logs and it was on a site where a small cabin once stood. The damn place was as big as some castles.

Dewin had two docks, one a covered one with balcony overhead. It had cut-outs for three boats and was at the far end of the wooden sidewalk lining the shore. A big cabin cruiser was under the balcony, moored in a center slot. The other, public dock was a straight metal one where a man now walked toward us, gesturing us to a mooring.

When we got closer, I saw it was the same guy who scared me the night before. He took the line Able tossed him and secured our boat to the dock then reached out a hand to help me.

I hesitated before taking it, but decided I didn't want to land on my butt in the water. I let him pull me onto the polished wooden dock. "Mr. Court, I believe," I said, unbuckling my life jacket and dropping it back in the boat.

His flat gaze didn't show any recognition. "Mr. Mervyn is waiting for you upstairs." He waited while Able opened a large tackle box near the driver's seat and drew out a cloth bag. "Need a hand?"

"Nope, I'm good." Able shucked out of his life jacket then jumped onto the dock beside me, timing his step with the swaying of the boat.

"You know the way?" Court eyed me warily, probably looking for my gun.

"Yep." I walked down the wide dock, Able next to me. Court busied himself with Able's boat, checking the lines before following several yards behind us. I glanced back once and intercepted his speculative gaze.

I glared at the building towering above us. "There's a central portion that's got the living room and kitchen and a couple of bedrooms." We started up the polished wooden staircase leading to the house above. "Then a north wing and a south wing. Those have two bedrooms each. There's a movie studio in the basement and a game room and God knows what else. I think the main house has like six bedrooms and six bathrooms or something. Then there are two guest cabins that sleep four or five people in each."

"Just a nice little weekend getaway," Able said.

"I'm glad you didn't forget how to find me," a voice said from above.

We looked up. Dewin stood on the deck that wrapped around the entire house. His dark tweed coat and dark pants made him blend into the shadows from the trees.

"It's hard to forget, Dewin," I said. "I can hear your stereo most nights and your lights are bright enough to land a 747."

He laughed. "You always were prone to exaggeration."

"Bullshit," I muttered, walking up the last few steps.

Dewin met us on the landing. "I'm glad you could come, Vivian. Thank you, Mr. Leroy, for driving."

Able reached into the bag he carried and pulled out a bottle, handing it to Dewin. "I thought you might enjoy this. It has a rather distinctive flavor."

Dewin read the label. "Warlock's Revenge Reserve Whiskey." He smiled briefly. "A brand I am not familiar with. How apt."

"Apt?" Able asked.

"It's his name. It's Welsh for wizard or warlock." I took a peek at the bottle's label. It appeared to be hand-lettered. "Where did you get it?"

"It's private stock. I've heard it said that it will make you feel like you've turned back the hands of time." Able handed the cloth bag to Court, who waited two steps behind us. "Put this back on my boat, would you?" Able didn't wait to see if Court did as he asked, but instead he moved to stand with Dewin on the deck. "You have a beautiful home. Perhaps a bit large for the site, but still lovely."

Dewin raised one eyebrow at this quiet criticism. "I fell in love with the location and felt my house had to be worthy of it."

"Yeah, right." I brushed by them and went to the

door on the deck leading into the living room. I glanced back at the lake. The sun was setting, sending long fingers of dark orange light into the bay. As far as the eye could see there were trees and water and quietude. What would happen if this land was developed? There would be houses and docks and boats and screaming children and sunbathers and hunters galore.

I shuddered to consider it.

I pushed open the glass French door and went inside. Two long leather couches were in front of me facing each other, a slab of textured slate on a carved pedestal between them to serve as a coffee table. A massive native stone fireplace was directly ahead with arched doorways on either side of it. Oversized armchairs on my left were in a "nook" about the size of my living room back in Linn. They faced floor-to-ceiling bookcases full of neatly organized volumes, all with similar leather bindings. On the right was another "nook," this one holding a round poker table with six chairs.

Faye Morgan and a younger man and woman stood near the fireplace with drinks in their hands, talking. "Ms. DuLac. I'm so glad you were able to come." Morgan set her glass on the mantel and came to meet me. She wore low heels, a dark green pencil skirt and a matching sweater set. It sounds demure, but on her it was as seductive as a backless evening gown.

"Who can turn down such a royal invitation?"

She appeared startled at my sarcastic comment but recovered her poise quickly. "This is my nephew, Morris Dredding and Eve Lake, Associate Director of Marketing for Scabbard Securities." The young man inclined his head. He was short and powerfully built with thinning brown hair cropped short and a long, narrow face. His expensive business suit was tailored, showing off his large chest. The girl next to him had thick blonde hair that hung to the middle of her back and delicate features, like a porcelain doll. Her dark blue dress clung to her slender body, highlighting her stylishly narrow waist and hips.

"Nice to meet you," I murmured. I headed for the end table next to the couch on my left where the phone sat. That's when I saw the man sitting there. He was one of the handsomest men I've ever seen, with a rugged face, thick dark hair, pale blue eyes and a sculpted and muscular body well exhibited by his tailored suit. He reminded me of David Beckham minus the visible tattoos.

"And that's Brad Devere, a business associate." Morgan smiled at the man, who flashed perfect white teeth at me then at Morgan.

"Hey, there." I edged past him. "I need to make a quick call." I tossed my jacket on a nearby chair and grabbed the phone to call Sy as Able and Dewin came into the room.

Able stopped inside the door, his gaze fixed at the man on the couch. "What are you doing here?" he demanded.

Devere stood. "Hello, Arthur. Long time, no see."

The crackling hostility between the two men was almost visible in the air. "What is he doing here?" Able asked Faye.

"Arthur?" Morris Dredding's head whipped from Faye to Able. "You didn't mention Arthur was here."

"Brad and I are friends as well as business associates." Faye put her hand out and Devere took it, pulling her nearer to him, making it very clear just what kind of friend he was.

"I thought you and Lon were involved," Able said, his eyes fixed again on Devere.

"Lon died," Morris said. "A few months ago."

"What?" Able tore his gaze away from the big man next to his stepsister. "Hello, Morris. I haven't seen you in a while."

Dewin picked up my jacket and held out his arm. "Let me take your coat, Mr. Leroy." He gestured with the bottle to the bar on the right side of the fireplace. "I believe I'll sample this now. Can I get anyone else a drink?" He set the bottle on the bar then went through the doorway, returning a second later without our jackets.

The tension in the room eased slightly when Morris moved to the fireplace, introducing the girl to Able. I tuned out the conversation around me and dialed the phone still clutched in my hand. I reported to Sy that we arrived safely. "You call us when you leave," Sy reminded me. "And we'll look for your signal at your place."

"Okay. Thanks for keeping an eye on me."

"That's what friends are for."

I hung up and found Dewin watching me from across the room. "Vivian, do you want to sample this whiskey? Or would you prefer something else?" He held up the bottle of whiskey Able brought.

"I'll make myself a drink," I said, joining him. Able and Morris Dredding were deep in conversation near the fireplace, the girl standing nearby. She appeared to be listening to them but her gaze was fixed on Dewin and me. Faye Morgan and Brad Devere stood near each other at the windows, looking out on the lake.

"Let me make you something," Dewin said. "Cosmo? Martini? Vodka tonic? As I recall, you like all of those drinks." His dark blue eyes watched me intently. Dewin's gaze could be unnerving because it was so focused. I was accustomed to it so his intensity bounced off my indifference.

"I'll handle it." I moved to the long, polished wooden bar counter and eyed the bottles displayed on the glass shelves above. They were reflected in a six-foot long mirror that served as the background for the bar. I noticed my hair was looking a tad bit wild with my curls bouncier than usual. I gave a mental shrug. No one here cared about my appearance. I grabbed gin and vermouth and proceeded to make myself a martini.

"I'm pleased to see you haven't changed your ways and you don't go in for those flavored varieties that are so popular now. I made an apple martini for Faye earlier." Dewin shuddered dramatically. "You always were a purist." He held up his cut-glass tumbler and evaluated the amber liquor in the light coming through the windows.

"I don't see any reason to tart up a good gin." I poured a generous measure of very expensive gin into a tall glass filled with ice and added a dab of vermouth. I pulled a silver spoon out of a compartment and proceeded to stir. "Why are you merging with another company?"

"That's really none of your concern. You're no longer a stockholder." Dewin stood close enough that I could smell his aftershave, a spicy fragrance mixed especially for him by a shop in Cornwall. They created a special perfume for me the same day they made the aftershave for him. It was on our honeymoon, when we were touring England. Dewin still sent me a tiny and incredibly expensive bottle of it every Christmas. And on the day after every Christmas I replaced the empty bottle in my shop that served as air freshener.

"I may not be a stockholder, but I'm curious." I poured my drink through the strainer into a faceted crystal martini glass, slender and fragile-appearing. "You never struck me as a team player. It's hard to believe you'd give up control of your company."

"Who said I was giving up control?" He moved even closer, blocking my view of the room. "You look very beautiful, Vivian. Are you letting your hair grow out? I remember when it was long." He gently touched one of my bouncy curls, twining it around his finger.

I turned my head and my hair slipped away from his touch. "I heard you got divorced. I'm sorry to hear it."

The fine bones in his wrist flexed when his hand tightened. Dewin had long fingers that easily wrapped around the glass and I knew he had enough power to snap the sturdy crystal. "It was a mistake to get married, one that is best rectified sooner rather than later." His gaze went to Able, standing with Faye and Morris. Devere stood behind Faye, not part of the conversation but still participating by eavesdropping. "Arthur Leroy doesn't seem like your type."

I poked through the containers of condiments, finally selecting a cocktail onion. I skewered it with a small pick made of colored glass and eased it into my drink. "I don't think you really know what my type is, do you, Dewin?"

"I once knew." His voice was low and silky, his

gaze intent on me. "I once knew exactly what you loved and didn't love. I knew how your skin felt. I know how you loved to curl up in front of the fireplace after a long, hot bath." He smiled slightly, faint dimples appearing around the edges of his mouth.

I moved away, sipping my martini. "People change and times change."

"Really? Tell me. Are you still helping your family out financially? Isn't that what this ridiculous sword is all about?"

Able crossed the room to us, a faint smile on his face. "Martini?" I asked, holding my glass so he could see it.

He grinned, shaking an admonishing finger at me. "You know what happens when I have a martini."

I grinned, too. "I know all too well. I'm sure Dewin has something else that you'll find palatable." I glanced back at Dewin when I said it and saw a look of such steely hatred in his eyes that I put a hand on Able's arm, drawing him to a stop.

Dewin smiled, all sign of hostility gone. "What's your poison, Mr. Leroy?" He gestured toward the bar. "I'm sure I have it."

I trembled, chilled by the breeze wafting in from the deck. Morris and his girlfriend had opened one of the doors. Able walked to the bar. "How about a beer? Do you have any?"

"Of course." Dewin opened the fridge under the cabinet and gestured. "Domestic or imported. Help yourself."

Faye Morgan joined us, holding out her glass to Dewin. "Can you make me another?"

"Certainly." He went to the bar and for a minute,

he and Able were side by side. Able was several inches shorter than Dewin and he didn't have Dewin's smooth, fluid way of moving. There was something sturdy and solid about Able. Dewin was a falcon. Able was an eagle. The analogy flitted through my mind in the blink of an eye.

Then Able reached for one of the glasses on a high shelf and his sweater pulled up. I saw a gun tucked into a holster at his back.

I was so surprised I suppose I gaped. Faye Morgan saw it, too, and I was even more surprised when she said, "Why are you here, Arthur? Are you on a case?"

"A case?" I asked.

Faye turned to me. "Didn't you know? Arthur's a cop. Fraud, isn't it?" She made it sound like fraud investigation was tantamount to doling out traffic tickets.

I covered my stunned shock by taking a sip of my martini, almost choking on the expensive gin.

"Yes, I'm still with the FBI." Able poured his bottle of beer into a glass carefully. "And I really can't discuss if I'm on a case. I can say that I'm combining business with pleasure." He smiled at me when he said it.

I managed a weak smile in return. FBI? Investigation? My head was spinning.

"Odd about Gwynne, isn't it?" Faye took her martini glass from Dewin, who was now watching Able with wary interest. "She and Lenny died in that horrible accident and now her brother-in-law was murdered."

"Horrible accident?" I asked. "What happened?"

"They were in a car crash and were pinned in their car when it went over the side of a bridge. They couldn't escape and they drowned."

I shuddered. "That is horrible. And then someone related to her was murdered?"

"You knew about that, right?" Able asked me.

Now it was my turn to be puzzled. "How would I know that?"

"You got the sword from his widow."

This time I didn't care who saw my gaping surprise. "You mean Hector?"

Able nodded. "He was brother to the man my ex-wife married. Gwynne and her husband died in an accident a year ago. And Hector Knight was shot a month ago."

I set my glass down on a nearby end table. "Lib didn't go into details. She and I haven't been on the best of terms, but…" My voice trailed off. "I'm sure my brother Ari would have told me if Hector was murdered."

Able turned to Faye, sipping his beer. "Who said he was murdered?" He sounded curious, not about the fact of murder but about the details surrounding it. It was like talk of murder was a commonplace, everyday thing. Of course, for someone with the FBI, it probably was commonplace.

Able? With the FBI? The idea still had me metaphorically spinning.

Faye seemed flustered. "I assumed it was murder." She and Dredding exchanged bewildered looks. Devere murmured something to her and she nodded, brows drawn together when she frowned.

"He was shot," Able said calmly. "It doesn't mean murder. Are the police involved in an active investigation?"

"I don't know." Morgan sipped her martini then set it on the end table before taking a seat on the couch with Devere, who watched us with predatory intentness. "How do you fit into all this?" she asked me.

"Innocent bystander," Able said quickly. "She has the sword, that's all. I want it back."

"Innocent bystander?" Faye put her hand on Brad's, lying on the couch beside her. "You'd better be careful, Miss DuLac. People who come into possession of that sword have a habit of dying rather unpleasantly."

It sounded like a promise.

Chapter 7

"You didn't die," Able pointed out. "I gave it to you to use at the office and you passed it on to Gwynne. And what about Lon? How did he die? He had it for a while, didn't he?"

Faye sighed theatrically. "Let's not hash that over again, Arthur. I gave it to Lon for safekeeping."

Bright spots of color flared on Able's cheek bones. "Was that before or after he helped you get me voted out of the company?"

"He's dead now." Devere spoke with what I think was supposed to be sadness but which came out sounding like pompousness. I noticed the girl, Eve, disguise a grin by a ducking her head so her long hair slid forward, hiding her face. "Why rake up old gripes?"

"How did he die?" Able repeated, ignoring Devere and focusing on his stepsister.

Faye took a sip of her martini then set it back down. "An odd accident. He cut himself and the wound turned sceptic. He died of blood poisoning."

"Cut himself? With the sword? Wow. Maybe it is cursed." The words slipped out before I could stop them.

"Well then, you'd better be careful," Dewin said. "It might get you next."

"It won't harm anyone who cares for it correctly,"

Able snapped. "It's an antique and it needs to be handled carefully."

"It was a simple accident. He should never have been mucking around with that old thing in the first place." Faye made a ladylike snorting noise of disbelief. "I don't know why you care so much. That old sword hung in the conference room for years."

"It was the symbol of our company," Able said tersely. "My company."

"Scabbard Security—Cutting Edge Software," I said. "I remember it."

"Well, it wasn't in tune with our new image. When Gwynne asked for the sword, I figured, why not?" Faye smiled coldly.

Why not? Maybe because your stepbrother valued it. What a heartless bitch. "It hasn't harmed you," I said to Able. "Of course, that's because it's rightfully yours, I suppose."

Dewin cleared his throat. "I believe the sword was once used as a symbol for the company. So I suppose it was part of the company assets, much like a piece of furniture."

Both Able and I shot him equally incredulous looks. "It's not a chair, Dewin. It's a family heirloom. Honestly." I picked up my martini.

"That's not yours," Dewin said. "That's Faye's."

I checked the glass in my hand. An olive bobbed gently in the alcohol. "Sorry." I set it down and took my glass, the one with the onion. "Why didn't you tell me you were an FBI agent?" I asked Able.

"It wasn't pertinent."

"Wasn't pertinent?" I took a healthy swallow of gin. "I think I have the right to know who is talking

111

with me about heirlooms and who—"

"What I meant was that I was primarily here in a personal capacity, not a professional one." Able sipped his beer, looking away from me.

"Excuse me," Dewin interrupted smoothly. "Let's not talk about unpleasant things such as murder and—" He glanced at Faye, "—old family feuds. Vivian, both you and Mr. Leroy are in a unique position. You both were involved in the ground floor of our two companies and as such, you're very familiar with how the companies operate."

"It's been a long time since I worked at Dewin," I said, silently fuming about Able's subterfuge.

"But the basic product hasn't changed. We're still the premier Internet search engine and our code is used in thousands of software products." His gaze went to Able. "And your company has some of the best security software, used to protect data when it moves from one site to another."

"My former company," Able said. "I'm sure you know it was taken out from under me."

"And you got a nice check out of the deal," Faye snapped. "And you've also retained your stock."

"Is that when you joined the FBI?" I asked. "What do you do for them?"

"I was approached by the FBI when I left the company. I'm a consultant. I didn't lie about that. I do evaluate software for the government. I work on an as-needed basis."

I chugged some more gin, my mind racing. What was it Ari said about Dewin being under investigation? Good Lord, was that why Able was here? I looked at Dewin and realized he wasn't at all startled by anything being said.

In fact, Dewin appeared unfazed by the idea of an FBI agent in his midst. He sipped his whiskey, his dark eyes on me. "You understand the base code of our product. What would it take to merge the code with a security product that encrypts data when it's transported from one site to another?"

"Why would you want to?" I asked. "What would that buy…?" My voice trailed away while I thought about the idea. At the heart of Dewin code was a search algorithm that evaluated a user's keystrokes, storing not only specific keywords that were searched for but other words entered by the user in other programs. The algorithm filtered all the keystrokes, refining itself when the user entered a word into the search box. The end result was a sophisticated product tailored to each individual user.

But the code required massive amounts of space on the corporate servers to store all the data. That data was continually refined and discarded, the space reallocated to new data coming in. Old data was wiped to free space for new data, which was time consuming and expensive.

Dewin smiled. "I love watching your mind at work, Vivian. You see, don't you?"

I finished my drink, my gaze intersecting Able's. I saw the same intense look of concentration in his eyes that I'm sure he saw in mine. "If searching could be combined with data transfer and filtering applied before transferring…" His voice trailed away, too, as his mind sifted through possibilities.

"Both searching and secure transference would be accelerated," I said. "There wouldn't be a need for so much swap space. It would save time and resources."

"I think you begin to see the possibilities. I'd like you to consider what that might mean for both companies." Dewin set his empty glass on the coffee table between the two couches. "Although not right now. Now I believe it's time for dinner." He crooked his arm and extended it to me. "Shall we?"

I set my empty glass next to his and put my hand on his arm. "Who's cooking tonight?" I felt eyes watching us when we walked out of the room. When I peeked over my shoulder, I saw Eve Lake staring. If looks could kill, I would have been rendered into small chunks of eviscerated flesh. Morris touched her arm and she jerked away from him, following Dewin and me out of the room. Morris fell into step behind her, his plain face set in anger.

"I brought in a chef from Chicago because we'll be having several guests here for the week." Dewin led me through the arched doorway to the left of the fireplace. We walked along a long hallway then into a dining room about the size of my entire cabin. Like the living room, a large fireplace was lit and crackling to the left and ahead of us was a bank of windows overlooking the woods behind the house. A round oak table in the center of the room had seven seats around it.

"I suppose you brought in your food and booze from Chicago as well." I eyed the small, leafy salads at the place settings. Each one was a work of art, varicolored lettuce carefully arranged with wedges of tomato on top, the vibrant red color indicating it definitely did not come from a grocery store, where the tomato selections were of the pale orange variety at this time of year.

Dewin sighed. "It's hard to find good liquor in a town the size of Avalon. And let's face it, Vivian—the grocery store here is hardly up to my standards."

I didn't bother to reply. He led me to a chair at the far end of the table, with the windows behind it. "You don't mind taking the hostess seat, do you?" he murmured.

I started to protest but the others were coming in, all of them taking seats where they found their name cards next to the water tumbler, each one hand-lettered on what appeared to be a small piece of birch. I examined mine, which simply said *Vivian.*

Morris Dredding sat on my right and Able was on my left. Next to him were Eve and then Faye. Brad Devere was on Dewin's left. As I shook out my napkin, I considered the table arrangement. If Dewin was following formal seating protocol, and I had no doubt he was, then that made Faye and Morris the most important people at the table because they were seated to the right of the host and hostess. It was a subtle comment about the others sitting there. It also told me that Dewin was aware of the animosity between Brad and Able, which explained the width of the table separating them.

"How long have you been an FBI agent?" I asked Able while we all helped ourselves to salad dressing from small silver cruets next to our plates.

"I'm not exactly an FBI agent," he said. "I'm a consultant."

"To the FBI," Faye said.

"And to other law enforcement agencies," Able said. "I have an unusual talent or gift, I guess you could call it." He munched his salad, seemingly unaware of six pairs of eyes focused on him.

"What sort of talent?" Dewin asked when Able didn't continue.

"I have an eidetic memory when it comes to software code."

Dense silence filled the room, broken only by the snap of logs from the fireplace. "So you remember code you've read?" I finally asked, pushing away my salad plate.

"Not just remember it." Able glanced to his left and behind him when a door next to the massive sideboard opened. A white-coated young man entered the room carrying an empty silver tray. The man was blandly handsome, reminding me of a model from a Ralph Lauren ad: blond, attractive and interchangeable with any other young man who attended Harvard and wore fashionable clothing. Another young man cut from the same mold entered behind him with a silver tray, this one full of plates.

Like carefully orchestrated dancers, the first waiter removed our salad plates and silver while the other swooped in and set a plate in front of us. A third young man entered with a bottle of wine and poured everyone a glass of pale yellow liquid before vanishing behind the other two, all silent, all moving with amazing grace and efficiency.

The dinner was as artful as the salad. A slender filet of grilled salmon was in the center of the plate with a dark glaze drizzled on it. Four perfectly round small white potatoes nestled against the salmon and next to that were four white asparagus spears with grill marks as well. It was a simple but elegant presentation, especially when you considered that the salmon was probably flown in fresh that morning from Alaska, the white asparagus was only widely available from Europe and the potatoes were dotted with small dabs of truffle butter.

"You were saying?" I prompted Able after I sampled the salmon. "Memory for software?"

"Eidetic memory means you remember it exactly." This came from Eve, who had not spoken since we sat down. "My aunt has an eidetic memory."

I forgot she was even there. Her voice was low and husky, an odd contrast to her slender, sylph-like shape. "My aunt used to show us how she could read a magazine article once then remember it, word for word."

"I can read code and remember it precisely," Able said. "I can compare two chunks of code and tell you if they're duplicates."

"It's a useful talent," Brad Devere said. "It came in handy a few times, as I recall." His tone of voice clearly said this was a boring topic, unsuitable for intelligent dinner conversation.

I focused on my food, using that to keep yet another stunned look off my face. Software code was incredibly complex. Any good program had dozens if not hundreds of people working on various pieces of it. In many ways, software design was like clock design. There were millions of moving parts, all of which had to mesh together in one coherent, cohesive fashion.

If one person could read through an entire block of software code and grasp it in its entirety that would be a huge asset. It would be an incredible advantage to anyone in software development.

I ate my food mechanically, barely tasting it. It

would be an asset not only to software development but to anyone who was investigating software piracy. Of course, it would take a long time to read through complex code and comprehend it. The product code was usually broken into subprograms and all of those would need to be read and understood, as well.

"How long does it take you to read and grasp what you read?" I asked Able.

Dewin laughed. "Trust you to consider that. We've moved on to other topics."

I glanced around the table, realizing that everyone, myself included, had finished their meal. What was discussed while I was woolgathering?

Not woolgathering, I decided. I was evaluating. I met Dewin's amused gaze and knew he was thinking the same thing. He knew how my mind worked.

"I don't really read." Able swirled the wine in his glass. "It's like a camera. I sort of take a snapshot of what I see. I process it later."

"What do you mean, you process it?" Eve asked. She glanced at him sideways, under her eyelashes, almost a flirtatious look then she shifted her gaze to Dewin, checking to see how he felt about that.

I ignored the romantic overtones while my mind buzzed with speculation. Holy moly, Able would be a walking encyclopedia of software code.

"I suppose it's like a camera," Able said. "I have the image in my mind and when I want to, I can recall it. Sort of like you can store an image in a digital camera and whenever you want it, you can print it."

"Could you recreate it?" Morris asked. "Could you create the code?"

The Graceful Boys waltzed in and whisked away

our plates, replacing them with a beautifully designed dessert and more wine. The sugar crust of my crème brûlée was swirled into the shape of a heart, an artistic touch I'd never seen before. Dewin smiled at me across the expanse of table, his eyes flicking from me to the dessert. I glanced at Able's small custard cup. His didn't have the design.

"Recreate it?" Able savored a bite of creamy custard. "Yes, I could."

I cracked the shell of sugar and dug in. The wine served with the dessert was a rich port, the dark ruby color a testament to its age and its taste. Trust Dewin to have the best. If he was in financial trouble, he certainly wasn't showing it at the dinner table.

"Of course, most code isn't worth replicating," Able continued. "It's surprising how poorly designed a lot of code is."

"That's because it isn't really designed," Faye said. "It just happens organically."

Able leaned back, looking at her behind Eve's back. "When did you become an expert in code design?"

She didn't acknowledge his sarcasm, but just smiled at Dewin before meeting Able's amused look. "Not the expert you are, Arthur, but I have familiarity with how things work. I've had to learn in order to manage my company." Her glance went to Brad and they exchanged an amused look.

Able's mouth flattened into a hard line. "Your company," he muttered.

Morris raised his port glass. "This is very good. It must be tricky bringing in wine because so many wines shouldn't be jostled in transport. The landing on the lake can be quite rough and I imagine the crossing can be rough sometimes, too."

His changing-the-subject tactic worked, but not in a way that I appreciated.

"That reminds me," Able said, turning to me. "It's ironic. I mean—your name and all. You're afraid of the water?"

I shot him a glare. "Yeah. Ironic."

"Afraid or something," he amended.

"I almost drowned once. I don't consider that ironic." I took a sip of port, savoring the rich flavor.

"You didn't almost drown," Dewin said. "You did drown."

I transferred my glare to him. "That's old news."

"How did it happen?" Able spoke to Dewin, not to me.

Dewin was happy to comply. "It was a year after we were married. We were in Majorca, weren't we?" He didn't wait for my confirmation. "My father owns a house there. All of Vivian's family was there. We were on the swimming platform. Vivian dove in and was swimming. Then a friend of her brother, Rodrigo, came up underneath her and pulled her down."

"What happened?"

"He grabbed my legs and pulled me under." I crossed my arms, suppressing a shiver. "Water immediately flooded my lungs. I passed out."

Dewin continued the story. "I noticed that Rodrigo came up but Vivian didn't. I got worried and dove in."

"You and Archer," I pointed out. "My brother," I said for the benefit of the others.

Dewin nodded. "Me and Archer. Vivian was starting to drift to the bottom."

"They had to give me CPR." It was hard to speak. I stared at my empty custard dish, remembering the choking, gasping feeling then the sudden blackness. "I used to love the water. I loved swimming in the lake when I was younger." I wiped a tear from the corner of my eye. "Rodrigo took that away from me." I met Dewin's gaze. "He said it was an accident, but I always wondered."

Dewin sipped his port then set down the glass. "Rodrigo was a mean son of a bitch, but he's dead now and can't bother anyone again, thank God."

"Rodrigo crashed his car about three years after what happened," I said. "I always wondered if it wasn't karma payback or something."

Dewin finished the last of his port. "What goes around comes around. Does anyone care for coffee? We can go back to the living room." He stood.

Able glanced at his watch. "We should probably be going. I don't like boating at night when I'm not too familiar with the territory."

I checked my watch, too. It was almost eight o'clock. Where had the time gone?

Dewin rested his hands on the back of his chair and regarded us. "I can have Bailey guide you so there's no need to rush."

I started to protest but Able said, "Given the fact he attacked Ms. DuLac in her own home, I don't think that would be wise, do you?" He stood and came to my chair, pulling it back as I rose. "You're ready to go, aren't you?" he asked, touching my shoulder in a gentle caress.

There was an inviting tone to his voice that made me shiver. "Yes, I am." I pushed my chair in, intercepting a speculative look from Faye and a furious look from Dewin.

"An attack?" Eve asked. "Really?" Her tone of voice clearly said, *Who would attack you?*

"Really." Able and I joined the others in leaving the dining room, pausing in the hallway separating it from the living room. "Can you turn on the outside lights?" I asked Dewin. "We'll go out through the side door."

"Are you sure I can't talk you into staying? I'd like to discuss the merger in more detail. I think you have some unique perspectives that could help us make this a success."

"It's getting late," I said. "I'm liable to fall asleep after such a good meal."

"You can't," Able chided. "I need you to point out the landmarks." He took my hand, squeezing it lightly. "We'll need our jackets."

"They're there." I pointed to the wooden pegs by the outside door where our jackets and several others were hanging.

Dewin's eyes narrowed. "Are you sure you won't let Bailey guide you?"

Able's eyes narrowed, too. "Yep, I'm sure. Let's go, Sunshine." He glanced at Faye and Morris, who stood in the entrance to the living room. Eve and Brad had already preceded them into the room. "Good to see you again. Stay in touch." His casual, dismissive tone clearly said it wasn't of any immediate importance to him if they did or didn't.

"Don't be such a stranger, Arthur," Faye called out. "We are still family, you know."

"How could I forget?" he muttered without

glancing back. He put on his jacket, holding mine for me.

"Nice meeting you," I said over my shoulder while I slipped into my windbreaker. "See you around, Dewin."

He stood in the middle of the hall, the chandelier overhead catching the gray highlights in his hair. "I'm sure you will, Vivian."

Lights came on, flooding the outside steps so they were bright as day. Beyond them the woods and the lake were dark as only a night in the forest can be—impenetrable and dense. Able and I were halfway down the stairs when I stopped. "Damn. I'm supposed to call Sy and tell him we're leaving."

Able reached under his sweater and pulled out his phone. "It'll probably take us longer to go back because it's dark. Figure half an hour or so."

I dialed the number while I carefully walked down the stairs, Able ahead of me. "We're leaving the palace," I told Kay when she answered. "Should be back to my place in a few minutes. We're taking it slow because Able hasn't been around here much."

"Okay, we'll look for your signal. How did it go?"

"I'll fill you in tomorrow. It was interesting."

She laughed. "It always is with him, isn't it? Drive carefully."

We reached the dock which was as brightly lit as the stairs. I almost jumped out of my skin when Bailey Court materialized out of the blackness to my right from the matching dock where the cabin cruiser sat. "Do you want me to guide you?" he asked.

"We're fine." Able stepped into the boat and held out his hand for me. "Cast off our lines, would you?"

Court hesitated and I thought he'd argue then he shrugged and did as Able asked. I took a deep breath and forced myself into the bobbing boat, staggering to the passenger chair and plopping down. Able pressed my life jacket into my hands and I tugged it on while he busied himself with lights and controls. Within minutes we were backing up and turning around to face into the cove.

"Are you sure you know the way back?" I asked, buckling on the jacket.

"Yep. It's not just code I can remember. It's pretty much everything." He peered over the bow of the boat. There were three lights in front, one on each side and one pointing straight ahead. I peeked over the side and saw nothing but blackness and water. I closed my eyes and prayed.

The boat moved forward rhythmically, rising and falling with the waves. Most people would say the lake was wakeless, but it never felt that way to me. I *always* felt the waves. If I kept my eyes closed, I could pretend I was in a rocking chair on solid land. I could pretend there weren't untold depths of water under me.

"He's still in love with you," Able said several minutes later.

I opened my eyes a crack. Dark silhouettes loomed on my left combined with a thick smell of leaf mold and the sound of waves on rocks. We were rounding Dewin's peninsula. "I know. There's not a lot I can do about it." I swallowed hard, remembering that Able had a beer, a couple of glasses of wine, and a glass of port. He appeared capable while he steered us through the water, but was he really?

Too late now to think about it, I decided. Hope for

the best.

"I wonder if it's love or if it's control," Able mused. "I get the feeling there are very few people or things that Dewin Mervyn can't control. You're one of them."

I tried to laugh but I think it came out more as a grunt. "Dewin is just used to getting his own way. It pisses him off that I left him. I'll bet if we'd stayed married, he would have eventually left me. I'm the one that got away, that's all."

"It's probably a combination of the two." Able hummed softly as he steered. "I wonder where he got the waiters. They were a matched set."

"They probably came with the chef." That thought made me consider the cost. And that made me think about Dewin's supposed financial difficulties. And that led me to ask, "I know you wouldn't tell them, but will you tell me—are you here in a professional capacity?"

Able glanced quickly at me where I huddled on the chair. "I told you. I can't say."

"Well, that probably means yes, then. What are you investigating? Or who?"

He turned the wheel and we moved past the outcropping and chugged onward, past the smaller bay then around my peninsula and into my bay. "This is a personal trip for me. I told you, I want the sword. What price are you going to ask?"

"I told you I don't negotiate on open water." I clung to the chair when the boat crested a wave caused by another boat far out in the lake. Their lights cut through the darkness, a thin beacon through stygian darkness. We bobbed crazily, the boat slewing from side to side and front to back like some kind of crazy carnival ride. I knew it was a gentle motion and I knew logically that we were not in danger of capsizing, but I still felt nauseous with fear.

"Think about it overnight, then," Able said, twisting the wheel again. The boat quieted somewhat and my stomach quieted, too. "That sword has been in my family for generations. Faye had no right to get rid of it when they did the corporate makeover years ago. I did everything I could to recover it then, but they blocked me at every turn. They're not going to block me now."

He sounded grimly determined. I suppose I could understand how he felt. To have his company taken away from him then to have a personal family heirloom taken, too. "I'll be fair," I managed to say around the lump of fear that almost choked me. "I need to get it appraised and evaluated to make sure there isn't any damage. That's an unusual scabbard and I'm not sure what kind of care it's had."

"As long as I have the right of first refusal, you can take all the time you want. I'm just glad I was able to find it and it's in good hands. Yours." Able fiddled with some controls, once again turning the wheel. "I'll come in to make sure there're no boogie men."

"What?"

"We're here." He threw the engine into reverse and nudged the boat against my dock.

I stared in disbelief at the lights of my cabin above us. "That was a lot faster than I thought we'd be."

"Twenty minutes, give or take." Able cleated our lines then helped me out of the boat. I left the life jacket on my chair and led the way up the steps to my cabin, grabbing a couple of logs from the stack under the deck as I went.

"Why don't you let me go in first?" he suggested after I tapped in the security code on the French door lock.

I didn't argue, but just opened the door and stepped back. He went in and I followed, leaving the logs near the fireplace. Able went into each room, flicking on lights while he went and even going out the back door and peering outside. Then he came to where I was arranging logs in the fireplace. "All secure," he said.

"Thanks for checking and thanks for getting me out of there so early." I straightened, turned—

And went right into his arms.

"I got you into the mess in the first place." He kissed the tip of my nose lightly. "It's the least I could do." He released me and went to the door. "What time can we start negotiations in the morning?"

"You name the time." I followed after him. "I'm an early riser."

"Let's meet for breakfast. I know you want to have your appraiser look at it, but I'd also appreciate the chance to examine it in good light." He smiled and pulled open my door, stepping out onto the deck. "Let's meet at eight o'clock in town, okay?"

"That sounds good. Thanks again, Able." I leaned forward and it seemed like the most natural thing in the world for our lips to meet in a lingering kiss, a kiss that left my stomach fluttering.

He pulled back, gently touching my face. "Good night, Sunshine. I'll see you tomorrow."

I stepped out on the deck and watched him go down my steps, jumping into his boat. He waved then backed away from the dock, turning to head into the

J L Wilson

channel between the mainland and my bay. As he made the turn to go north, he flicked his lights on and off. I waved and went back into my cabin.

That reminded me to flick my bedroom lights on and off twice, pause, then repeat it. I saw an answering signal from across the lake at Sy's house. As I turned to go back into the living room, I spied a small rectangular box on my bed's pillow. I took it with me to the living room where I lit the fire, poured myself some wine then opened the dark green cardboard box.

An enameled pin, about three inches long in the shape of a sword in a scabbard, lay on white satin cloth. The haft of the sword was topped by a small red gem and the scabbard had four blue gems along its length. I pulled it out of the box and noticed a tiny clasp around the sword haft. I flicked it with my thumb and the little sword slid easily out of the scabbard.

The sword shone in the firelight. I tested it on a splinter of firewood and found it was quite sharp on both edges as well as its point. I tilted it toward the light to examine it more closely. The gem in the haft appeared to be garnet and the ones in the scabbard looked like amethyst. Garnet was the birthstone of my birth month, but amethyst was the birthstone of my astrological sign.

A note was tucked into the box's lid.
Saw this and thought of you.
                    A.B.L.

Where had he found such a thing? And what were the odds he would find a piece of jewelry that had my birthstones on it? I cozied into my chair, drowsing in front of the fire. It was a sweet gesture from a sweet guy. More to the point, what were the odds someone like that would come into my life? I sipped my wine, giving daydreams free rein while the fire burned low.

A sharp crackling from my two-way radio startled me so much I dropped the pin. "Are you okay, Vivian?" Kay's voice said, echoing into my bedroom. "Vivian? Call back if you can."

She sounded panicked. I scooped up the pin from the rug where it landed and took it with me into the bedroom. "I'm fine. What's happening?" I said into the receiver. The clock on the bedside table said ten-fifteen.

"Oh, thank goodness you're okay. I just wanted to check on you. Sy wanted me to call. The Shack was broken into. Alarms went off at the police station, but he can't get there because he's with the paramedics out at Moneybag's palace. They got a sick woman they're bringing in to the hospital."

"What? A break-in? Someone sick?" I walked out my bedroom door onto the side deck. Cold air enveloped me, my breath creating bursts of fog. I spied bobbing lights in the distance, but they were far enough away that the sound of the motor was muted. "Who is it, did they say?"

"Some woman visiting there. They said she's in a coma, having trouble breathing. Somebody named Morgan. Anyway, Sy wanted me to call. He said he can come get you and go to the Shack with you once he's done with the paramedics."

"No, let the police handle it," I assured her. "No reason for me to come in tonight. He's got his hands full without ferrying me back and forth." I strained to see the lights of the boat. "I was just there an hour or two ago. She was fine then." I walked back through my cabin to the front deck, but the boats were out of sight.

"I wonder what happened."

"Sounded pretty bad," Kay said. "The paramedics said they weren't sure they'd get her in time. Hold on. Sy is calling in." After a long pause she came back on the line. "Well, that's crazy. He just said that she's dead. They think it's food poisoning."

Chapter 8

I immediately felt sick to my stomach, then reasoned that I felt okay just a few seconds before. It was all my imagination. At least, that's what I told myself.

"That's crazy," I said. "She was fine a little while ago."

"I wanted to tell you about the break-in and make sure you're okay. I need to get back to the dock in case they need me. I'll tell the police you'll come to the station first thing in the morning."

"If the lock was broken, can they chain it for me or something?"

"I'll see what I can do. Have to go now. If you want anything, you buzz us."

"I will, Kay. Thanks." I put the radio back in its charger and turned out all the lights in the cabin. Then I walked into the living room to stare out my door at the blackness outside. My eyes gradually adapted to the night and about five minutes later I saw lights far out in the darkness on my right, two boats cutting across the lake, one with a flashing light aboard. That must be Sy's boat with his emergency beacon lit, traveling from Dewin's house to the shore.

I went back to my chair. I wasn't overly concerned about the break-in. I had adequate insurance for all the items inside as well as the building, including Able's sword. That reminded me. I wanted to do some research. I went to the bookcase and retrieved my Sotheby's and Christie's catalogs from recent auctions then pulled out the paperwork that came with the sword.

Thirty minutes and one more glass of wine later, I had a good idea of the sword's value. Of course, it would need to be appraised by my guy in Duluth, but if what I found in the catalogs was true and if the paperwork was on the up and up, that sword was worth a lot of money. Actually, the scabbard was worth more than the sword. It was a very well preserved example of a reproduction of the Excalibur scabbard from the Arthurian legends.

The Victorians were obsessed with Arthur and the Knights of the Round Table and an ornate sword with scabbard was often part of the role playing that went along with the obsession. Many Victorian collectors paid a pretty penny for replicas of the famous Excalibur. According to the paperwork, the sword had been in the Leroy family for far longer than that, with the earliest documented owner being Able's many-times-great-grandfather, Arthur Leroy, who came to America in the early 1800s as a small child.

I put my homework aside for the time being. Once it was authenticated, I could consider a fair price but until then, all I could do was make an educated guess about its worth. Of course, Able was so anxious to have it, I could probably ask for the moon and he'd try to get it.

That led me think about the other news of the night. Faye Morgan was dead? That seemed impossible. Of course, if she had a food allergy or something, I suppose that could make someone dangerously ill. But she would have said something to Dewin ahead of time if she had any concerns. We all ate the same food.

I got ready for bed, my mind jumping from one thought to another. It took a long time to fall asleep and when I did, I tossed and turned. When I finally did doze off, I had a nightmare about a man with a sword chasing me. His hand touched my arm, his fingers closing on it and turning me—

I woke up gasping. It was still dark outside but that didn't mean it was night. The high land of the peninsula blocked sunlight at this time of the year, when the sun was low on the horizon. I rolled over and peered at the clock. Six-twenty. My mind started to churn through all the events of the previous night.

Faye Morgan was Able's stepsister. Would he need to be on hand to help the police? I jumped out of bed, my active mind demanding an active body, but I stopped in mid-step. Wait a minute. Able was the police. Or was he? He said he was a consultant with the FBI, so that must mean he had some kind of law enforcement background. Didn't it? Either way, he probably wouldn't be able to meet me for breakfast. He would probably be busy because Faye was a family member.

But I could still get an early start on the day. I had to meet with the police, call the appraiser, go to the Shack and do inventory and call Ari from the store to see if he had any more information about the so-called consortium who wanted to buy land. I dug out my old winter parka from storage and hung it out on the deck to air then I went to get ready for my day.

The air was crisp and frosty, but the sun promised

warmth for later in the day. I pulled on my flannel-lined denim jacket and decided to leave my parka to air out during the day. By seven-thirty I was motoring across the lake through a pristine October morning. It was chilly, the frost on the seat in the boat giving me a cold butt. I pulled on mittens before crossing and I was glad I did when I got into the main channel. When I moved away from the protection of my bay, the west wind sent cold tendrils through the boat.

Winter wasn't far away but today I could enjoy the brilliant red foliage on the far shore, the colors so vibrant they were surreal. Autumn hues in the North Country were like something seen in a photograph, so popping with saturation you know it must be fake. I focused on the leaves and didn't think about the cold water underneath me and the unknown depths below.

I pulled into the dock at Sy's and Kay came out to meet me, a bulky gray cardigan enveloping her thin body. "Glad to see you're okay," she called as soon as I was close.

"I'm fine," I called back. I tossed her the front mooring line. "What happened last night?" I asked while we secured my boat to the dock.

"The call came in a little before ten o'clock. The emergency people in town had to evacuate someone from the house out there." Kay gestured toward the lake.

"I thought Dewin had a dock farther west of here that he used." I put my life vest and scarf back into the boat and tugged my jacket closer when the wind blew in from the north.

"He has one, but the emergency services use Sy because he's really closer for them to get to Dewin's place," Kay explained, walking with me up the steps to their house. "Sy had the boat out and ready for them when they got here. As soon as I heard she was sick, I called you to make sure you were okay. I figured it must be something she ate."

"I think we all ate the same thing," I said. "I feel fine. Maybe she was allergic to something in the food."

"Sy said they had her down on their dock when they arrived. She was hardly breathing. They got her in our boat and he came back to the mainland as fast as he could, but it was too late." Kay shook her head. "The sheriff is there today along with one of our local police officers. I saw them going out earlier."

"I suppose they'll have to investigate." I stopped with Kay at her back door. "Will they do an autopsy? Or run tests or something?"

She shrugged. "Probably. We're pretty limited here in town in terms of facilities, so I guess they'll have to work with law enforcement in Duluth. That's the county seat and the Sheriff is based out of there. It must be serious if he came all the way here and didn't just let one of his deputies here handle it. Or maybe John Reeve asked for the help. Heaven knows, we're not equipped to deal with a sudden death like that here."

A gust of cold air made me shiver. "It feels like the weather is turning."

"It's mid-October," Kay said, tugging her cardigan sweater more tightly around her. "First snow is just around the corner." Her sharp blue eyes went to my pale blue sweater, barely visible under my denim jacket. "That's a nice pin. I don't remember seeing it before."

I glanced down at Able's little sword. "It's new. Is

Sy around?"

"He's got his truck in the shop again this morning." She shook her head. "I swear I don't know why he just doesn't buy a new one. That old thing is on its last legs. Anyway, he'll meet you at the store when it opens. What are you up to today?"

"I'm heading to the police station first to check in with them about the break-in, then to the Shack to do inventory and make a few phone calls. I may have to drive to Duluth this afternoon to see my appraiser."

"That reminds me. Able called and left a message for you." She dug in her jeans pocket and pulled out a slip of paper. "He said he's still planning to meet you but at eight-thirty, not eight. He has to meet some people at the hospital." Kay's mouth puckered. "Said he had to do the official identification since he was related to her."

"So was Morris Dredding," I said, skimming the note which said just what Kay had said. "I wonder why he didn't do the ID."

"Is that the nasty young man with them last night?" Kay crossed her arms, obviously cold. "Big chest, not much hair?"

I nodded. "He's her nephew, I think." The thought of one male guest made me remember the other one. "What about Faye Morgan's boyfriend? Did he come on the boat, too?"

"No, just Dewin and the muscle boy." Kay sniffed. "I'll give Dewin credit. He seemed concerned but willing to stay out of the way and let the medical people do their job. But that other one interfered every time somebody turned around." Her voice changed to a high-pitched, mocking tone. "Keep her steady. Don't jostle her. Are you sure she needs an IV?" Kay waved a dismissive hand. "He was more trouble than help."

"That's odd. He didn't seem particularly close to her last night." I shrugged and shivered again. "You go inside and get warm. If anybody needs me, I'll be at the Shack or the store. I have my cell phone."

Kay went inside, pausing in the doorway. "Fat lot of good the mobile phone does here."

"Able's phone works fine. He must have the right carrier for the woods." I waved good-bye and went to my Cooper, sighing when I saw the haze of frost on the windshield. I dug out my scraper and went to work and soon was driving to town, the rising sun bright in my face.

I decided to go to the police station first to read the report about the break-in and file any necessary paperwork. Avalon had five full-time police officers in the summertime when the tourists were in town, but after Labor Day three of those officers worked as paramedics and only helped out the full-time officers as needed. The police station shared office space with City Hall in the block north of my store. Any prisoners requiring more security than a simple locked cell were transported to Duluth for processing.

John Reeve was the senior man on the force and someone I had worked with in the past. To my surprise, he was there and not out with the Sheriff at Dewin's house. I was told John was busy but he left a report for me about the break-in with the part-time officer manning the main desk.

I skimmed it quickly. The lock was jimmied and the padlock cut. When the door was opened but the security number not entered, the silent alarm went off at the police station. Coincidentally, right after the alarm sounded the call came in to go to Dewin's house. John noted the times on the report: *Alarm, 9:45. Prepared to respond but called to Mervyn residence at 9:51. Directed on-call backup officer to warehouse while others responded to emergency. Officer arrived at 10:15. Found front door pried open, lock broken.*

I couldn't fault them for focusing on Faye Morgan at the expense of my property. I jotted the name of the officer who went to the scene, more to thank him than for any other reason. The guy was a retired Fish and Game officer who helped out during the off-season and he lived just a few blocks from the Shack. Given the times reported, there was only thirty minutes or so for someone to muck around inside the building.

When the officer arrived at the building he found the door open, lights on and no one on the premises. He secured a chain on the door to keep it shut then reset the security panel with a new passcode before coming back to the station to watch the desk until the others could return.

I signed for the new security code and I also initialed the report, getting a copy of it to give to my insurance people for the claim. I told the officer I would be at the Shack most of the morning and I assured him if I found anything missing, I'd file a report with them.

"Although I don't know how you'll be sure about that," he said doubtfully. "You've got a lot of stuff in there."

"I'm working on inventory this week, so if something is gone, I'll figure it out." I patted my trusty messenger bag, which held my lists of goods. "It was probably just a prank or something. I'm not too worried."

"I know John wanted to talk to you about that dinner party last night," the officer said while I tucked the report into my bag. "He'll probably come out to the warehouse later to get your statement."

"My statement? What statement? I had dinner there then I left."

"Just routine." He sounded so pompous I wanted to laugh, but he appeared so serious I didn't dare.

"I'll be at the warehouse or the store most of the day," I said. "John has my mobile number so all he has to do is call if he needs to see me." As I left the small one-story building, I spied Able's car in the parking lot in the back. I had some time before I had to meet him, so I decided to go to the Camelot and grab a table.

When I crossed the street, I saw Brad Devere peeking into the windows of my store. He saw me at the same time. "Just the person I wanted to see," he said when I got closer and paused near the Camelot's doorway.

He didn't look like a boyfriend in mourning. He seemed more like a male model in his dark jeans, stylish navy blue sweater and dark denim jeans jacket. His dark hair was tousled and fly-away looking, but I suspect it was mousse not the wind that caused that style.

"I'm sorry about Faye," I said. "My condolences."

He put on a suitably sad look. "I just came from the hospital. They're still trying to determine the cause of death. So sad. Such a beautiful life, cut short."

What a bunch of trite bullshit. I almost said it out loud but caught myself in time. "How is Dewin taking it?" I asked. "I'm sure it's shaken him."

Devere hesitated, like he didn't know what sort of emotion to show me. "He's distressed, of course. I'm sure anyone would be, under the circumstances."

"What circumstances are they? What happened, exactly?" I smiled, acting like I was merely concerned, not avidly curious.

"Faye didn't feel well after supper. She said she had a headache. I assumed it was just stress. She's so worried—she was so worried—about the merger." Devere glanced to his right, at the city hall. "Seeing her brother was quite a shock."

"I take it they're not close," I murmured, moving around him to try to reach the door to the cafe.

"Oh. I thought you knew." He turned, blocking my entrance, either accidentally or by design, I'm not sure which. "I suppose it's not a secret. Arthur and Faye aren't on the best of terms. Or, rather, they weren't on the best of terms. Arthur had to be removed as CEO of the company and he blamed Faye for that. He shouldn't have blamed her. He should have blamed his father."

"His father? Isn't he ill? Able mentioned that he was sick."

"Sick? Luther?" Devere laughed and it didn't sound forced. "He's as strong as an ox and twice as healthy. The old man has a controlling interest in the company and he's the one who dictates who stays and who goes." He nodded thoughtfully. "I suppose now that Faye's gone he'll want to step in and help manage things. He did that initially when Arthur was fired."

He made it sound like Faye had just left on vacation and wasn't lying on gurney in a hospital or wherever she was. What a callous bastard.

I looked past Devere. Able was walking toward us

from city hall. He wore a red-and-black plaid flannel shirt, jeans, and a heavy canvas jacket. Unlike Devere, Able appeared right at home in the north woods and it wasn't just his clothing. There was something about his casual acceptance of the small town and its environs that told me Able enjoyed it here.

The thought came and went in the time it took to blink. "He was fired?" I asked, since Devere seemed to be waiting for me to say something.

"Asked to leave," Devere amended. "I'm sure Arthur and his father almost came to blows about that."

Able saw me and smiled. Then he saw who I was talking to and he began to hurry. "What about Mr. Dredding? Isn't he CIO? Wouldn't he be in line for an upper management position?"

"Being a CIO isn't in the same league as CEO," Devere said with a condescending smile. "Morris is young and untried. I doubt if the shareholders would approve him. No, I was Faye's Executive Vice-President. As such, I suspect I'll be asked to step in and provide leadership in her absence."

"Really?" I blinked widely at Devere, trying to project a picture of innocence. Able was just a few steps away from Devere, who was unaware of his presence. "Maybe the shareholders will ask Able to come back," I said. "After all, it might be good to have an experienced person at the helm during a merger. You know—have someone objective in place, someone whose judgment won't be clouded by grief."

"That's ridiculous." Devere's pale blue eyes were flinty hard, like chips of ice or stone.

"Oh, so you're not grieving?" I asked.

"No, it's just that—I'm a professional and I won't

let my emotions get in the way of my responsibility to the company. Anyway, I doubt if anyone would want Arthur back. He didn't leave gracefully."

"Really?" Able's tone of voice was acidic enough to leave scars. "I have a different memory of that event."

Devere turned so quickly he almost tipped over. "What are you doing here?"

"Why wouldn't I be here? Did you expect the police to arrest me?" Able shifted his gaze from Devere to me. "Brad made sure the local police were aware that Faye and I have had our differences in the past."

"They asked us who was at dinner last night and when I mentioned your name, the police officer told me he was aware you and Faye weren't on the best of terms. I simply confirmed it. It's not like it's a secret, Arthur." Devere shrugged, the picture of nonchalance.

Able's lips thinned into a tight line. "You know, Brad, I must have been either stupid or crazy to have you or Lenny as my best friends. But to answer your original question, I'm here because Vivian and I have plans today." He smiled at me, but I could tell he was still pissed off. "I asked Barb at the cafe to put together breakfast to go for us. Hope that's okay?"

"That sounds great. I don't know about you, but I have a lot of things on my To Do List today." I edged my way around Devere and reached for the door, but once again he blocked me.

"Whatever Arthur offers on the sword, I'll double it." His eyes went to my sweater and he frowned when he saw the pin, revealed when my jacket shifted.

"And I'll double it again," Able said before I could reply.

"Why?" I asked Devere.

"That's none of your business. I want it and I'll do anything to get it." His gaze locked on Able, standing behind me. I could sense a fight in the offing if I didn't act fast.

I pushed Devere to one side and grabbed the Camelot's door. "The sword is mine now. And I'll decide who I sell it to. Money isn't everything."

Devere's lips curled in a snarky smile. "Right." He took a step back to let me past then moved forward again when Able followed me. "Your father is on his way here."

Able didn't pause, just brushed past him. "I know. I talked to him this morning. I expect him at any time."

I turned, holding the door open. Devere's eyes had widened and his jaw was slack. Then he recovered and strode away. "I wonder how he's getting around," I said, thinking out loud. "If he came in on the plane with the others, he doesn't have a car here. Or did he drive?"

"He probably drove." Able went to the front counter and I followed. "Brad hates flying. There's no way he'd get in a small plane."

I considered that while Able paid for our breakfast sandwiches and coffee. If Devere drove to the lake then he had to have access to a boat, also, in order to go back and forth to Dewin's home. Of course, Dewin had several boats, ranging from a big cabin cruiser to smaller utility boats like mine. Devere was probably using one of those and tying up at Dewin's private dock, the same way I was using Sy's dock.

"Penny for your thoughts," Able said, handing me a paper cup of coffee that matched the one in his hand.

I shook my head. "Just woolgathering. Were you at

the police station?"

He nodded. "I had to do the official identification of Faye's body then the local police wanted to talk to me. I talked with the Sheriff last night at the hospital."

"Really? They called you?"

"I'm Faye's next of kin. Morris came in with her on the boat, but when the police went through her—" Able hesitated. "Her purse, they found that I was listed. They called me around one in the morning. She was already dead." He handed me two small paper sacks and headed for the door. "Morris assumed he was next of kin, but that wasn't what she listed on the emergency card in her handbag."

"Good heavens, you must be exhausted. That's a long drive going to and fro." Based on what Able told me earlier, his cabin was at least three miles north of mine. Add that to the drive into town and it was at least an hour's worth of travel, one way, at night on a dark lake and along dark country roads.

He held the door for me. "I stayed overnight at the hospital. When the officer called, he told me what happened. I knew I'd have a lot of paperwork and other details to work on, so I just grabbed a nap on a couch in the visitor's lounge."

"Well, don't feel you have to come with me to look at the sword today," I assured him. "I'm not going to sell it immediately, so it won't get away from you. I need to have it officially appraised and evaluated."

"No, that's fine. I'm done with the police for now. I have time." He started walking toward City Hall and his car. I lagged back.

"Why did you lie about your father?"

He stopped. "I didn't exactly lie. I just sort of

avoided the truth." He resumed walking and I fell into step with him. "My father is Luther Leroy."

Now I stopped. "Seriously?"

He nodded.

"Luther Leroy? One of the richest men in the world? The man who owns television stations and ranches and islands and—" I sputtered to a stop.

"Now you know that I won't be outbid on the sword."

"That's assuming you have access to your father's money," I pointed out.

His cheeks darkened with color. "My father won't be outbid. He's as anxious as I am to find it. Your car or mine?"

"Let's take both. That way if I want to stay and work, you can leave." I didn't give him a chance to agree or disagree, but instead made a beeline for my car, parked in the City Hall parking lot not far from his. I also wanted time to digest the fact that I was hanging out with the son of an honest-to-God billionaire. Dewin was wealthy, but he wasn't in the same class as Luther Leroy.

I hopped into my Mini Cooper and set the paper sacks on the passenger seat then put my coffee cup into the cup holder in the console. I was buckling my seat belt when Able slipped into the car, deftly grabbing the paper sacks and sliding into place.

"Let's take your car. Hold this." He handed me his coffee and buckled his seat belt then took the cup from me with a smile. "You're mad at me, aren't you? I can tell."

"Of course I'm mad. You've lied to me from Day One." I concentrated on driving, using that to avoid looking at him. "You told me your father was dying, you didn't tell me you worked for the FBI, you spun this whole stupid story about wanting to buy the sword and you didn't tell me you were related to the woman who was trying to negotiate a merger with Dewin, who just happens to be my ex-husband. You used me to get close to him, didn't you? You're investigating him, aren't you?"

Silence. I glanced to my right. Able had a suitably hangdog expression, complete with big brown puppy eyes.

"Oh, quit it," I snapped. "This isn't a joke. You did it, didn't you? You used me to get close to my ex-husband."

"Actually, I used you to get close to the sword, which also happened to bring me closer to your ex. I plead guilty to that." He stared out the car window, frowning. "Remember I told you about my friend who taught me how to fold the cloth for your present?"

I nodded. "So?"

"He was a programmer at Dewin Software. He told me that he thought something illegal was going on."

"And?" I prompted.

"The official police report said he committed suicide, but I think he was murdered." Able swung his head to regard me, his eyes hard and cold. "I'd like to find out who did it."

"You think someone in Dewin's company did that?" It boggled the mind. It was a software company, for heaven's sake. This wasn't the Mafia.

"Or Dewin did it himself."

I laughed out loud. "Dewin? Murder someone?" I shook my head. "Not in a million years."

Able was silent for a moment. "I won't argue with you about that. I'm going to get to the bottom of what happened." He hurried on speaking when I started to argue. "And there's a reason I didn't mention that I was related to my father."

"That is?"

"I'm not him," Able said flatly. "I'm not a billionaire. I have a job like anybody else and I'm just a regular guy, like anybody else. When people find out I'm related to him, things change. They treat me differently."

"Poor little rich boy?" I muttered.

"I suppose you can say that," he snapped. "I'm here to get the sword and to make sure the company I founded gets a fair shake when it comes to this merger."

"So you do admit you used me to get close to the action."

He sighed loudly. "I just didn't tell you about it, that's all."

I fumed about the whole thing for a minute to two then shelved it for later consideration. "What's the deal with you and Brad Devere? It sounds like you two have history."

He choked on his coffee. "You could say that," he gasped. "Brad, Lenny and I all worked at the company. Lon was there, too. We were all in on the ground floor. Brad was in marketing, Lenny and I wrote code and Lon was in project management."

"One of your supposed best friends runs off with your wife, one undermined you to take over the company and one slept with your stepsister on the way to becoming CEO." I shot him an incredulous look.

"You don't have very good luck when it comes to choosing friends."

"I greatly underestimated Faye's appeal," he muttered. "Once she got her claws into them, they were goners."

"Oh, please. You act like she's a witch or something and she cast a spell on them. Why is that whenever men act stupid, it's a woman's fault?" I turned at the stop sign and sunlight angled into the car, flashing off something metallic in the distance— something at my storage building.

"You weren't there so you don't know what happened. They had no upper management ambitions until Faye got her hands on them. My father insisted that I give her a job at the company to please my stepmother. From that moment on, Faye did everything she could to undermine me."

"Is your father still married?" I turned into the lane for the Shack, my eyes zeroed in on the door, which appeared ajar.

"No, Yvette died." Able peered ahead. "What's wrong? Is the door open?"

I pulled to a stop. "Stay here." I reached behind me for my messenger bag resting on the back seat.

"Why is the door open? I thought you locked it." Able tucked his coffee cup into the other cup holder.

"I had a break-in last night. The police said they shut it, but it looks like it's been broken into again." I pulled out my gun and reached for the door handle. "I can handle this."

Able shot me an exasperated look. "You are the most annoyingly competent woman I've ever met. How can a guy be a hero around you?"

"I'm used to handling my own problems."

Able leaned forward, reached behind him and pulled out his automatic. "Give me a chance, would you?"

I didn't argue but opened my door. He did the same thing and we both stepped out of the car just as a man came around the side of the Shack.

Chapter 9

I raised my gun. Able moved forward, his gun up as well. As he walked, he edged in front of me. Damn it, he was still trying to protect me. I moved slightly to my left so he wasn't in my line of fire.

Dewin stepped from the shadows to the left of the door, his dark pants and long dark trench coat making him blend into the darkness of the doorway. He stepped into the sunlight, blinking at the brightness. When he saw us, he immediately raised his hands. "Wait a minute! Whoa!"

I lowered my Glock. "What are you doing here?" I demanded. Then I realized that Able still had his gun aimed at Dewin. "What are you doing?" I whispered.

"He hasn't answered yet," Able said calmly. "What are you doing here, Mervyn?" he called out.

"I saw that the door wasn't locked. I thought someone broke in." My ex-husband lowered his hands and walked forward slowly.

"Is everything okay?" Another man came from the side of the building behind Dewin. He was much older, with thick silver hair and a craggy, weathered face. He and Dewin were the same height and but the older man was slightly stooped with age. His dark jeans and flannel shirt appeared new and crisply pressed, like a tourist who dressed in what he thought was the appropriate clothing for a North Woods Adventure. His gaze went from me to Able then to Dewin, obviously uncertain about what was happening.

I grabbed my bag out of my car and tucked my gun away. "Nothing's wrong. I had a break-in here last night and I wasn't sure what to expect when I got here." I glanced at Able and frowned when I saw him still holding his gun, although it was now lowered. "I think you can stand down."

He holstered his gun and strode forward. "What time did you get here?" he asked the older man.

"I flew in to Mr. Mervyn's bay early this morning. It's good to see you, Arthur." The old man nodded to Able, who still watched Dewin like he expected some sudden movement.

"Where's your car?" I asked Dewin.

"Eve needed the car to go shopping so she dropped us off. She and Morris will come back to get us."

Shopping? There was a grocery store, drugstore and my shop in town and not a whole lot else in a thirty-mile radius. Oh, well. It wasn't my concern if Dewin wanted to loan a ninety-thousand-dollar car to his latest girlfriend. I slung my bag over my shoulder. "What are you doing here, Dewin?"

"Mr. Leroy asked to see the sword. I assumed you had it stored here. I called Sy to find out your schedule and he mentioned you were coming here to do inventory. When we got here, we found the door open." Dewin shrugged as though to say, *Anyone could see.*

"I don't appreciate you trespassing."

"We weren't trespassing. We assumed you were inside." Dewin turned to the older man. "This is Luther Leroy, Faye Morgan's stepfather. Luther, this is Ms. DuLac, the owner of this building and the proprietor of the store we saw in town." Dewin performed these introductions with his usual graceful charm, ignoring my bad temper.

I stuck out my hand. "Sorry for your loss."

"Thank you." Leroy took my hand and gave it a shake. "Mr. Mervyn has told me a lot about you. From what he said, you're an extremely gifted programmer."

I moved forward and the two men parted to let me undo the chain holding the door closed. "It was a long time ago. I doubt I could write a subroutine now to save my life." I flipped on the light switch and moved to the nearby security panel where I typed in the new code. When I was sure the alarm was deactivated, I turned on the overhead heaters, which chugged into life.

I blocked the doorway when Dewin started to follow me. "If you don't mind, I'll do a preliminary examination without bumping into people," I told the three men.

"That's ridiculous," Dewin said. "You'll never know if anything was taken." He glanced into the crowded building. "Your insurance company won't even bother investigating a claim."

"Let me know if you need help." Able turned to leave the building. After a brief hesitation, his father joined him.

I stared at Dewin. "Leave."

"But—"

"Now."

He jammed his hands into his coat pockets and followed the other two men to stand outside in the sunlight, his hunched shoulders making him look like an angry black crow.

Dewin was right, of course, but I still wanted to do

a quick pass through the building, just to see if anything appeared out of place. I worked my way along each aisle, pausing at the painted spots and snapping quick pictures. If anything was obviously missing, I'd be able to compare my photos to the most recent set of images.

Five minutes later I was back at the front door. The three men stood facing the door and I got the feeling Able and Dewin were arguing. Both appeared annoyed. Luther Leroy looked amused. "Come on in," I said, gesturing. "I assume you want to see the sword?"

Leroy nodded eagerly and started forward, but Dewin moved ahead of him to walk beside me, leaving Able to walk with his father. I wended my way through the building, navigating the aisles of furniture and boxes, taking my time to look at everything.

"What happened last night, Dewin?" I asked, keeping my voice low. "She seemed fine when I was there."

"I don't know. Faye and Brad went to the west guest wing shortly after you left. Dredding, Eve and I stayed in the great room, talking."

I heard a faint inflection or softening in Dewin's voice when he spoke the girl's name. She was probably thirty years younger than Dewin, but he never let that stand in his way before. I mentally shrugged it off. How he spent his romantic moments were of no concern to me. "How long did you stay there and talk?"

"An hour or so. Dredding left before Eve did. They were staying in the east wing. It was just a few minutes after he left that Devere came in and said Faye was ill. As soon as I saw her, I knew we had to get her to the hospital." Dewin's face was pale in the bright overhead light, but perhaps it was just in contrast with his dark coat, the collar pulled up around his dark hair. "I never realized before how isolated we are on the peninsula."

"It's a damn big lake. There's no fast way or easy way to get around. I remember when Mom would come out here alone. It drove Dad crazy with worry sometimes, especially in the wintertime."

"The women in your family are intimidating that way." Dewin laughed ruefully. "I can't imagine living here alone and yet you seem to get along just fine."

"You're alone here a lot."

"No, I'm not. I always have a caretaker or a chef or staff with me. Not like you." He touched my shoulder, pulling me to a halt. "I still miss you, Vivian."

I gently moved his hand away. "We've been divorced longer than we were married. You miss our youth and our past. You don't miss our marriage." I continued into the warehouse, pausing once to widen the aisle by nudging a box out of the way.

"You're wrong. I miss you. I think I was a better person for being around you."

"What is it with you men?" I asked, only jokingly rhetorical. "You always seem to want to give women either the blame or the credit for how your lives turn out. For heaven's sake, if you want to be a better man then be one. You don't need me to show you how."

He laughed softly. "You never pulled punches."

"Why should I? What's the worst that can happen?" I reached the back of the building and the workbench where the pine box still sat. I set my messenger bag on a nearby table. "I'm sorry if you're not happy, Dewin, but it's up to you to make your own happiness. It doesn't come from other people."

"She sounds like she's been talking to you,

154

Arthur."

I turned to Leroy and Able when they joined us. "Is that your philosophy, too?" I asked Able.

"Something like that," he said wryly. "I discovered it when my best friends turned out to be not very good friends. I decided then that it didn't make sense to dwell on the defects of others when I could just as easily dwell on my own."

Dewin started to touch the pine box but I blocked him with my arm. "I want to get some pictures." I snapped a few shots with my phone. It was warm under the heating duct so I shucked off my jacket and laid it on a nearby table.

"That's a beautiful pin," Leroy said, his eyes fixed on Able's gift.

I touched the little sword on my left shoulder, pinned to my pink sweater. "Thank you. It's unique."

"Yes, it certainly is." Leroy approached the workbench, his gaze alternating between the pin and the pine box. "Have you seen it?" he asked Able.

Able stepped forward, too. "Yesterday. It's in good shape."

"Did you handle it?" The elder Leroy was curiously insistent, as though the condition of the sword was critical.

Able heard it, too because he nodded immediately. "It's fine. Not damaged."

"Good. I was hoping that—wait, you can't do that." Leroy moved in front of Dewin, who was reaching into the box while my back was turned so I could set the lid of the box to one side. "You shouldn't handle the sword. It's an antique."

"No one is handling the sword until I can take

some more pictures," I snapped. I was getting tired of all these males hovering around me like a bunch of nervous Nellies. I took a picture of the sword in the packing material, then moved the material aside and took a picture of the sword in the velvet surround.

I set my phone to one side and reached into the box. "That's rather heavy," Luther said, leaning forward. "You might want to let Arthur—"

I angled my body so I could keep him behind me, politely but firmly. "I've handled swords before." I lifted the sword in its scabbard out of the box, barely able to keep it upright when I realized how heavy it truly was. My wrist wasn't strong enough to hold it solo, so I used both hands to lift it in front of me.

"Be careful," Able said softly. "It has an odd balance."

I glanced at him, surprised to see the intent look in his eyes when he watched me with the sword. "It's heavier than it looks," I admitted.

He grinned. "Most swords are, especially if you've been using it for a long time. After a while it feels like a bag of rocks."

I let the sword in its scabbard drop to the palm of my left hand and I brought it closer to me for examination. The pommel was a solid piece of metal, worn but still bright. An engraving in the silver was faded but it appeared to be a dragon, drawn in such a way that its tail wrapped around the ball of metal that was the pommel itself. "It's beautiful craftsmanship," I murmured.

I maneuvered the sword into the box but held onto the grip, drawing the sword itself out of the scabbard. The metal left its surround smoothly and easily. It was appreciably lighter weight, which told me the scabbard was as solid as I thought, although the blade was still heavy and difficult for me to balance.

I turned and caught a glimpse of Luther Leroy's face. He was so stunned his mouth gaped open. Then he saw me looking at him and he quickly smoothed out his expression, the sharp look in his eyes changing to one of mild curiosity.

"I've handled weapons before," I said, figuring he was anxious about me holding the sharp blade.

"That's obvious. It's just that I haven't seen anyone but Arthur wield the sword for a long time." He eyed me nervously, his dark eyes flickering from my wrists to the tip of the blade.

"I'm not really using it. I mean, it's not like I'm chopping up any enemies or anything." I glanced sideways at Dewin when I said it. He backed off a step in mock terror. Or at least, I think it was mock.

"It's been in our family for generations. I was heartsick when Faye gave it away." Luther stepped forward to stand next to the box, looking down at the scabbard. "It's a precious piece of our history."

"Maybe Faye had no idea how you valued it," Dewin said.

"Bullshit." I raised the sword but it was hard. My wrists were barely up to the task. "Of course she knew. She probably did it out of spite."

"You didn't know my stepdaughter, did you?" Luther asked with a small smile.

"Not really. But she talked about it last night. She knew how Able cared about the sword." I lowered it carefully. "From what I've heard, anybody who uses it is cursed." I angled the blade so I could see it better in the light. When Luther didn't answer, I glanced at him and once again saw that stunned look in his eyes. He managed to hide it better this time, though, and he recovered faster.

"You've heard about that?" he asked.

"We were talking about it last night," Dewin said, edging closer to me to peer at the metal blade. "Everyone who handles the sword has died a violent death."

I shot him a reproving look. "Not everyone. Able is still alive. But we decided that's because he's the rightful owner of the sword."

Dewin returned my look with one of his own. "We didn't decide that. You did."

"And I was right." I carefully laid the flat edge of the weapon in my left hand, lifting it so the light from the windows shone brightly on it. "There's lettering here."

"It's hard to see unless you know where to look," Able said. "I'm surprised you saw it."

"I have good eyesight. What's it say?"

"*Rex quondam*, on one side. *Rexque futurus* on the other." Luther spoke the Latin words solemnly, like a benediction or a blessing.

"The once and future king?" Dewin asked. He smiled at my surprised look. "The benefits of a classical education."

"So does that make you a king?" I grinned at Able, remembering our earlier conversation about *Spamalot* and *Monty Python and the Holy Grail*.

"Not unless some watery tart comes along and tosses it to me," he said with an answering grin.

"Who are you calling a tart?" I held out the sword.

Luther Leroy's eyes widened and he and Able exchanged a surprised look.

"Thank you," Able said softly. He took it from me and raised it fluidly, making it look like a small fencing rapier in his hand. I knew how heavy it was and I had a new appreciation for his muscular control. The sword glinted, sparkles of light thrown off it. For an instant it glowed with a life of its own.

"I have no idea what you're talking about," Dewin complained. "What's all that about a tart?"

"*Spamalot*," I said. "The play? The movie? *Monty Python and the Holy Grail*?" He shook his head. "It's a plot point," I said. "You'd have to see it to understand."

Able twisted the sword so it pointed downward, the blade almost touching the ground. He pivoted, his feet sliding into a fencer's defensive posture. "Brad Devere made an offer on the sword," he told his father, turning the sword right then left, only his wrist moving and his arm and body still as stone. My arms ached to watch him.

"And as I explained to Mr. Devere and to your son, I am currently the legal owner of the sword because I purchased it from my sister to sell it for her. I plan to get a fair price for it, once I've had it evaluated." Mentioning my sister made me remember that I needed to call Ari. Did he know that our brother-in-law was murdered, if indeed it was a murder?

"Brad's doing that just to be an ass," Luther muttered. For a minute he and Able appeared exactly alike, with a disgusted and slightly bemused expression.

"He told me that he's next in line to be CEO of Scabbard Securities now that Faye Morgan is dead," I said.

Both Luther and Able chuckled at the same moment. "Over my dead body," Luther said. "I'll see the company liquidated before I let that idiot take charge."

I glanced at Dewin to see how he handled all of this insider talk. As I expected, he pretended not to listen. He peered down at the scabbard in the pine box, his long fingers tracing the lines of the design in the old leather. He caught me watching him and he winked. I smiled at his conspiratorial expression.

"Can you do that?" I asked Luther.

"Of course I can," the older man said. It wasn't arrogant, just a simple confident statement of fact. *I am powerful. I can do what I want.* He sounded as regal as a king.

"What I meant was do you have legal control of the company?"

"I'm a majority stockholder." He said it the same way someone would say *I'm God.*

"There have been hostile takeovers before." I joined Dewin at the box, peering down at the scabbard. "And I've known Boards of Directors to override what stockholders want." I met Dewin's eyes when I said it and I saw my memories in his eyes. When we took our company public, we had a hell of a fight with the Board to do what we wanted. "Things don't always go as you plan."

"I have experience in these matters," Luther said dismissively.

Something in the way he said it just rubbed me the wrong way. I straightened and stared at him over the box. Dewin put a hand on my wrist, his fingers gently pinching my radial artery. "Patience, Vivian," he whispered.

I automatically drew in a steadying breath and held it for three counts, calming my racing heartbeat. Dewin always knew how I got pissed off by events and people out of my control. We had worked out this system where he would touch my wrist and simply say the one word, *Patience.* Whenever he did that, I trained myself to take a mental step back and regroup, defusing my incipient anger.

"Experience is a great teacher," I said. "Some lessons are harder to learn than others." I smiled at Dewin, thanking him for reminding me of my lesson in handling arrogant bastards.

He released my wrist. "I am pleased to see that you are still unafraid. It was always one of your more exasperating and endearing traits."

"Nothing will change that, I guess." I turned away from the intense look in his eyes, only to encounter a similar intense look in Able's eyes.

"Except water," he said.

I turned to face him. "What?"

"You're afraid of water." His voice was a challenge.

"I'm afraid of drowning. Yes." I admitted it regretfully.

"But that isn't intrinsic to you," Dewin said smoothly. "You had to learn that. You almost died and that taught you fear."

Something was going on between the two of them and I was caught in the middle. I think I realized it at the same time Luther Leroy realized it. "You almost drowned?" he asked, his voice overly curious and insistent.

"I did drown," I corrected. "Dewin gave me artificial respiration and saved my life."

"Dewin and your brother." Able's gaze went from me to Dewin and back again, daring us to contradict him. "Isn't that what you said?"

I glared at him. It was my story to tell, not his. "Yes, Dewin and my brother saved me."

"How traumatic," Luther murmured. "Were you young when it happened?"

Able's phone rang, muffled in the pocket of his shirt. He turned to one side to take the call, lowering the sword to his side. Dewin watched him and I could tell he itched to get his hands on the blade, to try it out. Dewin always had a competitive streak a mile wide and seeing Able handle the sword probably had him thinking he needed to try it, too.

"It's for you." Able held out his phone to me.

"What? For me?"

"You used my phone yesterday, remember? Whoever you called is calling you back."

"Oh. It must be Ari." I took the phone and moved away, going to the back of the warehouse away from the three men.

"Say hello for me," Dewin said as I passed him.

I didn't acknowledge his comment. Ari hated Dewin and Dewin knew it and delighted in forcing Ari to be polite. That happened quite often because Dewin used to be married to our brother's sister-in-law. "What's up?" I asked into the phone.

"Do you know who this phone is registered to?" my brother whispered theatrically.

"Yes. Arthur Leroy." I turned to look at the men. Able was holding the sword out for Dewin to examine

162

it. The blade didn't waver so much as a hair. I admired his strength. Luther saw me watching and I couldn't quite interpret his expression, which was a mix of speculative curiosity and downright surprise.

"Oh my God," Ari said. "Do you realize he's the son of—"

"I know," I interrupted. "Luther Leroy. So?"

"So? Luther Leroy is one of the richest men on earth."

"And he's standing here looking at Lib's sword." I kept my voice low and my eyes on the men who were now examining the scabbard Able pulled out of the box. The sword was still in his hand, held down at his side. It seemed as natural to him as a cell phone with a businessman. I blinked, wondering where the hell that thought came from.

"What?" My brother's excited shout jerked me back to the here and now.

I smiled smugly. "Yep. I have one of the richest men in the world interested in that sword. So I think I can guarantee Lib a good price for it."

"You're kidding. What's he doing there?"

"Hold on a second. Somebody's coming in." I glimpsed shadowy figures moving through the warehouse, briefly lit then unlit by the uneven lighting. "Who's there?" I called out.

Able turned in one sinuous movement and raised the sword, his elbow close to his body and the blade at a forty-five degree angle. It was a fencer's position of defense, enabling him to attack quickly if needed. It happened so fast I barely realized what he was doing.

Eve Lake stepped out of the aisle hiding her from view, her denim skirt swirling around her legs. A short, tailored denim jacket showed off her narrow waist and ankle-high boots with tall heels made her long legs seem even longer. She was like a runway model until you saw the sharp intelligence in her baby blue eyes, eyes that widened when she saw us. "What's wrong?"

Morris Dredding pushed past her, stopping short when he saw Able with the sword held at the ready. "What's going on?" he demanded. If Eve was a lithe greyhound, he was a bulldog, all muscles and power in his jeans, T-shirt and windbreaker.

He moved in front of Eve but it wasn't to protect her. He headed for Luther Leroy, his hand outstretched. "Mr. Leroy? I'm not sure if you remember me. I'm Morris Dredding. Faye was my aunt. My mother is Margo, Faye's older sister."

"Hold on, Ari," I said into the phone. "There's a whole crowd of people here all of a sudden."

"Call me back," he said. "It sounds busy there."

"That's an understatement," I muttered, touching the End icon on the phone face.

Able sheathed the sword in the scabbard and laid it back into the box. As he turned, our eyes met and he smiled that slow, sweet smile, all trace of his previous bad humor evaporated. "It's a good weapon," he said softly.

It was a simple statement of fact, an appreciative comment from a man who understood weapons. I doubt if anyone else in the room saw the sword in that light, as an item of combat. Anyone else here saw it as an interesting antique or a thing of value. Able understood it in its context. A small piece of the puzzle that was Arthur Leroy fell into place for me.

Luther and Morris shook hands, Luther looking

polite and somewhat confused. I nodded toward them. "I take it your father wasn't very close to all of your stepsisters?"

Able turned to see what I was looking at. "Margo is quite a bit older than Faye. She was on her own by the time my father and—" He hesitated, as though looking for a word. "By the time my father and stepmother married."

While we watched, Dewin went to Eve's side. He stood very close to her, his head bent to hers. She kept her eyes focused on his. Dewin moved so he stood between her and Morris Dredding, subtly nudging Dredding away from her.

"He seems to be recovering from his divorce nicely," Able said dryly.

Dewin looked at me over Eve's shoulder, a speculative glance that let me know he was evaluating my reaction. "Yeah, Dewin never did let the grass grow under his feet." I raised the phone. "Can I use this again? I need to call Ari back."

"Sure. No rush." Able touched the sword in the box. "Remember, I get right of first refusal."

"I won't forget." I found Ari's number in the call list while Able joined his father and Morris. "Hey, I'm back," I said into the phone, once again moving to the back of the building for some privacy. "It's not my phone, so I probably shouldn't talk long."

"I can't believe Luther Leroy is there. What's he doing there?"

"The CEO of Scabbard Securities was killed last night." I briefly recited the few salient facts I knew about Faye Morgan's death. "She was his stepdaughter so I guess he came here to claim the body."

"Wow. That makes sense now."

"What makes sense?"

"I did some digging about that consortium you told me about." Ari paused and I heard the rustling of papers then he returned. "They're trying to buy up land all along the lake. Guess who is the majority shareholder?"

"Dewin," I said. "No surprise there."

"Not Dewin. He's not involved at all. Luther Leroy."

"What?" I peeked furtively over my shoulder where Luther, Able, and Morris were talking. "Why's he doing that?"

"I don't know. Why don't you ask him? But hey, there's something else you need to know, about the son, Arthur."

"What about him?"

"Did you know that Hector was murdered? At least, the police think he was."

"I've heard that," I said. "Why didn't Lib tell me?"

Ari made an exasperated noise. "She told me that she thought Hector killed himself and she was ashamed."

"Ashamed?" I rolled my eyes. "Why?"

"You know how she is with all her high society friends. If they found out he killed himself, she was sure she'd be treated like a pariah. Add to it the fact that he mismanaged most of their money and she's hurting financially and—well, you know how she is."

I did indeed know how Lib was. She cared more about superficial appearances than she did about substance and she always had. That explained why she married Hector Knight, a handsome, brutish, arrogant bastard who had a high society name and little money.

She gave him what she had inherited and managed to save and he gave her the social connections she so craved.

"Do the police have any motive for somebody killing him?" I asked. "I can't imagine why anyone would want to do him in except the fact that he was a bully and a boring asshole."

"That's what I wanted to tell you. They interrogated Arthur Leroy. They think he might be involved. Hector was shot and Leroy was the last person to see him alive."

Chapter 10

I almost laughed at the melodramatic tone of his voice. Of course, Ari was a lawyer and they're given to melodrama. It's the nature of the job, I think.

"That's ridiculous," I said automatically. "Why would Able want to kill Hector?"

"Able? Who's Able?"

"Arthur Leroy. What motive would he have?"

"Hector was a major shareholder in Scabbard Securities. He inherited the shares from his brother, who died—"

"Yeah, I know. In an awful car accident." My stomach lurched. To be trapped underwater like that, unable to get out. I swallowed hard, biting back the fear. "I heard about it. Able—Arthur—wouldn't kill somebody over stock options."

Ari ignored my protestations. "Here's the thing about that company. Ninety-five percent of the stock is held by family members and those members cannot sell the stock to outsiders. In the event of death, the stock has to revert to the other family members. The people who own the stock are Arthur Leroy; his ex-wife Gwynne and her husband Lenny Knight. Faye Morgan and her nephew Morris Dredding. And Luther Leroy."

"But Hector isn't a family member. How did he inherit the stock from his brother?"

"There's a court case pending about that. When

168

Arthur Leroy's ex-wife and her husband died, the husband's brother—Hector—was left in charge of the estate. He refused to turn the stock over. Arthur Leroy initiated the lawsuit."

"Even if he did, that doesn't mean he'd—"

"Everything okay?" Able asked from behind me.

I whirled, almost crashing into a crate of antique picture frames. Able grabbed me, arms going around me to keep me upright. For an instant we were face to face and chest to chest, locked in an embrace. Then he loosed his hold and I stepped back shakily.

"Ari, I have to go now," I said into the phone. "I'll call you later and we can talk about that."

"I don't like you there with all those people," Ari said. "You need to—"

I touched the End icon and handed the phone to Able. "He's a real talker," I said with an apologetic shrug. "Sorry about that."

"No problem." Able tucked the phone back in his pocket. "You know, I just realized that we never had our breakfast together."

"You're right. I forgot all about it." The sack with the food was probably cooling in the car, along with our coffee.

"How about lunch? I need to spend time with my father this morning, but I should be free by lunch."

"Okay. I'm doing inventory here then I'm going back to the store. Why don't I meet you there at noon?" I could use the landline in the warehouse and call my appraiser. Maybe I could call Ari, too, and find out more about Hector's death.

"Can I get a ride to town with you?" Able asked his father, who stood by the crate containing the sword, gazing down at the antique blade.

Luther appeared startled. I got the feeling he had been lost in thought while he stared at the sword. "It's Mervyn's car, but I'm sure that's fine. We need to talk to the Sheriff and the coroner and make arrangements for Faye." For an instant, his face softened and his eyes took on the hazy look of memory. "I can't believe she's gone. I first met her when she was a rebellious teenager trying out all kinds of odd things at college."

"She was so damn sure of herself," Able said, his fingers smoothing the velvet surround in the box.

"That's a side effect of being a teenager," I said. "When you're that age, you think you're immortal and always right."

"Immortal?" Luther nodded thoughtfully. "Yes, Faye always did act like she was protected by a guardian angel. I suppose she was, in a way. Her mother spoiled her terribly, especially after Faye's father died." His gaze went first to Able then to me. "I was just thinking about her mother, Yvette. She was such a beautiful woman, so graceful and charming."

I nodded and in doing so, I saw a bitter, sour expression in Able's eyes.

"Faye was like her in many ways, but in so many ways she was like her father." Luther sighed, a long-drawn breath of loss.

"He was arrogant and self-centered, too," Able muttered.

His disparaging words seemed to break Luther's mood of melancholy. He straightened, shooting Able a reproving look then he smiled at me, his handsome face once again affable and benign. "I hope you'll come to a quick decision regarding the sword. I'd like to get it back in the family." He nodded apologetically at Able. "Not that Gwynne wasn't family, of course."

"Right." Able smiled sardonically. He and his father started back into the warehouse and I fell into place with them. We'd gone only a few steps when Luther stopped, staring at the far wall on the right.

"Where did you get that?" He picked his way through boxes to stand in front of the tapestry hanging on the wall among framed landscape paintings. Luther stared at the cloth, hands clenched at his side.

I took an alternate path to the wall so I ended next to it, facing Luther. "An elderly woman gave it to me to sell, but she died." I smoothed the fabric affectionately. It was smallish, only four-by-five feet, but it was unique. She took a simple woven blanket and hung it on a heavy wooden dowel carved with dragons, elves and fairies cavorting in leaves and trees. The dowel was as fascinating as the wall hanging itself, which was embellished with embroidery and needlepoint to make it look like a quilt composed of twenty individual one-foot squares. Each square depicted a different scene from the Arthurian legends.

"Who was she?" Luther's gaze darted here and there to take it all in.

"She lived on the other side of the lake in Lancelot Bay. She would come to the shop now and then. She made the best jams and jellies. We used to sell them in the store. The last time she came in, she brought me the blanket and told me to find it an owner." I smiled at the memory of the wizened little lady who had pressed the blanket into my arms so insistently. "I had it up for display in the store most of the summer but nobody took an interest in it. Sy moved it here last month and I

171

was going to take it home with me to try to sell back in Iowa." I wasn't sure Luther even heard me. He was like a man in daze, staring at the different scenes, each one simply executed in vibrant colors.

I glanced at Able to see what he thought about his father's fascination and was surprised to see he was equally transfixed. Both men stood about a foot away from the tapestry, their eyes fixed on the designs.

"She left a note describing each scene. I didn't know some of the story, I guess. She had a couple that I had never heard. I mean, everybody's read about the sword in the stone and the Round Table and all that, but she had more than the ones you see in a Disney movie." I gestured toward the front of the warehouse. "I have the document in the file cabinet if you want—"

"I'll buy it." Luther turned and walked back through the boxes without a backward glance.

I started to protest. It wasn't really for sale. Elaine, the old woman who made it, told me to find it an owner, not a buyer. Maybe I was splitting hairs, but I felt a certain obligation to find it the right home. Then I glanced at Able. He smiled while his gaze went from square to square like a child looking at a kaleidoscope, delighted by the varying colors.

"It's beautiful," he murmured. "She captured the feeling of each event." He touched the cloth gently, reverently. "My father has just the right place to hang it. I'll bet it goes in his study where he can look at it every day." He shifted his gaze to me and any doubts I had vanished when I saw his happiness.

"I'll get it down and bring it to the store," I said. "Along with the documentation."

"Thank you." He fell into step with me and we

walked through the building, stopping where Dewin, Morris, and Eve stood.

"Arthur and I need to handle some business in town," Luther was saying to Dewin. "Can you give us a ride? I'm sure Arthur can give me a ride to your house later. In fact, I'd appreciate it if he would because we need to discuss the future of the company and the merger. We canceled the meetings, of course, but Dewin and I felt we should still discuss it since the officers of Scabbard Security are all here. I'd like you there, too, Arthur."

"I'm not associated with the company anymore."

"But you're a stockholder. Your opinion matters." Luther turned to me. "And you, too, of course."

"You don't need me there," I said. "Like I said, it's been years since I wrote any code. I'm sure there have been a lot of changes since I worked on the software."

"I'd appreciate your help nonetheless," Luther said. "Dewin has told me how he values your opinion. I'm sure we would all benefit from it. In addition, your late brother-in-law was involved in a lawsuit regarding the company, so perhaps you would want to attend. What you learn might be of help to your sister." He resumed walking to the front, Morris falling into step with him.

Once again I felt a flare of anger at the assumption he made that I would be happy to accommodate him. I started to snap a refusal then I saw Able's silent, pleading look. I sighed. "Sure," I said to his father's back. "Why not?"

Dewin grinned at me. "When gods command, mortals must obey," he said softly.

"Yeah," I said. "Something like that."

He moved to Eve's side and she slipped her arm

through his, pulling him close to her. She smiled sweetly at me but I saw the smug satisfaction in her eyes when Dewin's arm rubbed against her breast and his leg touched hers.

"Sorry," Able said in a low voice. "He's used to getting his own way."

"So is a two-year-old child, but that doesn't mean he always gets it."

Able laughed out loud. "Touché."

We reached the front door and I hung back while they all filed out. Eve was the last to go and she paused, turning so she blocked my view of the four men grouped around Dewin's Porsche. "I thought you should know that Dewin and I are very serious about each other. I plan to make sure he forgets all about you."

"You won't hear me complain about that." I edged to one side so I could see Morris Dredding, who was focused on whatever Luther Leroy was saying. "I thought you and Morris were together."

She made a charming little gesture with her hand, like waving away an irritable fly. It was somehow aggressive and ladylike at the same time. "Morris and I are friends. He understands my attraction to Dewin."

I doubted that. I saw the way Morris watched her with Dewin the night before. But hey, it wasn't my problem. "I'm sure if anyone can make Dewin forget the past, it will be you," I murmured. "Have fun." It was a clear invitation to leave and she took the hint, striding to the men on her high-heeled boots with her skirt whipping around her legs.

Although I closed the door against the chilly autumn air it started to swing open again. I checked it more closely and realized that not only the lock but the closing mechanism itself was damaged. I wedged a box against it to keep it closed and went to the landline phone on the workbench against the right side of the building.

I called my insurance agent, a locksmith and my appraiser, making appointments with the first two for the afternoon. The appraiser was out of the office so I left a message, asking him to call me back and let me know his availability.

Next I walked to the back of the building and retrieved my inventory list from my messenger bag. I spent the next two hours roaming throughout the building, checking off items on my list. I had a barcode inventory system for items in the store and for most of the items here so I didn't need to do much actual physical inventory. This was more of a spot check on the larger and older items that hadn't made it into the barcode database.

When I finished my check, I settled in an old chair at the back of the building and got out the provenance papers for the sword. I compared the photos to the item in the box, verifying for myself that this was, indeed, the same sword. I read through the history again, intrigued by how the sword bounced around America.

Ownership of the sword was given to the eldest male in the family at the discretion of the previous owner. Some handed over the sword at death. Others, like Luther Leroy, handed on the sword much earlier. The records showed Able took possession when he was thirty years old, eight years after being honorably discharged from the Army. A brief biography of each owner was included and it wasn't until I read it through for the third time that I saw the striking similarities in each man.

All the men in Able's family served in the military at one time or another. All the men had one son. They each learned to actually use the sword, some of them participating in tournaments and competitions and usually winning when they did. Another odd similarity was that the names in the family alternated generations, from Luther to Arthur then back again. It made for somewhat confusing reading.

According to what I could glean from the documents, Able was the fourth Arthur in America. From the way he talked, Able was no longer very close to his son. Did he name his son Luther? Would Able hand over the sword to young Luther? Did the younger man know the sword's family history? Did he care about it, the way Able cared?

"Vivian? Are you in here? It's John Reeve."

The voice from the front of the building startled me out of my musings. "In the back, John," I called, bundling the papers into the envelope. I tucked it into my messenger bag and met John, meandering his way through the aisles.

"Have you found anything missing?" John was a small man, short and compact, with thick gray hair and a weathered, lined face that made him look older than his forty years. He and his father before him were the local law since I could remember.

"Nope. Let's face it—anything anybody could steal out of here wouldn't be worth much. The pricey things are what fetch the big bucks." I tapped a massive carved oak headboard that matched the equally massive dresser next to it. "Anybody who lives in town knows that. Why would somebody bother to break in when they know it would take a truck to haul out anything worthwhile?"

"Maybe it wasn't a local person." John turned slowly, looking around the space. His dark jacket, khaki shirt and dark pants were like camouflage, letting him blend into the shifting light of the space. He went full circle, finally facing me again, his green eyes calm and impassive. "Maybe it was just a distraction."

"What? Why?"

"Can you tell me what happened last night at Dewin Mervyn's house?"

"Happened? Nothing happened. We went there, had drinks, had dinner and came back around eight or so." I shrugged. "Everything was fine when we left. How did she die, John? Was it food poisoning?"

"We're not sure yet. The Medical Examiner in Duluth will do the autopsy and run tests to help us figure it out." John pulled a small notepad and pen from his pocket. "Step me through your movements last night, okay? I want to get a good idea of who was where when."

"Didn't Able tell you?"

"Able?"

"Arthur Leroy."

"I'd just like confirmation." He glanced around the space, spying a grouping of dining room chairs. "How about we sit down and go over it?"

"Sure, but I doubt I can add anything to what Able told you." I grabbed a clean rag from the workbench and dusted off two chairs then John and I settled down, his belt with the gun and the cop gadgets thumping against the chair back when he sat.

With calm and simple questions, he had me go through everything we did the night before. I described the boat ride, Bailey Court greeting us at the dock and meeting Dewin on the steps. "He was waiting for you?" John asked, his pen poised above the pad balanced on his knee.

"I think he was on the deck, watching as we came in. Able gave him a host gift and we went inside."

"What host gift?"

"A bottle of booze. It was some kind of whiskey. Anyway, we went into the great room or living room or whatever it is. Faye and the others were all inside." I described where they were standing and how I called Sy to report in.

"Smart move," John said without looking from his notepad.

"Sy and Kay have always kept an eye on me," I said. "I'm lucky they're still living out so near to me."

"They'll have to drag Sy kicking and screaming away from the lake," John said with a wry smile. "He's an old-timer, like a lot of us."

I smiled, pleased at being considered an old-timer. "Anyway, I called Sy then I fixed myself a drink."

"You fixed yourself one?" John made a note. "Didn't Dewin do that? Doesn't the host usually do it?"

"I suppose, but I didn't give him the chance to do it. I know how I like my drinks." I thought about the previous evening. "He made one for Faye, I think. And he showed Able where the beer was stored. But otherwise I'm not sure if he made drinks for anybody."

"What kind of drink did you make?"

"Martini. Dewin and I chatted while I made it, mostly about the merger of his company with Faye

Morgan's company."

"How well did you know her?" John had his head down while he jotted a note.

"I didn't know her at all. I met them all last night for the first time."

"Except for Arthur Leroy. You knew him. And Dewin, of course. From what I've heard, he knew them all quite well." John glanced at me to gauge my reaction.

"He did?" I frowned, trying to remember if Dewin said anything about that. He acted friendly, of course, like a host, but not particularly close to anyone. Except to the girl, Eve. Dewin seemed close to her. "I didn't know that."

"They've been in discussions about this merger for a long time. From what he told me, he's spent a lot of time with all of them in Chicago."

Well, that explained how Dewin and Eve knew each other. John watched me, his sharp eyes on my face. "Last night was the first time I met them," I said.

"Except for Arthur Leroy," John repeated.

"I met Arthur—" I had a hard time saying the name. I was so accustomed to thinking of him as *Able*. "I met Arthur a few days ago at my store in Iowa. He's interested in a sword I'm selling for my sister, Lib."

John smiled. "How's she doing? Haven't seen her or your brothers for a long time."

"Archer and Leo are doing fine. They're back in Iowa. Ari is out East, working at some fancy law firm. Lib's husband died and sort of left her in the lurch so I'm helping out by selling the sword for her."

"I heard he was shot," John said, looking up at me through his lashes after he jotted something in the little notepad.

"You heard? From who?"

John straightened in his chair, tapping the notepad with his pen. "From Luther Leroy," he said. "He's got information about everybody who's here and he gave us copies of it."

"What? Does he have information about me?"

John nodded. "A pretty damn big dossier on everybody, you included." His lips twitched into a brief smile. "Big files on everybody, even his stepdaughter and her nephew. Interesting reading."

I flopped back in the chair. "Why me? He didn't know I'd be here."

"You're, um, associated with Dewin," John said, hesitating while he chose his words with care. "I suppose that's why. Or maybe because you have that sword he wants."

"But I just got the sword. How could he have time to…?" My voice faded when I realized what I was saying. Luther Leroy was one of the richest men in the world. He could probably assemble a detailed dossier about anybody within days, if not hours.

John nodded again. "Yep. He's probably been keeping an eye on that sword and when it was given to you, he did some research. And maybe sent his son to get it for him."

It all made sense, except I doubted Luther sent Able after the sword. From what I could tell, Able was after it for his own reasons. That reminded me. "Did you know that Able—I mean Arthur—is a consultant with the FBI?"

"Yep. We had a little chat with some of the people he works with." John leaned back in his chair and regarded me, frowning thoughtfully. "What are your thoughts on this? I've known you a long time and I think you're a pretty good judge of character."

"Except for Dewin?" I asked with a grin.

He tucked his notepad into his shirt pocket. "A person's allowed a few mistakes when love is involved. There's nothing wrong with Dewin Mervyn that a big dose of humility wouldn't solve."

I took a second to gather my thoughts. "I guess the question is why would someone want to deliberately kill Faye Morgan? Who has anything to gain by that?"

"Good question. There are all kinds of motives in the world. Love and money are right at the top. And besides motive, we need to consider means and opportunity. I'm not sure about the motive and we won't know about the means until we know what killed her. And once we know what killed her, we'll have a better idea who had the opportunity." He stood and I got to my feet, also. "Until we know what's going on, you watch out for yourself. Any one of those people might have been involved in her death."

"Does that mean you've eliminated me as a suspect?" I followed him while he walked back to the front door.

"I doubt if you or Arthur Leroy would be considered contenders because I doubt if either of you would have the opportunity." He stepped through the open door. "Of course, my opinion might change once we get the toxicology report."

"Good to know." I nudged the box on the floor toward the door to keep it closed.

"You call somebody about that?" John asked, nodding to the broken handle.

"Yeah, they'll be out this afternoon." I leaned in the doorframe. "Why would someone break in, John? That makes no sense. Nothing is gone. Nothing even seemed touched."

He frowned. "I'm not sure, but I think it has to do with what happened at Dewin's last night. You watch out for yourself, Vivian. Somehow, I think you're smack in the middle of all this." He tapped his pocket again.

"I have Sy and Kay keeping an eye on me. And Arthur," I added. "I'm covered."

He looked skeptical. "Remember what I said about a lapse in judgment where love is concerned."

"What's that mean?" I demanded.

John paused on the way to his squad car, parked near my Cooper. "Dewin seemed to think you and Arthur Leroy are involved."

I managed a credible chuckle. "It's been months since I saw Dewin and he sees me for a few hours and decides I'm in love with somebody?" I shook my head. "Since when did he become psychic?"

John nodded. "Yeah. Odd, isn't it?" He went to the car then turned to look at me. "Are you going out to Dewin's place later on with the others?"

I shrugged. "I was summoned by the great Luther Leroy and I don't dare disobey."

John hesitated for a second, eyeing me thoughtfully. "It's not a secret, I guess. Dewin knows. I might see you out there later. We're trying to get a search warrant for his property."

"What? A search warrant?"

"I told you. Be careful." He got into the car and drove off, leaving me staring behind him.

Holy moly. What were they looking for with that search warrant? I shook my head and returned inside. I retrieved my messenger bag and started to leave, but hesitated by the crate containing the sword. I hated the thought of leaving it behind. Granted, no one bothered with it while the building remained unlocked last night, but it still worried me to think of it here, unprotected. I decided to take it to town and store it at the shop until the lock was changed and I could be sure it was secure.

I got the tapestry down from the wall and carried it to the workbench near the sword. I rolled up the tapestry on its dowel and wrapped it in a clean old sheet before putting it on top of the sword. Then I wrapped the whole thing in a worn blanket, tying the ends securely.

I took it and my messenger bag out to the Cooper where I tucked the sword into the hidden cargo hold under my trunk liner and tossed my bag into the back seat. A piece of rope from a bin inside the Shack worked to tie the door to the warehouse shut.

A few minutes later, I hopped in the car and was at the store promptly at noon. I parked next to Able's car in front and went to the trunk to get the sword. Then I spied Luther and Able inside the shop, Luther leaning on the counter and looking out at me.

If I got out the tapestry for him to view then I'd have to reveal that I had the sword with me. I could imagine him having a hissy fit about me lugging it around so cavalierly, just wrapped in an old, albeit clean, blanket and tossed into my car. I pretended to reach into the trunk to arrange something then I slammed the lid and went inside.

"I'm sorry, I didn't have time to get down that

tapestry you wanted," I told Luther when I entered. "I can do it after lunch if you'd like."

"That's fine. Bring it to the house tonight, would you? I have to meet Dewin now." He held out his hand to Sy. "Pleasant chatting with you. I appreciate the advice." He passed me going to the door. "I'll see you later." Then he was gone.

"What advice?" I asked Sy, taking Luther's place at the counter.

"I told him how Dewin never uses any local people for the work done out at his house. If a man is going to have a home here, he should use the local workmen for jobs." Sy nodded emphatically, his white buzz cut almost vibrating with surety.

"Is your father building a house here?" I asked Able. Maybe Luther's involvement in the consortium wasn't such a secret after all.

"I doubt it," Able said with a frown. "He's not really the outdoors type. He complained about a residential property he has in Shanghai that isn't being managed properly. Sy pointed out that there's nothing like having a manager living on the premises to ensure things get done right. That led to discussions about other residential properties, like Dewin's and how he's been managing his."

Sy crossed his arms on his flannel-shirted chest. "Bringing in a fancy chef and staff to cook and serve meals. Hiring an outside cleaning service to keep the place going. Like we aren't good enough to wait on him."

"I doubt he even thinks about it," I said.

"You're probably right. I heard you're going out there again tonight." Sy pursed his lips, regarding me worriedly.

"I was summoned," I said gloomily.

"We won't stay long," Able said quickly. "I promise."

"Hmm. Was everything okay at the Shack?" Sy asked. "I'm sorry I couldn't get there last night to meet the police."

"You were too busy to worry about it. I couldn't tell that anything was disturbed. I called the hardware store and they're sending someone out to put on a new handle."

Sy nodded. "They called here and said somebody could go out there at twelve-thirty." He glanced at the Betty Boop clock on the wall. "You folks go on and get some lunch. I'll lock up here in a few minutes and go out to the Shack. By the time you're done with lunch, the new lock will be in place."

"Sounds good. I'm hungry. How about you?" I nudged Able.

"Ready when you are. I checked earlier and the cafe looks busy."

"We can go to the White Hart," I said. "It's a bar down the street. They have good food and I wouldn't mind a beer."

He smiled. "Lead on."

We emerged into a brilliant autumn day, the faint aroma of wood smoke and leaves in the air acting as a perfect accompaniment to the blue sky, vibrant foliage colors and brisk air. All of those aspects combined to offer us the quintessential fall day in Northern Minnesota. Even the gray clouds piling on the horizon only served to accent the amazing azure sky.

The Hart was across the street and just a few steps

north of the shop. In addition to booths and bar stools, a seating area was near a window above the street. Able and I took chairs there, giving me a good view of my car. I didn't expect anyone to rob me, but I didn't want to take any chances, either.

We ordered burgers and beer, sipping in silence for a few minutes. "I guess I never really expressed my sympathy," I said. "Faye was your stepsister, after all. I'm sorry for your loss."

Able lowered his beer mug. "Loss?" He shook his head. "Politeness has kept me from saying anything before this. She's no big loss. If I had my way, I probably would have killed her a long time ago."

Chapter 11

I almost choked while I swallowed some beer. "What?" I gasped. Holy moly, did he mean what I thought he meant?

He saw the stunned look on my face and his eyes widened. "No, I didn't mean it that way. It's just a figure of speech. I never would have killed her although I have to admit, I wished her dead a few times."

I started breathing normally again. "Why?"

Able took his time to answer, sipping his beer while he sorted out his words. "I don't have the same happy memories my father has of Faye and her mother. Faye was far more than a rebellious teenager, like my father called her. She was a lying, promiscuous, conniving witch. Faye didn't care who she hurt if she could get what she wanted. My father had to bail her out of jams more often than I can count and he had to smooth over a lot of ruffled feathers from the stunts she pulled."

"You obviously saw things he didn't," I said, at a loss for how to respond to such raw anger and bitterness.

"She was very careful to show Luther only what she wanted him to see. Faye always made it seem like she was the victim. Faye knew I wouldn't go to my father and complain. He was so in love with her mother he wouldn't have believed me." Able took a swallow of beer, his hand trembling when he set down the mug. "She came on to me once. It was right before my father married her mother."

"No offense, but that's kind of weird." I made a face. "I mean, it's not like you were really related, but you were, kind of."

He nodded. "It didn't matter to her. Or her mother." His mouth twisted, forcing back words that shouldn't be said.

When he said *her mother* I heard a subtle inflection, a twist of extra bitterness. "Her mother the beauty?" I asked lightly.

He grimaced. "Her mother the harlot, you mean. She cheated on Luther every chance she got. My mother died when I was little and he threw himself into his work. In fact, he didn't see anything but work for years, until he met her—Yvette."

Again, I heard that inflection, the way his voice dropped into a lower tone when he said her name. Small clues seemed to drop into place. "The daughter tried to seduce you and when she failed, the mother succeeded?"

Able almost dropped his mug. As it was, a lot of beer sloshed over the side when he set it down. His cheeks were red and so were the tips of his ears. I touched his arm sympathetically.

"I was stupid," he muttered. "I was married with two kids and I wasn't happy. Gwynne and I were having problems and—" He took a long swallow of beer. "No excuses. I was stupid. Luckily my father didn't find out and Gwynne didn't find out. Otherwise there would have been hell to pay."

This intimate chat was interrupted when the

barmaid delivered our burgers, big juicy patties that demanded two hands to hold them and full attention to prevent juice spillage on our shirts. As we ate, I had a sudden thought that made me pause in my chewing.

Why did I believe him? I really didn't know Arthur B. Leroy well at all, yet I was willing to believe every word he said. I just met him a few days ago and knew very little about him. He lived in Des Moines, he worked for the FBI as a consultant, he had a phenomenal memory, he was a good kisser, he—

I set down my burger, blinking in surprise. That one kiss was no basis for the evaluation of a person's kissing ability. I mean, granted, it made my knees slightly wobbly and left me somewhat gasping, but was that so important?

I shelved evaluations of romantic prowess for the moment. I was convinced Able was a Good Guy in every sense of the word. For some strange reason, I felt I knew him as well as I knew Dewin. Actually, better than Dewin because he and I had been separated for so long. No, it was as if Able and I were friends with years behind us instead of just days.

"Penny for your thoughts," he said, breaking into my musings.

"I was wondering why I trust you so much. I barely know you, but I do trust you." I nibbled on a French fry and glanced at him for his reaction to my honesty.

He stared out the front window, his face thoughtful. "Maybe we knew each other in a previous life. Or maybe you just have good instincts about people." He glanced at me, his dark brown eyes mischievous and laughing. "I trust you, too."

"Yeah, but I have more at stake than you do," I

pointed out. "After all, you're the one driving the boat when we go out on the lake."

"And you're the one who knows my darkest secret." He leaned against me, giving me a playful push. "My weakness for martinis and beautiful, curly-haired women."

Any response I might have made was interrupted by my insurance agent, Alvin Selwyn, a plump, jovial gentleman who worked at the Shield Insurance Agency a block away from Main Street. He came in the back door and worked his way through the crowded bar to us. "I ran into Sy and he said you were coming here for lunch. You don't mind if we chat, do you? I have to drive to Duluth this afternoon so I was hoping we could go out to the warehouse earlier."

I dabbed at my lips with a napkin. "That's fine. We're almost done with lunch." I checked my watch. "Sy is out there now. Give me twenty minutes and I'll meet you there."

"Are you sure? I hate to rush you." Alvin eyed my half-eaten burger and half-consumed beer. "I don't have to be in Duluth until two-thirty, so there's time."

"Not a problem," I assured him. "You head on over. I'm having a new lock put on and the police already gave me a new security code. I went through the place this morning and did a quick look-around and I don't think anything was disturbed, much less taken."

He shook his balding head sadly. "Probably some kids out on a prank. Your insurance covers the damage to the door, of course, and you've already met your deductible because of that wind storm in the spring. I have some paperwork in the car. We'll fill that out and you'll be reimbursed before you know it."

"Good to know there won't be any problems. I got a report from the police, so I'll make a copy for you."

Alvin's head bobbed happily. I'm sure he was relieved there wouldn't be any tedious claims work to do. "I'll see you there, then. Thanks for being so flexible." He bustled back the way he'd come, pausing to chat with a few patrons on the way.

"What's on your schedule for the afternoon?" I asked Able.

"I'm driving to Duluth, too. I have to arrange for Faye's body to be moved when the medical examiner is done with it. My father and I are her next of kin, so we need to handle that."

"I'm surprised her nephew isn't doing it. After all, they worked together. I guess I assumed they were close." I smiled wryly. "It sounds like you and she weren't on the best of terms so it's odd that you have to handle it."

"My father should handle it, but to be honest, he's more upset by her death than I thought he'd be."

"I suppose it raised memories of her mother, whom he obviously loved." I took another bite of my burger then pushed the basket away. Heaven knows, I didn't need the calories.

"There's that, I suppose. And he's getting older. We all seem to forget that he's in his seventies. It's been a big strain on him."

Seventies? I was surprised. Luther Leroy looked and acted far younger than that. But he would have to be that old to have Arthur for a son. "It's too bad you can't delegate some of the unpleasantness to her nephew, though."

"Morris isn't the most capable person around,"

Able said, picking his words with care. "The only reason he has a job is because he's family. It's probably better if my father and I handle it and since he's busy with Dewin, I get to deal with the paperwork." He finished the last of his burger, washing it down with the last of his beer. "I should be back by four o'clock at the latest so I can drive us to Dewin's house tonight."

I sighed. "Do I really have to go? I have nothing to contribute to a merger discussion."

Able pulled out his wallet and laid a twenty on the table. "I'd appreciate it you'd come." He took my hand and squeezed it lightly. "I really would."

I sighed again. "Okay." Then I brightened when I remembered the tapestry in the trunk of my car. "I have that wall hanging for your father. Maybe I can negotiate a good price on it."

Able laughed. "Don't forget, you need to give me a price on the sword, too."

"The appraiser can't get here until tomorrow so you'll have to wait." I slipped off my bar stool and we went outside, crossing the street to my car. The air felt colder. The wind had shifted direction and instead of a gentle breeze coming from the southwest, it felt like a gustier wind was coming from the north. "Where do you want to meet later?" I asked, my hand on my car door.

"I parked at the public dock, down the street there." Able gestured to our left. "Why don't you meet me there at four-thirty? I'll call you if I'm going to be late."

"My mobile service is iffy here," I reminded him.

"I'll call the store and leave word if I can't get in touch with you." He glanced at his watch. "I have plenty of time."

I touched my sweater. "I should probably go back to my cabin and change clothes before we go."

"Why?" Able eyed me, up then down. "You look great."

I tugged my denim jacket closed on my cowl-neck sweater. "I suppose you're right. After all, I did wear my good jeans." I grinned, running a hand over the dark fabric on my thigh.

Able took my hand and tugged me closer to him. "Don't change a thing," he said softly. Then he kissed me, his body pressed against mine where I leaned against my car.

It took a few seconds for me to remember that we were standing in Main Street, with all the windows facing out and probably more than a few patrons watching us. Then I figured, *oh, what the hell,* and I put my arms around him and participated with a lot of enthusiasm.

We broke apart several dazzling moments later. "That was fun," he murmured.

"Yes, it was." I managed to turn and slide into my car. "But maybe we shouldn't be having so much fun in front of the entire town."

He grinned. "That sounds like a promise of privacy later."

I successfully got the car started, once again thanking God for a keyless ignition system. I doubt if I could have gotten a key into the ignition slot. "It's a big lake," I said out my opened window. "Lots of room for privacy."

He watched me back out, smiling.

I was glad for the drive to the Shack, using the ten minutes to calm my rattled hormones. I hated to admit how much I enjoyed that brief kiss. I'd been living my celibate life for so long that I wasn't sure if I wanted a man intruding on it. At least, that's what I'd been telling myself until I met Able.

I had a few flings in my past, but they were long behind me. I wasn't the sort of person who indulged in one-nighters or love-em-and-leave-em behavior. I just wasn't cut out for brief affairs so I avoided the whole thing by not having affairs at all. What if Able did want some kind of relationship? He lived in Des Moines, I lived in Linn. Two hours separated us. Granted, not a big deal given the Interstate.

Now that I thought of it, maybe that wouldn't be so bad. He could have his life, I could have mine, and we could get together now and again. I took the last parking slot at the Shack, pulling in next to Sy's pickup. The other slots held Alvin's car and the locksmith's. I grabbed my bag from the passenger seat. I decided to cross any romance-bridges when I got to them. Maybe this was all just a bunch of harmless flirting on his part.

Happy to postpone my thoughts, I went to talk to the locksmith, who was just finishing his work when I arrived. I took possession of a new set of keys and went inside to find Sy and Alvin seated at my battered old desk, having a cup of coffee. I filled out the necessary paperwork then Alvin walked around and took a few pictures, 'just for formality sake,' he said.

"What happened to that old needlework that used to hang there?" Sy asked, nodding toward the bare spot on the wall.

"I sold it to Luther Leroy. That reminds me. I forgot to get the papers for the tapestry." I rummaged in a file drawer and found the folder with the old woman's descriptions of the panels on the wall hanging.

"What's he paying for it?" Sy asked.

"We didn't talk price. I get the feeling with Luther Leroy, you don't bother dickering. He names a figure and you take it."

"That's a bit high-handed, isn't it?"

"It's not like that. What I meant was he'll probably offer me ten times its value and I'd be crazy not to take it." I tucked the folder into my bag and walked to meet Alvin, who was working his way toward us.

"I didn't know you had Internet security in here," he said, his voice rife with accusation. "That can help lower your premiums, you know. Did the police get anything from the video feed?"

"What do you mean?"

He turned. "Back there. The camera."

Sy and I followed him to the middle of the building, to a cluster of wooden furniture. He pointed at a free-standing china hutch. "I wouldn't have seen it except when I turned, it caught the light. That's a good place for it. Where are the others?"

I peered at the top of the ten-foot hutch. Sure enough, a small black teardrop shaped device sat on top of the walnut cabinet, blending in with its surroundings. It was about three inches tall with a small circle of glass in the middle.

"People usually do four or more. A building this size, you could easily have six. Of course, I suppose with the security panel, you don't really need that many."

Sy was quicker on the uptake than me. "We just did four," he said, steering Alvin to the front of the building. I followed them, looking over my shoulder at the gadget perched high above us. "It's just set to go straight to video because I can't be monitoring a screen all day." He laughed very convincingly. "It's not like anybody's going to haul out a bed without somebody seeing it."

"Well, it will still lower your premiums. You should have told me." Alvin paused at the front door. "I'll get that paperwork processed, Vivian, and we'll get you a reimbursement for your lock. I'll come out another day when I have time and I'll get pictures of your cameras and I'll see what I can do for your premiums."

I nodded, barely hearing what he said. It felt like I was in a spotlight, standing there with a camera behind me pointed at who knows what and being watched by who knows who. "Sounds good, Alvin. Thanks." I stepped outside the building to stand next to Sy. "What the hell is happening?" I whispered around a smile at Alvin, who was getting into his car.

"Somebody broke in last night, not to take something, but to leave something behind, it looks like." Sy smiled at Alvin then turned his back on my insurance agent to speak to me. "Somebody put that camera in there. Do you think there are others?"

"Probably," I said, waving to Alvin while he backed out. "It took about twenty or thirty minutes from the time the alarm sounded until somebody got here. That's plenty of time to walk through and set a few cameras." I tugged my jacket tighter. It was definitely colder, although the sky was still blue with just a few scudding gray clouds on the western horizon. "I'll bet it's all done with WiFi or satellite," I said, thinking out loud. "I'm sure there's a way to track it back to the source but I'm not exactly sure how to do it."

"Who would do it?" Sy asked. "Why?"

"Well, whoever did it now knows that we know." I dug my hands into my coat pockets, shivering when a chill wind whipped around the corner of the building. "We should tell John Reeve. Let's go back to the shop and I'll call him."

"Wait a minute. Whoever put that there may not know that we're on to them. It depends if they're looking at the video or whatever it is. That camera might not even be on. Maybe it gets turned on or off."

I thought about that. I researched a video surveillance system a year or so ago. The ones I was interested in were motion activated. But others could be set on a timer or turned on remotely, at any time. All you needed was the right equipment and a smart phone.

"What do we have to lose?" Sy asked. "Let's find the other ones. Once we know where they are, we can go back, call John and maybe he can track it back to whoever set it up."

I shook my head doubtfully. "That takes some serious computer work. I doubt if John has anybody on his staff that can do it."

"He's got the computer club at the high school helping him out," Sy said. "You'd be amazed at what those young'uns can do. Come on. Let's do some of the footwork and see what our thief was so interested about."

I considered it. "Okay. It shouldn't hurt anything." We went back inside.

"Now just act natural," Sy said in a low voice. "Whoever is watching may not have the sound on. Or maybe they're not watching at all right now."

I nodded nervously. Of course, the minute he said to act natural, I felt like I was on a stage and I forgot all about how to act naturally, almost tripping over my feet while we walked. Sy led the way to the back of the building, talking while he meandered.

"Can't believe somebody wanted that old wall hanging. How long has it been here?"

"A few years," I mumbled, my eyes darting right and left, looking for other cameras.

He shot me a reproachful look and wiggled his fingers slightly. "How long?" he prompted.

"I got it a few years ago from an old lady who lived on the other side of the lake," I said, elaborating for our unseen visitors. "She used to love to come in the store and look around."

"What was her name?" Sy roamed through the aisles of furniture, boxes and bins, his brown eyes searching high and low.

"Elaine," I said. "I think her last name was Pella or Pelles or something like that. She lived alone."

"I remember her," Sy said, moving down the aisle. "I think she was divorced or maybe a widow." He gestured furtively to the left, near the wall where the tapestry had hung. I moved in what I hoped was a nonchalant fashion that way, pretending to stop and look at a box of old cast iron grates.

"There," Sy breathed. "Up on the picture of the sailing ship."

I straightened and walked on, pausing once to look back and let my gaze sweep over the wall. Yep, there it was. Tucked in the dark reaches of the wall was a small glitter of light from the lens.

We continued pacing through the entire building,

pausing to chat here and there. By the time we left an hour later, we found five cameras all situated at strategic areas.

It wasn't until I was following Sy back to town that I realized someone might have seen me package the sword and take it out of the building. I immediately checked my rear view mirror, as though someone might be lurking behind me on the sleepy town streets. The only car I saw was a faded green sedan which turned off before we reached Main Street.

Sy and I went to the police station, but we were told John was gone for the afternoon. I belatedly remembered the search warrant and wondered if that was what was occupying him. In the end, Sy and I decided not to file a report but wait until we could talk to John in person. Neither Sy nor I would be going back to the Shack until we talked to him, so it didn't matter if someone continued to watch on those stealth cameras.

We went to the shop and Sy insisted we do a complete sweep, as he called it, checking the shop for any electronic devices. It was easier said than done because there were a million places somebody could hide such a thing. In the end, we did a combination of inventory and investigation, working our way through any immediately accessible spots where someone could have placed a device.

We stopped at a little after four and I used our tiny bathroom to wash my face and hands and make an attempt to tame my flyaway hair. I gave it up as a lost cause and left with Sy by the back door where our cars were parked.

"I heard on the news that we might get snow tonight," Sy said, locking the shop behind us. "I hope you brought your warm coat if you're going out tonight."

I thought of my parka, hanging on the deck. "I have a blanket in the car," I said. "I'll bundle up in that. We shouldn't be out late."

"You call us again like you did last night." He stopped with his hand on his pickup door handle. "I don't like that you're going out there again. I got a bad feeling about the lake tonight."

I wanted to laugh off what he said but I didn't. I trusted Sy's bad feelings and I knew what he meant. I hated the thought of going back to Dewin's house. *Awkward* didn't even begin to cover it. It felt creepy. Shouldn't at least some time be spent mourning the dead woman? Or shouldn't her death at least be acknowledged somehow?

"I'll be careful," I said. "Able is a good navigator and we won't stay out late."

He nodded but I could tell he was still worried. That's okay. I was worried, too. He drove off with a wave and I drove in the opposite direction, heading for the public dock on the outskirts of town.

Able was already there, sitting in his car in the parking lot. He got out when he saw me coming. I parked next to his car and pulled out my messenger bag. That's when I remembered I still had the damn sword in the trunk of my car.

I didn't want to leave it here especially on the chance someone saw me take it via a clandestine video feed. I made a fast decision while Able walked toward me. "I have that tapestry for your father," I said, opening the trunk. "Do you have a tarp we can wrap it in?" I pulled out the wrapped sword and wall hanging, as well as my old and frayed camp blanket.

"Sure." He took the bundle from me and nodded toward my blanket. "Smart idea. It's going to be cold on the lake. Do you have a heavier coat?"

I shook my head. "I didn't plan for a change in the weather. Silly me."

"I have a heavy jacket in the boat. That and the blanket should keep you warm."

I wrapped the blanket loosely around my shoulders and followed Able to his boat, docked not far from us. He helped me in then he hopped in, unmindful of how the boat bobbed with his weight. I took the seat next to the captain's chair and he pulled a heavy black plastic tarp from a compartment in the side.

He spread the tarp on the bottom of the boat and put the tapestry/sword bundle at one end, rolling it up in the plastic and tucking the ends in halfway through the process, the same way you'd roll a burrito. "It's heavier than it looks," he said while he manhandled the bulky fabric.

"I rolled it around an old oak bedpost. I didn't want to wrinkle the fabric."

"Makes sense," he said.

He bought the story. I breathed a sigh of relief. Given how protective they were of the sword, if they knew it was here, lying near my feet in Able's boat, they'd probably read me the riot act. Although, now that I thought of it, they didn't bat an eye when they found out the Shack was broken into and the sword was left unprotected, so to speak.

"Here you go." Able pulled a heavy windbreaker out of another compartment and handed it to me. I pulled it on, happy for its additional flannel-lined warmth on top of my denim jacket.

Able piloted us away from the metal dock, his gaze moving from side to side. The water was choppier today, with big dips and swells near the shore where the waves lapped on the rocks. There was also a lot of boat traffic tonight, mainly fishermen coming in from a day on the lake. I suppose the cold weather and setting sun were driving them homeward.

I didn't know this part of the lake very well, although I docked here now and again when I had business on the east side of the lake. This area of six docks was at the end of a long chunk of land jutting into the lake and near a wide channel separating the east and west ends of the lake. We were about ten miles northeast of Sy's dock, which meant our trip would be longer today. I glanced once at the whitecaps, gritted my teeth and focused on my breathing and keeping my stomach under control.

I clung to the seat, my feet resting on the wrapped sword while I sought a topic to keep my mind off the water underneath us. "You know about law enforcement stuff, right?"

Able shot me a quick look while we left the dividing channel and entered the lake proper. He slowed, letting a faster boat go by. "I know probably more than the average guy, yes."

"John Reeve told me they were going to do a search at Dewin's house."

He nodded like this was the most natural thing in the world.

"Does that mean they think Faye was murdered?"

Able moved us forward again and I kept my eyes on him, not on the lake. The deep lake. The cold lake.

"She was reasonably healthy and she died suddenly. She had no known allergies and she had all the symptoms of poisoning. I guess it's not too far-fetched to consider murder."

"Who has a motive to kill her?"

He grinned. "Besides me? Just kidding. Let's see. Morris might kill her so he could be CEO, although if my father has anything to do with it, that won't happen. Brad could kill her just because Brad is an asshole."

"Can you be serious, please?" I tapped the bundle under my chair. It felt surprisingly comforting to have it there. I rested both feet on its solid bulk, as though the sturdiness of the sword could morph into a steadier boat.

"Seriously? I don't know. Murder is a risky business." He steered adroitly into the center of the lake and headed southwest. The setting sun was an indistinct glow in the gray clouds on the horizon. The sight of the clouds made me huddle deeper into Able's jacket, which smelled vaguely of fish. I didn't care. It was warm.

"What do you mean it's risky? Don't you think that's why she was killed here? I mean, wouldn't a murderer assume that a place like this has a small police force, so the odds of getting away with it are better?"

"You think like a murderer," he said with a sidelong glance at me.

"Or maybe I just have a practical mind," I countered.

"Maybe," he said doubtfully. At least, I think it was doubtful.

"I thought a lot of murders don't get solved. That's what it sounds like if you watch enough TV shows.

There are all those cold case shows."

"If you believe that then you must believe that crimes are solved in an hour or two." He steered us into the wind, the boat bobbing even more.

"Of course not. But if murder's so risky, why do people do it?" I realized I wasn't being logical, but I was anxious to keep the conversation going. I wanted anything to distract me from the rise and fall of the boat. I was thankful I wasn't out in my smaller utility boat. If we were moving this much in Able's boat, it made my stomach lurch to think what mine would be like. Thank goodness I didn't have to worry about it tonight.

"Most murders are spontaneous, spur-of-moment events. Somebody gets in a fight, they get so angry they're not thinking straight and before you know, a gun is pulled and somebody dies." He glanced at me and raised an eyebrow. "Sound familiar?"

"You make me sound like a gun-toting desperado. I told you, all I would do was fire warning shot."

"Warning shots can go astray. Premeditated murder doesn't happen as often as you see on TV because it's hard to get away with it. There are a lot of variables that have to be considered."

"Motive, method and opportunity," I said, pressing down hard on the sword when the boat rode up one swell and down another.

"Exactly." Able pointed to the left. "There's Sy's place. See the flag?"

I peered through the windshield, spying the black-and-gold Iowa Hawkeye flag in the distance. I breathed a sigh of relief. We were only twenty minutes or so from Dewin's house. I belatedly remembered my boat was at Sy's, waiting for me. Maybe Sy could pick me up in the morning from my cabin. I would need to talk to him tonight about that.

Able put the boat engine into neutral. "I think it's time we talked."

Chapter 12

"What are you doing?" I asked, looking around frantically.

"We need to talk." Able said it with a sense of finality, like something momentous was about to happen.

I didn't care. All I wanted was to get moving. "Okay. Get us to land and we'll talk." I gestured toward the steering wheel. "Start the boat. Get us moving."

"This is more private. Nobody can eavesdrop here."

"Eavesdrop? On what? For heaven's sake, keep driving, would you? We can talk once we get to shore." Then his words registered. "Eavesdrop? Did you know someone bugged my warehouse?"

Able nodded. "When I was told about a break-in, I thought it might be something like that. I went through the place last night and found them."

"What? Why didn't you tell me?"

"I needed time to track them back to the person who put them there."

A wave rocked the boat and my stomach lurched. "Can we talk about this on land?"

"I lied to you."

I stared at him, open-mouthed. We were stranded in the middle of the damn lake and he was confessing. What the hell? "About what?"

He stared at me as if I could read the truth in his eyes. "I used you to get close to your ex-husband."

"Dewin? Why?" I knew why but I wanted to hear him say it.

"He's under investigation. I needed the opportunity to get close to him, to try to evaluate his involvement. And I needed to know if you were involved, too."

"What? Me?"

"He's made no secret of the fact he still loves you. Maybe your indifference to him was just a front. Maybe it was a perfect disguise for what was going on. Maybe you and he were still lovers and you were working with him."

My panic turned to indignation then to sarcasm. "And what did you find out, Mr. Secret Agent? Did I prove to you I'm not still Dewin's long-lost love?"

Able smiled slightly. "Yeah, you did. I decided you weren't involved."

"Involved in what?" Maybe if I played along, he'd start the stupid boat and get us moving again.

"We were told by an informant that the software code being developed by your company is being auctioned to the highest bidder."

"It's not my company anymore," I said automatically. "Wait a minute. What do you mean it's being auctioned? You make it sound like a bunch of guys are all in a room somewhere, huddled around a computer monitor and waving their numbers." I held an imaginary auction paddle in one hand.

"You're not too far wrong. The same thing happens, but it's all electronic. The seller establishes a high-speed Internet feed with closed-circuit cameras. The buyers are given the IP address to log in to the feed. The code is demonstrated and the buyers submit closed bids electronically to a secure email address."

I tapped first one foot, then the other, on the sword bundle, using the action to propel my brain away from my fears of drowning and into the realm of software piracy. It could work, I suppose. A person could set up an Internet Protocol address, which designated a specific computer. There were private networks that had private IP addresses, but typically the addresses were assigned by a public entity that managed such things on a global scale.

"Criminals have been doing it for years," Able said, correctly interpreting my silence for skepticism. "Closed-circuit feeds are hard to track back, especially if it's dynamically routed. I heard about one case where a kidnapper used it to show the family pictures of the victim, to prove she was still alive."

I had a vague understanding about that, too. IP addresses could be static and unchanging or could be dynamically allocated from a block assigned to a group or corporation. I had no idea how it was done. That fell into the area of network management, something I avoided like the plague because it required a whole other level of software understanding that I didn't possess.

"The Feds can track it, though, right?"

"How close are we to Canada?" Able asked.

I looked north, the setting sun sending fingers of light bouncing over the lake, rippling with the waves and the clouds on the far horizon. "Ten miles, maybe less."

"There are international laws about tracking back computer network protocols. Some countries allow it.

Some don't."

"Canada allows it?"

He nodded. "But if the originating address is in a non-participating country, Canada will honor that. The U.S. has other laws regarding that eventuality."

"So if someone originated the signal in Canada but bounced it to Bosnia or some other country that doesn't allow trackback…" My voice trailed away while I considered it. "Do you have proof?"

"Not really. My friend told me his suspicions then we got new information from someone on the inside. Someone who refuses to be identified. But it's someone who I think is here this weekend."

"Wait a minute." I tapped the bundle again, reassured by its solidity. "That means it must be Morris, Eve, or Dewin, right?"

"Or Brad." He grimaced. "I hate to think that bastard is a good guy, but it's a possibility. And you forgot one other person."

I frowned, puzzled.

"Faye."

"Oh." That's right. I forgot her. Then a realization hit me. "Oh. Do you think she was killed because she was the informant?"

He nodded, finally—*finally*—nudging the motor so we puttered forward. "I was asked to investigate because of my connection to the family and the company. We had to make it look good. I couldn't just appear when they were all here. That would have been too suspicious."

"So you used me." I sat it flatly and tried to sound non-accusing, but I'm not sure I succeeded.

"It was a perfect opportunity." He focused on

steering, for which I was grateful. Not only were we moving again, but I didn't have to look him in the eye. "You had the sword and I wanted the sword. It would make sense that I would follow you here where, lo and behold, everyone was gathered."

I mulled that for a minute. "So what do you think about Dewin? Do you think he's the mastermind behind it all?"

Able shook his head. "I think he's a dupe. I don't think he has any idea that the software code he might be handing to Scabbard Security will end up on the black market."

"That's a snap judgment from someone who's spent like two hours with the man," I said. "Do you have any facts to back it up?"

He was quiet for a minute then he said, "No offense regarding your taste in men, but he doesn't strike me as being intelligent enough to manage such a thing. Or maybe intelligent isn't the right word. I don't think he's energetic enough, if you know what I mean."

I did know what he meant. Dewin always took the easy way if he could. Arranging a black market auction of cutting edge software would require a calculating nature and someone who was savvy about the software involved. Dewin was crafty but in a more overt way. And I doubted he had the software ability to pull it off. "So that leaves Brad and Morris."

"And Eve," Able said, turning the boat so we were now going north, into the bay where my cabin was located.

"Eve?" I forgot all about the waifish child-woman who clung to Dewin's side. "She's just a girlfriend, isn't she?" I hated that I sounded so dismissive, but she hadn't exhibited much personality except that of a hanger-on.

"She has a Ph.D. in Computer Science from Carnegie-Mellon University. She's no lightweight."

"Holy moly," I muttered. "I had no idea. Does Dewin know?"

"I think he must. She used to work for him."

"What?"

Able nodded. "She worked for Dewin Software until about a year ago, in the Marketing division. She changed to Scabbard Security late last year."

I wondered what other secrets Able had up his sleeve. "You set me up, that first night at the shop, didn't you?" I accused.

Able blew out a long breath. "Yeah, I figured if you were in debt to me for helping you out of a jam, you'd trust me faster. I had a friend pretend to follow you for a couple of nights." He grinned. "Darren almost peed his pants when you drew your gun."

"Is he just a friend or is he with the FBI, too?"

Able laughed. He seemed totally at home out here on the water, easily handling the bouncing boat through the choppy waves, the wind riffling his hair and the cold air making his cheeks glow with color. I thought I had never seen such a carefree person as the way he was at that moment. "Yeah, he's with the Agency. He didn't expect a female shopkeeper in Iowa to be packing heat."

I laughed, too, and for an instant I was just as carefree. The cold air whipped my curls around my face and I was huddled for warmth into Able's jacket, but I didn't mind at all. I was safe and secure with him even though untold depths were beneath us.

The thought chilled me into sobriety. I glimpsed my cabin on the right, nestled on its small peninsula. The dock lights had come on, activated by twilight to outline the short length of the planking. One light glowed in the living room, set by the timer it was plugged into. The sight was comforting but also far away, like a life preserver just out of reach.

"Us female shopkeepers can surprise you."

"No kidding." Able grinned again. "You've surprised me more than once, that's for sure."

The warmth in his voice made me understand that the surprises weren't all unpleasant. That was a nice thing to consider, but we were still out on the damn lake and the waves were kicking up faster and higher. I struggled to find a new topic to divert my attention. "Why was your father so interested in this tapestry?" I asked, tapping the bundle with my left foot.

"My father has always been fascinated by the Arthurian legends," Able said. "From what I could see on that wall hanging, whoever did it was fascinated, as well. A couple of those panels represent little-known aspects of the myth."

"Myth or legend?"

"I guess it depends who you talk to. It's a family legend for us. I suppose it's because of the sword. My great-great-many-times grandfather brought it with him from England when he emigrated here."

"Plus a lot of men in your family are named Arthur," I said.

"You did your homework. I suppose all of that is on the papers that came with the sword." He glanced at me quickly but returned his focus to steering. The wind coming off the rocky land near us eddied and swirled into the bay, making the boat rock from side to side and front to back. I fought to keep my emotions and my stomach under control, but inwardly I was close to either screaming or barfing from fear.

"I need provenance so I can determine price. There's quite a complete history with it." I peered ahead anxiously, looking for lights from Dewin's house. We had passed the overhanging promontory on the right and the high land on the left blocked most of the sun's meager light, already obscured by dark clouds.

"We've always kept the documentation current," Able said. "It's our history as well as the sword's history." He, too, stared intently forward, bent slightly to get a better view through the windshield. "Where's the dock? I thought we'd be there by now."

For an instant, I panicked. Had he forgotten the way to the house? Were we lost on the lake? Then I remembered passing my cabin and I relaxed. "Just around the point," I said with more assurance than I felt. A wave pushed us closer to shore. "Be careful, there are rocks here."

"I know." He jiggled the wheel, his hand gripping it as if the engine was fighting him. The boat struggled to go left, away from the shore. I longed to point out the rocks and the shallower water, but I knew that he knew. I glanced once at the set, determined look on his face where all trace of carefree laughter had vanished. I subsided back in my chair, both feet firmly on the sword and my hands clutching the sides of my seat.

I suddenly realized I wasn't wearing a life vest. I wanted to go scrambling into the boat to look for one, but I was too terrified to move. The boat heaved and rolled, fighting the wind and the waves. Able pulled the wheel firmly to the left, drawing us with maddening slowness away from the crashing shore.

We changed course, heading northeast and the waves quieted. Able let the boat settle into the new course. We rounded the peninsula and there were the lights, high on the bluff overhead. "I think my life flashed in front of my eyes," I said, my voice cracking with strain.

Able steered us toward the dock, still fighting the current, but it was less forceful now. "I wasn't going to let that wall hanging go down. My father would never forgive me." Then he shot me a quick grin. "Not to mention the fact you'd never forgive me if I let you get wet."

"Get wet?" I slapped him on the arm. "We almost capsized."

"It wasn't that bad." He drove to the nearest dock, still eyeing the waves pushing us around crazily. The far dock had three boats moored. The big cabin cruiser we saw the previous day was still there as well as two long aluminum utility boats and a smaller cabin cruiser with *Cook County Sheriff's Department* stenciled on the side.

"They must be doing that search warrant," I said while Able eased the boat next to the plain metal dock, edging in on the driver's side of the boat to stay in the relatively quieter water between the two docks.

"They might still be searching." He focused intently, trying to put us close without bumping too hard. "And it depends on how specific the search warrant is. Some can be broad in reach."

I took advantage of Able's distraction to ease out

of my seat and kneel on the floor of the boat, keeping my back to him. I dragged the tarp-covered bundle in front of me and out of his sight.

"Hold on! You can't tie up there!" A man hurried down the steps to us, gesturing us away from the shore.

"Wait here," Able said. "I'll be right back." He jumped out with the mooring lines in hand and tied us up then went to meet the man at the base of the steps.

"Thank you, whoever you are," I muttered, feverishly undoing the bundle and extracting the wall hanging in its covering sheet. I set it on my chair then I slid the sword against the back of the boat near the motor and covered it with the tarp. The light from the dock's lamps didn't reach far enough to shine into the boat and the black tarp blended with the interior.

I was standing and waiting when Able approached. "Who was it?" I asked, handing him my messenger bag then the wrapped wall hanging.

"A deputy. I explained we were invited guests." He set the tapestry on the dock then reached down to help me. "And I flashed my FBI badge at him."

"You have an FBI badge?" I slung my bag on one shoulder before scooping up the tapestry.

"Yep." Able jumped into the boat and unrolled some canvas from the back of the boat, covering the passenger area. He unrolled it to the front, snapping it in place while he went. Then he hopped out, leaned over, and snapped the last of it into place. He moved to take the wall hanging from me. "I can carry that. It's heavy."

"No you don't." I shifted away from him, cradling the bundle. "I want to make an entrance and impress your father. Show me your FBI badge."

"What?" Able followed me along the dock.

"Show it to me. I've never seen one."

"It's like any badge."

"I've never seen any official badges up close." I kept moving, hoping to distract him from noticing how light the bundle now was.

I think I succeeded because he pulled out a wallet and flipped it open. I stopped at the foot of the stairs to examine his official photograph on one side of the wallet and the gold-tone badge on the other. "Wow. You really do have one."

"I told you I work for the FBI."

I started up the stairs. "You said you were a consultant. I didn't know consultants got badges and guns." When he didn't answer, I paused to look back at him. One look at his face and I knew. "Oh, don't tell me. You lied about that, too?" I kept walking while he stammered out a reply.

"I didn't exactly lie. I just didn't tell the complete truth. I am a consultant to other departments in the Bureau. And I do work in the Fraud Division. Sometimes."

"Oh, be quiet," I said, half-irritated and half in jest. "You're just digging the hole deeper. Hello, John." I smiled at John Reeve, who waited for me at the top of the steps.

"What do you have there, Vivian?" He held out his arms.

"It's a rather valuable wall hanging. Do you have to examine it or something?"

He nodded, taking the bundle and turning to go inside. As he did, he spotted Able on the step behind me. John's eyes narrowed.

"Mr. Leroy drove me," I said. "You know I hate being out on the lake at night."

"I thought maybe Mr. Leroy figured the local cops couldn't be trusted to handle his sister's death right." John's tone of voice was so bland it was insulting.

"She was my stepsister," Able said. "And I have no problem with how you're handling it. None at all."

John stared at Able, skepticism almost oozing off him. "Wish I could say the same for your father."

Able sighed loudly. "Is he being an asshole again? Excuse me," he said to me. "I need to have a talk with my father." He strode across the deck to the living room door and disappeared inside the mansion.

John unrolled the wall hanging with my help. "All okay?" I asked when he held it high and it was finally revealed.

"Fine." He started to roll it back up but I took it from him, draping the tapestry across my arms.

"It shows best when it's hanging. I'll have Dewin take down one of his million-dollar paintings and we'll hang this in its place." I started for the door, but John stopped me with a hand on my arm.

"There's supposed to be snow tonight. Don't stay here too late or you could run into problems on the lake."

I peered at the sky, the dark blue of sunset almost vanished behind heavy clouds. "Snow? How much?"

"Doesn't matter how much. When the weather turns, it can get tricky out on the water. Be careful, Vivian."

"Thanks, John. I'll make sure we leave early." I went to the door that led inside, a man in a black winter coat with an insignia on the breast opening the door for me.

I nodded my thanks and entered the house, coming into the living room where we assembled the night before. Luther and Able stood at the fireplace in the same place where Faye and Morris stood the night before. Luther had changed from his Northern Woods flannel shirt to a heavy navy turtleneck sweater, which highlighted his white hair and tall, slender build.

Several lamps glowed around the room, casting pools of light on selected pieces of furniture. Brad Devere and Morris Dredding were in the reading nook to the left, seated in the matching leather chairs, drinks on the table between them.

Devere turned when I entered and smiled. I'm sure that smile had melted many female hearts because of his dimples and the way his blue eyes seemed to latch on to mine. His pale blue sweater might have seemed effeminate on another man, but on him it accented his broad chest and muscular build.

He started to get to his feet, then he intercepted a look from Able, who watched him from across the room. Devere shrugged and leaned back in his chair, seemingly relaxed. Morris didn't move. He stared fixedly at the bookcase, a large glass in his left hand resting on his knee and his right hand tapping the arm of the chair. Like Able, he wore a flannel shirt and jeans, but Morris was more rumpled, somehow, not as tucked-in and pressed as the other men.

"Where's Dewin?" I asked the room at large.

"He's with the police," Luther said. "They're searching the bedrooms."

"I'll bet he's fit to be tied." I could imagine Dewin following the police, standing there with his arms crossed with a peeved expression, probably pointing out the value of every item they touched. They'd be lucky if he didn't sue them.

I spied a framed watercolor painting of a man in a boat on a lake, high on the wall behind the card table. "Help me with this, would you?" I asked Able, going to the picture. I dipped one shoulder and my messenger bag slid off to land on a nearby love seat.

"With what?" He and Luther joined me.

"I want to hang this up." I put the tapestry on the card table and pulled a chair from under the poker table to the wall. Once I had it positioned, I climbed up and reached for the picture, which was almost out of my reach.

"I believe that's a Wyeth," Luther said reprovingly when I grasped the frame.

"Nah. It's a copy," I said. Knowing Dewin, it probably *was* a Wyeth and knowing Dewin, it was probably insured for a million bucks, so I wasn't too worried about moving it. I managed to get it off its hook and turned with it in my hands. "It's a heavy sucker, be careful." I almost dropped it into Able's arms, overbalancing and tipping on the chair.

It was touch and go for a breathless moment, when I was sure I was going to fall backward right onto the table. Then somehow Able got his arms around my legs even as he held onto the bulky painting, easing it to the floor and stabilizing me. "I'm taller than you. Why don't you let me do it?" he asked.

"I've got it. Just hand it to me." I pointed to the table.

"You are the most exasperating woman. One day you're going to let me help you, Aquarius Dulac." He released me then handed me the tapestry.

"I do let you help me. I let you drive the boat." I unrolled the wall hanging and leaned toward the hook.

"Aquarius?" Luther asked in an odd, choked sort of voice.

I couldn't look at him because I was in the middle of hanging the tapestry. "There. That's just right." I squinted at the small light overhead, which was angled to illuminate the spot on the wall where the painting had hung.

"Aquarius?" Luther repeated.

I couldn't tell if he was struggling not to laugh or if he was just bemused by my odd name. "My mother loved the zodiac. I usually just go by my middle name, Vivian."

His mouth opened into an O of astonishment. "Vivian?" Luther looked from me then to Able, who smiled and nodded.

"Vivian," he confirmed.

"Now that we all know my name, I'll let you help me down from this chair." I held out my hand to Able, like a queen accepting the accolades of her subjects. To my surprise, it was Luther who stepped forward and took my hand, giving me a courtly bow while I scrambled down from the chair. Able took the painting to the far side of the room, well away from any area where someone would walk.

"Pretty amazing, isn't it?" I said, nudging the chair back in place. "Look at the colors. Even though it's old, the colors have stayed vivid. The handiwork is fine, too. She added so much detail to each panel."

Luther glanced at me with a small smile. "I'm prepared to pay an excellent price, my dear. You don't have to convince me of its beauty."

"Sorry. I don't want to let Elaine down, that's all. She spent a lot of time on this and I want to make sure you appreciate it."

His gaze swung from the tapestry to me. "Elaine?"

Across the room Able paused to stare at us while he leaned the painting against the wall. "Elaine?" he echoed.

I nodded. "She was an elderly lady who lived near here. Sy thought she might have been divorced or maybe a widow. Oh, that reminds me. I need to call him. Excuse me."

I left Luther alternately staring at the tapestry then me while I went to the landline phone. I dialed Sy's number and when he came on the line, I told him about the search warrant taking place.

"I'll bet Moneybags is enjoying that," he said with obvious satisfaction.

"I haven't seen him yet. I think he's following the police around, making sure they don't steal the china or something."

"I wonder if they'll find anything. Have you heard from your boyfriend about what killed her?"

"My what?" I peeked surreptitiously at Able, who was now talking to a big man who just entered the room from the direction of the dining room.

"Your boyfriend. I saw the way he was looking at you."

"You old busybody. He's just a friend. And no, he hasn't told me anything about what might have killed her. I did tell you he's with the FBI, right?"

The sputtering sound on the other end of the line told me that I forgot to tell him. "He's what?"

"He's a Fed. He said he's here investigating—" I stopped. Maybe I wasn't supposed to tell. "I'm not sure why he's here. Listen, I have to go. I'll call you when we leave."

"There's a storm coming in tonight. You make sure to leave early. In fact, you may want to stay on shore tonight. Have your boyfriend bring you back here. We'll make up the spare room for you. He can sleep on the couch. It might be a rough crossing in the morning."

"We'll see how it looks when I call. That might be best. Talk to you later." I replaced the receiver, momentarily worried. If snow was in the offing, I might take Sy up on his offer. I occasionally bunked in their spare room when the weather was iffy for crossing. I doubted if Able would stay, but I would suggest it.

I shoved that worry to the back of my mind. For now, I had a tapestry to sell. I went back to Luther, who was still contemplating the wall hanging, hands behind his back. Able had disappeared, presumably with the man I saw earlier, and Devere and Morris still sat in the chairs, apparently engrossed in conversation.

That's when I remembered the other member of our party who was absent. Where was Eve? Surely she wasn't still on the shore, was she? The way she was clinging to Dewin, I couldn't imagine her letting him out of her sight.

That reminded me of our conversation the night before. One nagging question lurked in the back of my brain all day. "Why did Faye give the sword to Able's ex-wife?" I asked Luther. "Surely she knew how much it meant to her stepbrother."

"Gwynne could be very persuasive," Luther said. "In a way, that's how she and Arthur ended up together.

She knew Brad and knew Brad worked at the company. She convinced him to introduce her to Arthur so she could ask Arthur to help her father. Her father had a small software business near bankruptcy. She wanted Arthur to buy him out."

"Did he?"

"Yes, he did. Arthur took their software and managed to make a profit of it within three years." The old man sounded proud and somewhat surprised.

"And he got the daughter in the bargain," I murmured.

"I suppose you could say that." Luther's mouth quirked up in a smile.

That made me think of another question I wanted to ask. "Why did you look so surprised when I handled the sword back in the warehouse? You seemed amazed that I was touching it."

"It's a very heavy weapon," he said smoothly. "I was worried that—"

"That's crap. There's something else going on. I saw the way you and Able looked at each other when I gave him the sword. What is it?"

Luther's gaze went beyond me, to the spot where Able had left the room. "It's an old family legend or well, a tradition I suppose you could call it."

"What is?" I prompted when he didn't seem anxious to continue.

Luther sighed. "It seems like there's always been a woman named Vivian involved with the Arthurs in our family."

"Well, that doesn't make any sense," I said when he didn't seem disposed to continue. "It's not a common name."

"I know," Luther said, his eyes flickering to the window, the bar, the table—anywhere but at me. "And often the woman is, um, involved with the sword, I suppose you could say."

"Involved how?"

He touched the wall hanging, tracing one finger along the design of Arthur lying on the shore of the lake, the gleaming sword held aloft in the distance by a hand parting the waters. "It's just an old legend, I suppose. When the heir accepts the sword from a woman he loves…" His voice trailed away.

I almost laughed out loud. Woman he loves? What a load of baloney. "What?" I prompted again. "What happens?"

"When he takes the sword, everything changes."

"What's that mean? Everything changes? What changes?"

He shrugged. "It's just an old family story."

Everything changes…that made me think of Sy and his lament that the lake shore might change. I decided I had nothing to lose by confronting Luther with my newfound knowledge. "Why did you form a consortium to buy land on the lake?"

"Who says I did?"

"I do." I met and held his flinty gaze.

Luther looked away first, his eyes going to the windows overlooking the now dark lake. "It's the only thing I can give him. He refuses money, property, homes, cars, jobs. But I can buy the land and hold it in trust and when I die, it goes to him. He loves it here and it would break his heart to see the lakeshore developed."

"I wish I could believe you," I said.

"Why can't you?"

"It's hard to believe a big businessman like you would do that."

"I'm not like most businessmen."

"Yeah. Right."

He laughed so loudly Devere turned to peer at us around the back of his chair. When he saw Luther grinning at me, he frowned and turned back, saying something to Morris that made the younger man turn to look at us.

"We're the talk of the town," I murmured.

Luther raised one eyebrow. "Let them talk."

Loud voices from the hallway made us both turn toward the fireplace and the arched doorways on either side. Able, Dewin and three other men came in with John Reeve. Dewin was the picture of the casually elegant host in his dark pants and dark green cashmere sweater. His dark gray goatee and curly gray hair framed his face in such a way that when the light caught him, his face seemed sunken, almost skeletal.

I shifted position, squinting at him. The light must have changed because when I blinked, he was just old Dewin, the devilishly handsome man I once loved. The men with him all wore dark windbreakers with sewn-on patches like Able's badge. One of them was the big man Able talked to earlier.

"The sheriff," Luther said in a low voice.

"That's insane," Dewin said, his voice so loud I suspected the deputy on the deck could hear him. "Why would he do that?"

"Who? Do what?" Devere asked. He and Morris joined them in front of the fireplace.

"I wonder what's going on." I tried to catch Able's

eye, but he gestured to his father. Luther walked across the room and I trailed behind him. Just as I reached Able, Eve came into the room from the hallway. Gone was the chic little girl-model. Now she appeared all business in navy slacks, a fitted navy jacket and a white blouse with a big white bow tied under her chin. The only giveaway that she was still a Style Queen was her high-heels, which added at least three inches to her height and made her already impressively long legs even longer.

She strode to Morris and grabbed his arm. "Why did you do it?" she demanded, her voice shrill. "Why did you kill Faye?"

Chapter 13

"What the hell?" I muttered.

"Ma'am, please." The Sheriff pulled Eve, none too gently, off Morris and thrust her at Able. He promptly handed her off like a hot potato to Dewin, who put an arm around the girl's shoulders and held her tightly against him.

"I object to this, Sheriff." Dewin sounded more annoyed than upset. "Mr. Dredding is a guest in my home. I've already called my lawyer to verify the legality of you executing a search warrant in the rooms of my guests." Dewin smiled briefly at Luther. "I apologize for the intrusion, Mr. Leroy."

I frowned at his rudeness. From what the sheriff said, Morris was the one who was inconvenienced, not Luther Leroy. Of course, Luther was probably a million times wealthier than Morris and a million times more important in terms of the merger, but it still wasn't like Dewin to appear like such a brown-noser.

Luther waved it away. "I'm happy to cooperate with the local authorities." He caught my eye and smiled. "I have nothing to hide."

"Lucky you," I muttered. "A lot of folks have a skeleton or two in a closet."

"I didn't say that," he corrected mildly. "I just didn't pack them for this trip."

"Feel free to have your attorney call the District

Attorney in Duluth." The Sheriff ignored Luther and me and our byplay. He reminded me of Andy Griffith with his big ears, plain face and the supposedly bland lack of intelligence in his downturned eyes. I say *supposedly* because I saw the way he evaluated Dewin and Eve together in one quick sweep of his eyes and he also noticed the way Able handed off the girl so quickly. There was a brain behind that facade.

"What's the problem?" I asked Dewin. Eve shot me a malevolent glance and burrowed even closer to Dewin.

"The police found something unusual in Morris' room," Dewin said.

"I thought he and Ms. Lake were sharing a room," I said without thinking through the implications of that comment.

The sheriff turned his attention to Eve. "Is that true, ma'am?"

"We were sharing a room until she decided another bed was better." Morris glared at Dewin when he said it, but I didn't see any real anger in the look. He appeared to be playing the appropriate role of wounded lover, but I didn't sense any true loss there.

"What was found?" I asked.

The sheriff turned his attention to me. "Who are you, ma'am?"

Able started to introduce me, but I interrupted him by saying, "I'm just a nosy neighbor. I live across the way." I gestured vaguely at the living room doors leading to the deck and the lake. I nodded toward John Reeve. "We discussed last evening's events earlier today."

John leaned closer to the sheriff and murmured

something I couldn't hear. When he finished, the sheriff nodded. "I'm not at liberty to discuss what we found. We're taking some items with us for processing but it will take a day or more to get the results. Until then, I want you all to stay in Avalon until we can evaluate what we've found," the Sheriff said.

"There's nowhere for us to go," Dewin pointed out. "We're on a lake and my plane isn't due to fly in until late tomorrow."

The Sheriff didn't bat an eye. "There are boats and Canada isn't far away. Officer Reeve has volunteered to stay here tonight to assist you if you have any questions about our search warrant and how it was executed."

What a tactful way to phrase it. Luther noticed, too. His lips twitched when he repressed a smile.

The Sheriff left via the deck door, Able and John Reeve with him. Dewin disentangled himself from Eve and followed them out. Morris stalked to the reading nook again and plopped down like a bag of sand, picking up his half-finished drink and swallowing it in one gulp.

Brad and Eve went to the bar. "Can I fix anyone a drink?" Devere asked.

Just make yourself at home, I thought. "No, thanks," I said. "I'll wait for Dewin."

Brad shrugged. He and the young model-turned-businesswoman fussed found with the glassware, heads together while they concocted a drink involving several different booze bottles.

Luther walked to the tapestry again and I followed him. "What do you think they found in Dredding's room?" he asked me, his back to the others and his gaze fixed on the wall hanging.

I duplicated his stance, hands behind my back and my face turned away from the room. "I guess it depends on what killed your stepdaughter. If it was a poison, they might have found traces of it. Although it would be a pretty stupid killer to leave evidence like that lying around."

Luther sighed. "I haven't spent much time with Morris, but he doesn't strike me as being particularly intelligent."

"Two people were sharing that room," I pointed out. "At least they were supposed to be sharing it." I turned when Dewin and Able re-entered the room, John Reeve behind them. All three men appeared mad as hell, although John hid it better than Able or Dewin.

Eve abandoned Brad and went to Dewin, putting a hand on his arm and speaking to him in a low tone of voice. He glowered at her and she stepped back, obviously surprised. Dewin ignored her and made a beeline for Luther and me. John and Able went to talk to Morris, who was slumped in his chair, apparently oblivious to the rest of us.

"I apologize, but the chef and the staff were detained on shore," Dewin said to Luther. "The police are questioning them. I'm not sure when or if they'll be here to fix dinner."

The wall clock read five-thirty. If the staff couldn't get here anytime soon, that meant a late supper. "Why don't we just make sandwiches or something?" I suggested. "Surely there's some food in the fridge."

"Of course there is," Dewin snapped, as though miffed that I would question his hospitality. I didn't believe him. He probably had no idea what was in his larder.

"That would be fine," Luther said. "In fact, given the circumstances, a light dinner might be best then we can start our business discussions."

"I want to leave early, anyway. There's supposed to be a storm coming in." I started toward the doorways to the left of the fireplace. "Where's the kitchen? I can get the food set out."

Dewin looked so relieved I almost laughed. "I'll show you." He led the way out of the room. Luther started to go with us, but Brad stopped him and the two men moved to one side to talk. Eve shot me a glare then joined Luther and Brad with an appropriately businesslike expression on her childlike face.

Dewin and I went to a doorway at the far end of the hallway, opposite the outside door that Able and I used the night before. He ushered me before him and I entered a room as big as my cabin's living room and bedroom combined. Heck, the island in the middle of the room was almost the size of my kitchen. Like the room, the gleaming stainless steel appliances were massive, the refrigerator occupying several feet of space to the left. Even the fireplace positioned against the outside wall was big enough to roast an ox.

"Let's see what you've got." I went to the fridge and pulled open the two French doors on the front. The interior was neatly arranged with meats on the left, condiments and jars on the right and fresh produce in the drawers. "Looks like they brought in enough food for an army."

"I was supposed to have a houseful of guests this weekend." Dewin hung back, watching me while I pulled out a small ham and set it on the kitchen island.

I delved back into the cool interior and emerged

with a container of egg salad, one of potato salad, some cold chicken and a head of lettuce. "Be useful. Find some bread and plates."

"Just like the old days," he said with a grin. "You're ordering me around."

"You're easy to order around." I poked some more into the fridge. "Why haven't you badgered me this week about selling my cabin? You haven't mentioned the so-called legal action you plan to take once."

His dark eyes widened. Then he shot me the fakest smile I've ever seen. "I decided to let bygones be bygones. I hardly have time to use this house. Why bother with your cabin?"

"Hmm." That was suspicious. Dewin was an off-and-on thorn in my side for years. What would make him change?

"I designed this kitchen with you in mind." Dewin opened the dark cabinet doors, pretending to examine the interiors while he surreptitiously watched me.

"I doubt you designed this kitchen at all." I pulled out a gallon of milk, a jar of mayo, a jar of Dijon mustard and a bowl of fruit and set them next to the ham.

"Well, I didn't personally design it, but I told the architect what I needed for you."

I pulled a carving knife from the block next to the stove. "And what was that?" I set the knife on the kitchen island and started searching for silverware.

"Something homey, cozy." He gestured toward the fireplace. "Someplace where you could curl up and read, drink a cup of coffee, relax."

I almost laughed out loud. This kitchen was like something from a professional television cooking show.

The only homey thing about it was the dark wood cabinets and the brick floor. "I'm sure Eve will enjoy it."

Dewin slammed a cabinet door shut and was at my side in three long strides. He took me by the arms and turned me so I faced him, his intense gaze just inches from me. "Eve is temporary and you know it. You're the only woman I've ever loved. I gave you everything you could possibly want. What more can I do?"

I stared into his dark blue eyes then gently pulled away from him. "You need to learn to love your life as it is. Don't go chasing after old dreams. Learn to love new ones."

"You're wrong, Vivian." He moved so I was pinned between him and the cabinets behind me. "I love you and I always will."

I found his undying love to be charming at one time. Then it was annoying. Now it was starting to piss me off. "You need to get a life."

He leaned into me, his body against mine. "You are my life." He lowered his head.

"Damn it, Dewin, get off me." I pushed at his shoulders but all he did was press more insistently against me while he tried to kiss me.

"Everything okay here, Vivian?"

I peered past Dewin to see John Reeve entering the room. Dewin reluctantly moved away from me, but stayed nearby. "Dewin was just trying to reassert his marital rights. I pointed out that he has none anymore."

John smiled wryly. "Some people have a hard time learning hard lessons."

"And some people shouldn't interfere," Dewin snapped.

"Oh, Dewin, grow up." I edged past him and went to the island. "We're setting out some food. You'll join us, won't you, John?"

He glanced at the fridge, then to the food on the island counter. "Let me check what you have there first."

"You don't think there's a problem with the food, do you?" Dewin gawked at John, anger forgotten by this turn of events.

John poked carefully at the ham, the platter of chicken and the bottles of condiments. "The forensics team already checked but it doesn't hurt to be careful."

"Careful of what?" I asked, watching him peer into the various jars. Dewin was still rooted to the spot, his eyes wide. "Dewin, why don't you find some napkins?"

Dewin tore his eyes from John and turned slowly, obviously at a loss. I sighed. "For heaven's sake, don't be so helpless."

My sarcasm succeeded in waking him out of his trance. He started opening drawers in the cabinets next to the giant stove. John smiled. "If it's okay with you, I'll make a sandwich then I'll camp out in the living room for the night."

"I have two guest cabins," Dewin said, his voice muffled while he rooted through a kitchen cupboard. "You're welcome to use one."

John shook his head, more at me than at Dewin, who still peered into the cabinet. "That's fine. Thanks."

"But I'm sure a cabin would be much more comfortable." Dewin emerged with a pile of linens in his arms. "There must be napkins here somewhere."

I strode to the cabinets and opened several, finding silverware in one drawer, paper napkins and plates in another. "I'm sure John would prefer to be in the middle of things, Dewin. Why don't you get the others and tell them we have the food out?"

"In the middle…" Dewin's voice died away. "Oh. Sure." He did an about-face and left the room.

"He's not the sharpest tack in the box sometimes," I said to John, who took the carving knives I found and sliced the ham.

"Not many people are when it comes to the police. It's out of their realm."

"Arthur Leroy seems to be taking it all in stride," I said casually.

"He has the advantage of a lot of experience." John put the slices of ham on a paper plate I held out. "He and Dewin almost came to blows a few minutes ago because of you. Dewin was acting all high and mighty, like he has your best interests at heart. Leroy pretty much told him to take a leap into the lake. I thought Dewin was going to hit him right there." John's weathered face crinkled into lines when he grinned. "I admit that I wish he would take a swing at Leroy. I'd like to see your ex take a dunking."

"If Able doesn't do it, I might."

"Be careful tonight," John said in a low voice, all trace of humor vanished. "The sheriff is pretty sure he knows what's going on, but we don't have enough evidence to take anyone into custody. I'm sure you're safe with Leroy, but stay alert."

"What do you mean? Is someone here the killer?"

John's gaze swung to the door, where Luther and Brad Devere were entering. "I can't say any more. Just be careful." He put a couple of slices of ham and bread on a plate next to some potato salad and left the room, passing Able who entered, Eve tagging behind him.

"Help yourselves," I said, gesturing to the kitchen island. I went to the window, peering out at the patio. Snow was starting to fall, just a few flurries drifting through the lights illuminating the intricate stonework. I turned to watch people pile food on plates. No one seemed worried about potential poisoning, which I thought was interesting. Either people were innocent about what killed Faye or the poisoner knew it wasn't in the food.

"Where's Morris?" I asked Able, who had a chicken leg and potato salad on his plate.

"He's not feeling very sociable. Aren't you eating?"

"In a minute." I watched the different interactions in the room. Eve and Brad sat in the big carved wooden chairs close to the large stone fireplace, plates balanced on their knees. Dewin fussed around with firewood, lighting several matches to no avail. Luther approached him and gave a few helpful hints and soon a blaze was going. "Your father is a nice guy," I said.

Able took a slice of ham and some potato chips. "He tries to do the right thing. It's one of his most annoying traits and one of his best traits."

"Why?"

"Hmm?"

"Why does he try to do the right thing?"

Able tilted his head to one side. "I don't know. I suppose because it makes him feel better to do it?"

I nodded. That coincided with my opinion. I doubted Luther did anything altruistically. I took a chicken wing, some egg salad and some coleslaw. "I'm going to fix a drink. Do you want anything?"

"I'll come with you." Able followed me out of the kitchen and back into the living room. "My father said he wants to talk to Dewin soon about the merger and he wants us to sit in." He paused at the floor-to-ceiling windows. "I'd like to leave before bad weather sets in."

"You're too late."

Both Able and I turned, surprised by the surly voice. Morris had apparently refilled his glass while everyone was in the kitchen, because a half-full tumbler of amber liquid was on the table by his side. He waved a hand to his left, toward the windows. "Take a look."

I walked to the window and peered out. "It's only flurries."

"Look again, down to the docks."

I tried to glimpse the docks through the darkness. "I can't see them."

"Too much snow."

"Or too dark." I went to the poker table and sat down with my back to the chilly view, spreading a paper napkin on the felt surface lest I spill.

"What do you want?" Able put his plate next to mine and went to the bar.

I started to say *martini* then changed my mind. Had the forensics people tested everything in the house? How could they know that the liquor wasn't poisoned? I tried to reason away my uneasiness, but I just couldn't. "A beer," I said. "Any kind."

Able pulled two bottles of beer from the bar fridge and grabbed two glasses. "I had this last night and suffered no ill effects." His dark eyes were mischievous when he set the bottle down on the table and twisted off the cap.

"Was she poisoned?" I asked in a low voice,

shooting a glance at Morris. The dour man seemed content to stare at the bookcase and nurse his booze, ignoring us.

Able nodded. "Her symptoms came on too fast and too hard to be anything else. They're doing a tox screen to see what it might be, but I'm betting on foxglove."

I stared at him blankly.

"It's a plant and very deadly. It can grow wild in a lot of the United States. Digitalis is the active ingredient."

I considered that while I munched my food. "I thought that was used for heart attacks or something. I remember hearing about it on one of those emergency rescue TV shows."

"An overdose can be fatal. A small amount slipped into a drink or food would kill someone."

"Where does somebody get it?"

"Some people grow it in their gardens as a decorative plant. The entire plant is poisonous."

"How do you know so much about it?"

Able focused on his beer, avoiding my gaze. "Faye dabbled with herbal teas and cures. When we were growing up, she studied the medicinal uses for flowers and herbs. When I joined the FBI, we had to take some basic courses and I remembered a lot of what Faye told me."

Brad and Eve came into the room, Dewin and Luther following. Brad was laughing at something Eve said. "He doesn't look like the grieving boyfriend," I commented.

"No kidding." Able scooted his chair closer to mine when Dewin sat down with us.

"When were you planning on addressing the board

about the merger?" he asked Luther, who paused at the bar next to Eve to make himself a drink.

"I was hoping Faye would address them next week, after she had a chance to talk with you this week. The sooner we can nail down the details, the better."

"Why are you merging?" I asked. "Aren't both companies doing okay on their own?"

"Of course we are," Dewin said a little too quickly.

"Merging the two companies makes a stronger, single company," Luther said smoothly. "Thank you, my dear." He smiled at Eve, who handed him an empty glass.

"Does the government have to approve it?" I bit into a tart dill pickle and my eyes started to water. "Man, that's sour."

Eve turned to look at me and laughed. "Be careful your face doesn't freeze that way."

I scowled at her while Luther poured a dollop of bourbon into the glass. He took it and a bottle of water from the fridge then made his way across the room to join us.

"I've checked with my legal team," Luther said, handing me a napkin so I could dab my tears. "Because the Department of Defense and the Department of Homeland Security use our software, they want to re-examine all Dewin Software code to make sure it's compliant." He glanced at Brad, who took a seat on the couch with Eve. "Our code is compliant already, certified by our senior officers. I believe there was a slight problem with Dewin code at the last governmental review."

A dense silence permeated the room. "What kind of problem?" I asked Dewin. "When I worked there, we always had a formal code handoff before creating release candidates for testing. The government reps reviewed the code then we went ahead with final testing before shipping."

"The process has changed." Dewin spoke confidently but once again I had the feeling he wasn't quite certain what he was talking about. "It was creating too much of a time crunch at the end. We don't release it for evaluation until we're ready to ship." His eyes were on Eve when he said it and some kind of message passed between the two of them.

"But that means that—"

Able kicked my foot under the table. I almost choked on the bite of pickle I had in my mouth. He patted me on the back. "Are you okay? Those pickles are sharp."

I nodded, bleary-eyed. What did that little eye-exchange between Dewin and Eve mean? She used to work with him—did she know about the change in procedure?

"Several of the search algorithms used in Dewin code were developed by you," Brad said. "How difficult do you think it will be to consolidate the two code bases?"

I shrugged. "It's been years since I wrote any code. I have no idea. But one thing might be difficult and that's merging the two corporate cultures. We ran a pretty loose ship and if what I've read about Scabbard Security is true, it's sort of the opposite."

Those innocent words kicked off a heated discussion about workplace philosophy. That led to more discussions about testing policies, software development tools and the overlap in personnel that would inevitably result from the merging of two companies. I didn't even realize how much time had passed until Morris lurched to his feet.

"I think I'll retire, if anyone cares." He stumbled out of the room.

"I forgot he was there," I said apologetically. "He's so quiet."

"That often happens with Morris," Brad said with a sigh. "Even when he's there, he's not really there."

I glanced at the wall clock then did a double-take. "Holy moly, it's getting late. We'd better get going." I swiveled around in my chair and almost fell out of it in shock. "I can't see the deck. What's happening?"

Able turned, too, but he wasn't as surprised as me. That's when I realized he'd been stalling, keeping the talk going while the snow snuck up on us. I almost hit him when it hit me. "It looks bad out there," he said calmly.

"Bad? It's a blizzard." Luther stood to peer at the windows. "I didn't realize it was getting so bad. We must be buffered from the wind here."

I pushed away from the table and went to the window. Luther was right. The overhang of the house and the high bluffs behind us kept the sound of the storm at a distance. The deck was covered with snow and I couldn't see beyond its railing, just yards away.

"You can't go out in the lake at night in that," Dewin said with finality. "We have plenty of room. You can stay here."

"I'd better call Sy. He'll be worried about us." I went to the phone near the couch.

Static on the line made it hard to hear him when he finally answered. "I'm glad you called," he said. "We were worried about you. You haven't left, have you?"

"No, we're still at Dewin's. Is it bad?"

Static overlaid whatever he said then I caught, "...warnings tonight, so don't try."

"I think we'll stay here tonight. Dewin has enough room to house an army, so we'll be fine. Don't look out for us, okay?"

More crackling then I heard, "...called in that he'll be making an arrest. Make sure to stay close to..." Then the line went dead.

Well, crap. What did that mean? I replaced the receiver and turned to talk to John Reeve.

That's when I realized he was nowhere in sight. I hadn't seen him since the kitchen, when he came in to make himself a sandwich.

I meandered away from the couch, heading back to the kitchen. "Everything okay, Vivian?" Dewin called out.

I waved in what I hoped was a nonchalant fashion. "Sy said the lake was rough so I guess we're stuck here tonight. I'm going to put the food away." I didn't wait to see any reaction to my words.

I hurried into the hallway and peeked into the kitchen. John wasn't there. I bolted up the staircase directly opposite the fireplace on the other side of the house. A long hallway stretched right and left. I went right and tried the first door on my right.

It was an empty bedroom with a large king-sized bed overlooking the woods behind the house, woods that were now blanketed with snow. I continued down the hall, trying the next two doors on the right and left. I glimpsed Morris going into one, so I avoided it. The other was a bedroom, tidy and empty. At the end of the hall was a large bathroom, probably shared by several of the bedrooms.

I went back to the staircase and passed it, going down the other end of the hall. Two more bedrooms and a bathroom. One bedroom was obviously the master, with a large fireplace, an even larger bed and several elaborately carved pieces of furniture overlooking the lake and a private balcony.

I raced back downstairs and came into the hallway just as Able emerged from the kitchen. "Where's John?" I whispered.

"John? The police?"

I nodded. "I can't find him anywhere."

Able gave me an odd look. "He's in the living room, isn't he?"

I stared at him, open-mouthed and followed him back into the large room. Sure enough, John sat in one of the armchairs in the reading nook, his back to the rest of us. I glimpsed his dark hair above the back of his chair. "I had no idea he was there," I said.

"You're not the only one." Able nodded toward Dewin and Eve, who were in low-voiced conversation not far from John. "I think they're arguing."

"Have you settled on a price for the wall hanging?" Luther asked, joining Able and me near the fireplace.

"No, I haven't. Elaine asked me to donate her profit to a local charity, so I want to get as much as possible." I smiled in what I hoped was a disarming fashion. "If you know what I mean."

Luther smiled, too. "How does forty thousand sound?"

I had a hard time not gaping at him. "It sounds pretty good," I managed. With a twenty percent commission, I'd net eight thousand dollars. Not bad for a night's work.

Dewin joined us, an iPad in hand. "Do you want to stay in the main house or a guest cottage?" he asked Able. "Brad is in the east wing and Morris is in the west wing. Luther has the other master suite and I thought Vivian could stay in the guest room next to mine. I can set up either Cornwall or Devon for you. Both are ready for guests because we were expecting a full house this weekend." He raised the iPad. "Everything is controlled remotely so I can get the heat turned on now for you."

"Cornwall?" Able asked me in a low voice.

"Dewin is big on English geography. Where's the help staying?" I asked Dewin.

"They stay on the shore."

"Where?" I asked.

"There's a perfectly reasonable motel in Avalon," Dewin said dismissively.

I snorted. The Avalon Inn was ten motel rooms that hadn't been updated in at least twenty years.

"Are you comfortable staying alone in the house?" Able asked me.

I started to say *yes* then I thought about it. Strange place, big storm, possible murderer on the premises. My gaze went from Dewin, who regarded me with smug anticipation, to Able, who smiled faintly. Sleeping in a room next door to Dewin?

"No," I said. "I'm not."

"We'll both stay in Cornwall. I've always fancied a trip there," Able told Dewin. "I assume there are several bedrooms in the cabin?" He smiled blandly.

Dewin shot me a frosty glare. "Of course there are. I'll make sure that all four are properly heated. That way you can choose the room you'd like."

John stood. "I'll escort them to the cabin if you'll point the way."

Dewin angrily tapped a few icons on the iPad. "I'll show you." He dropped the iPad on a nearby end table and strode out of the room.

"I'll join you in a minute," Able said. "I need to talk to my father first."

"Okay. Night, all." I grabbed my messenger bag and nodded to Brad and Eve then I hurried after John, who waited for me in the hallway.

"Make sure to lock up tonight," John said in a low voice while we followed Dewin into the kitchen and to a door set in the far wall. He didn't have time to say more because Dewin was waiting for us just inside the door.

Dewin handed me a flannel-lined nylon jacket with hood from the wall rack and he took a sheepskin parka, buttoning it before he pulled open the door. Wind swirled the snow around us, but it felt gentle and soft. Blizzard? This was a minor touch of winter, nothing to be feared.

Dewin led the way, kicking through the snow covering the brick walkway. Lights lit our way, hazy in the misting snow. He went up a set of steps, turned to the right then went up seven more steps. We passed out of the protection of the towering pines surrounding the main house. Wind tore at us, buffeting us from the overhanging bluffs. Dewin leaned into it, taking several more steps before throwing open the door of the two-story building that suddenly loomed up in front of us out of the storm.

John thrust me ahead of him and I stumbled into

warmth and light. "Bedrooms are through there," Dewin said roughly, pointing to the doorway opposite the door we'd entered. "Two on this floor, two above. Let me know if you need anything. There's a phone." He gestured to the kitchen on our left then he turned and vanished into the snow.

"Dewin, I'm sorry—" My words were lost in the howl of wind. I closed the door and surveyed my accommodations. The living room/dining room/kitchen were all one long space, about half the size of Dewin's living room. The kitchen occupied the wall on my left, birch cabinets above smaller versions of Dewin's appliances. The living room had the same Ikea-Danish modern furnishings, spare and utilitarian yet elegant. Although built of logs, the whole place had a modern feeling to it, with its simple lines and light, airy furniture.

John went through the far doorway and soon returned. "Empty," he said. "Will you be okay here with Leroy?"

I nodded. "I'm sure we'll be fine. I just didn't feel right staying in the main house with Dewin so nearby."

John smiled. "I can understand that."

We both turned when Able came into the room, shaking snow off his coat. "It's bad out there."

John nodded. "Take care of her. I'll keep watch in the main house."

"I'm sure nothing will happen tonight," Able said confidently. "The weather will keep everybody indoors."

"Maybe," John said. "Desperate people do desperate things."

Able smiled. "They aren't that desperate yet."

"Maybe." John looked at me. "Lock your doors."

"Will do." I went to the kitchen while Able and John spoke in low voices near the outside door. John nodded at something Able said then Able closed the door and locked it with the dead bolt.

"Nice guest cabin," he said, walking around the counter separating the kitchen from the dining nook.

"Look at this," I said, peering into the fridge. "Fully stocked." I turned and walked right into Able's arms.

"Finally," he said. "I have you alone."

Chapter 14

It was like a scene from a corny old movie. There we were, stranded, with a howling storm outside. Two almost-strangers, thrown together by adversity. Two ships passing in the night. Strangers in the night…well, you get the idea.

I went into his arms and we kissed with no hesitation, no uncertainty. I felt as if it was meant to be, like fate brought us to this place to be together. I drew away and peered into his eyes. Able returned my gaze, searching my face. "What is it?" I asked, tracing my fingers down his face.

"I feel like I know you so well. I can't believe I just met you a few days ago. It's like you've always been in my life." He ducked his head to kiss my fingers. "It wasn't until I saw you that I realized how incomplete my life was."

Oh, oh. This sounded serious. "You're only saying that to get my sword," I said teasingly. "Fancy words will get you anywhere with a girl."

He didn't smile in return. "I mean it. I know how I feel about you. I think you feel the same way but you just won't admit it." A little smile made one corner of his lips twitch upward. "I guess I'll just have to convince you." His arms went around me again and I sank into his kiss.

This time when we pulled apart, we had moved and

were now in the living room. Able's jacket was off, my jacket was off, my sweater was unbuttoned and his shirt was loose around his shoulders. "I think we need to get more comfortable," Able said, his breath hot on my ear.

More comfortable? That sounded—wait a minute. Suddenly every doubt I ever felt about myself surfaced. I was overweight, my skin was no longer supple but had that hail-damaged look of cellulite, I had a chubby waistline, my breasts were saggy—

Able kissed me and self-doubt vanished into passion. We made our way to a bedroom where Able eyed the accommodations. "Twin beds," he said with a laugh. "I don't think so. Come on." He tugged me up the narrow staircase and to the right into a loft, where a double bed was positioned in front of the windows. "This looks like our size." We tumbled onto the dark blue duvet, laughing.

I won't go into details. You've seen the movie, right? The one where the hero and heroine sink into bed, arms around each other, their eyes locked. In the next scene, they awaken in each other's arms, sunlight creeping into the room, in love.

It went just like that—kinda. Except for the love part, of course. I wasn't in love with him and he wasn't in love with me. We intersected briefly and we'd un-intersect once he bought his sword and went back to his FBI life.

And it was kinda like that except for the sunlight part. When I awoke hours later, the first thing I saw was dark windows with faint light coming in from the outside security light. The snow was still swirling around it, but it appeared to be lessened now. The next thing I felt was, *I need to pee*. Not the most romantic thought, perhaps, after an hour or two of lovemaking and a few hours of sleep, but it was a pressing need nonetheless.

I glimpsed a doorway that probably led to a bathroom when we first entered the bedroom, but I didn't want to wake Able, who had been very able indeed, just a few hours before. He even faced the dreaded condom issue by addressing it bluntly while we undressed each other. "I have condoms and I'll use them, but I can tell you now I'd rather not. I haven't been with a woman for years and I know I'm healthy. What about you?"

"It's been years for me, too, and yes, I'm healthy. I'm not worried about pregnancy. I'm on birth control to help control my hot flashes." I laughed. "Too much information?"

He laughed in return even while he drew me down to him in the bed. "Not at all."

I smiled at the memory while I propped myself up on my elbows and peered around my unfamiliar surroundings. The bed was to the left of the doorway to the stairs with a large window opposite us. Able was curled on his side facing away from me, breathing heavily. The bedclothes were tucked under his arm and I saw the curve of his shoulder in the half-light of the room. He was surprisingly lean and muscular, something I hadn't guessed about him. I thought he would be sort of chunky and maybe a bit flabby, but there wasn't an ounce of flab on him.

I wished I could say the same about myself, but apparently I didn't disappoint Able. I slipped out of bed and rooted around on the floor for something to cover my nakedness, not out of modesty but because the room was chilly. I found Able's shirt and pulled it on. The tails covered my butt and it was roomy enough for a bathrobe. Plus it smelled like fabric softener and man, a smell that was sort of nice.

I left the room, closing the door softly behind me. Across the narrow landing was another bedroom. I crept inside, avoiding the double bed that, like the other room, faced the window. The clock on the bedside table said three a.m., the digital numbers floating like ghosts in the air.

I peered out the window. The cabin was situated at an angle to the main house, with each guest cabin on the ends of a crescent behind the mansion. We were on the south crescent tip, with most of our view being the cove and the house because we were on the tip that curved into the land surrounding the property. The other cabin, the north one, would have more of a view of the lake in the distance.

Where was the bathroom? Surely each bedroom had one, didn't it? I spied a doorway and went through it into a small but luxuriously appointed bathroom. The room was cool but not cold. Dewin had presumably turned on the heat everywhere and I mentally thanked him for it. I did my business and washed up using the provided linens, basking in the feeling of warm towels when I removed them from the heated towel rack.

I went back into the bedroom and stared out the window at the house below. The window was roughly level with the roofline, allowing me to look down into the rooms. One light was on in the middle of the house. It was faint, like a nightlight or a lamp far from the window. Another light must have been on to the right, at the far end of the building. It was the kitchen, I realized. Someone left the light on there, too.

The snow had stopped, with just a few flakes drifting past the security lights lining the paths between the house and the cabin. I could clearly see the outline of the walk and I wondered if Dewin had it heated. Knowing him, he probably did. The patio behind the kitchens still had furniture out and it was blanketed in about two inches of snow. Usually I'd laugh at two inches of snow, but two inches of snow on a cold lake at night was a different matter.

I left that bedroom and went to the landing. The angle from the window was different here, giving me more of a view of the side of the house near the steps leading to the cove. I thought I saw movement outside, but it had to be an illusion of shadow on the snow when the wind swirled. I slipped back into the bedroom I shared with Able and peered out the window there. That's when I saw two figures emerge from the side door and head down the stairs.

"Able," I said. "Something's going on."

He was out of the bed in a heartbeat and at my side. "Where?"

I jumped away in surprise. Such an immediate response seemed unnatural. "There." I pointed. "By the side of the house."

Able peered out, seemingly oblivious to his nakedness, the cold, or me. "It's Brad and Eve." He got dressed so fast I barely knew what was happening until he sat down on the bed to pull on his boots. When he stood and reached for his gun, I realized what was going on.

"You can't go out there," I said. "You don't know what's going on."

"I thought they'd make a run for it. I wasn't sure if the snow would slow them down or not. Where's Reeve? Where's my father? They should have stopped them." Able paused and drew me to him in one tight hug that pressed me lengthwise against his body. "Stay here." He kissed me then was gone, racing down the steps.

Holy moly. Were Able, John, and Luther all in cahoots? Where was Dewin? He and Eve were supposed to be lovers. Surely he would notice if she slipped away. For that matter, where was Morris? What was his role in this whole tangled mess?

I peered out and down but didn't see Able, even though I heard the downstairs door close. I had enough light to see by and the snow wasn't an issue. Where was he? Maybe he went the long way around, taking the path between the two cabins and coming in to the main house via the north cabin.

I was wide awake now and no way was I going to crawl back in bed while Able was out, roaming around. I dressed in the dark, dragging on my jeans and tying Able's shirt around my waist. I grabbed my shoes and socks and went downstairs. The lights were still shining where we had left them on. I put on my footwear then grabbed a jacket from the floor where it was dropped earlier. I started to leave then hesitated. My messenger bag lay on a kitchen chair. Should I? Shouldn't I?

In the end, I decided I should. I took out my gun and the lightweight nylon holster and belt I seldom used. I slid the belt into my jeans' loops, threaded on the holster and was out the door in a few minutes, the jacket effectively covering the gun and most of me. It wasn't until I put my hands into the jacket pockets and pulled out a pair of oversized leather gloves that I realized I'd grabbed Able's jacket. He wore these gloves when he drove the boat.

I paused outside the cabin to get my bearings. The house was about fifteen or twenty yards below me, down a flight of stone steps. Ahead of me was the other cabin, barely seen through the dense pine trees lining the brick path connecting the cabins to the patio and then to the house. Old-fashioned miniature street lamps were set every six feet or so, low wattage light giving just enough illumination for me to see the footprints in the snow.

There were several sets of prints, our older ones half-filled with snow. Able's fresher prints were superimposed on top and I followed those. I got to the junction where the path branched to go to the other cabin and made my way carefully down the steps to the patio outside the kitchen and dining room.

That's when I saw the second set of footprints in the snow. They came out of the kitchen door, the door we'd used the night before. They went around the side of the house, disappearing along a curve in the lower path.

Able's prints went to the patio, I was pretty sure of that. I debated following his steps but decided not to. Odds were that he would be busy. I would only get in the way. I followed the other set of prints, discovering they led to the deck, which wrapped around the entire front of the house and ended here, near the kitchen door. The prints led to a break in the railing where I glimpsed stairs leading downward.

It was too precarious for me. This house sat on a bluff and if steps were going down, that meant they paralleled the ones that led up from the dock. That staircase was steep enough. Anything here on the north side would be steeper still.

I shuffled through the soft snow to the kitchen and tried the door. To my surprise, it opened. Of course, there wasn't any reason for it to be locked. The only people here were guests and I suppose Dewin trusted us. A night light was on at the stove, which gave me enough brightness to see my way through the room to the door to the interior hallway.

I peeked through the door. The hall was dark but a lamp was lit in the living room. I tiptoed into the hall and into the living room, coming in by the reading nook where Morris and Brad sat earlier. This end of the long room was dark. The fireplace glowed faintly from dying embers and a table lamp near the poker table was the only illumination.

Where was John? The last I saw of him he was going back to the house after escorting me to the guest cabin. I assumed he would be in the living room where he could keep an eye on the doings in the house. He should have been camped out in one of the big chairs or stretched out on a couch.

Maybe he was with Able. I nodded. That made sense. Able and John talked earlier. Maybe they worked out a plan and would meet somewhere if needed. The idea made me feel a lot better. If John was with Able then between the two of them, they'd take care of each other.

I inched through the mostly-dark room, bruising my shin on one of the gigantic coffee tables made from a slab of slate. I cursed softly and moved closer to the windows overlooking the deck, hoping to catch a glimpse of Able, who must be outside. The view was beautiful with the soft white snow draping the deck. The whiteness extended into the distance, blending with the whiteness on the trees. It was a disorienting feeling, like the house was suspended in space and the trees were supporting it.

Dewin's iPad sat on one end table and I picked it up, tapping the button to activate it. As I expected, the last application Dewin used was on the screen. I tapped the icon of the happy house and was prompted for a password.

Damn it, Dewin. Just make this hard for me. I tried his birthday then my birthday. Wrong password. I had one more chance. After that I'd be locked out. I tried Vivian325, which was my name plus our wedding date.

Voila. The screen cleared and I had clear access to the house controls. I tapped the light icon for Main House Living Room and the lights overhead blinked on, dimly lit. I tapped Deck and soft light glowed outside. I dropped the iPad on the end table and went to the windows. Security lights along the deck railing showed me its outline where it wrapped around the entire front, going to the left and the steps from the dock and to the right from the side near the kitchen. I moved through the room, glancing right and left, my gaze going from outside to inside and out again.

I was almost to the poker table at the far end of the room. Elaine's tapestry still hung on the wall, but the special lamps that highlighted it were turned off, probably by me when I was tapping icons on Dewin's iPad. The panels gleamed ghostly white in the faint glow from the end table lamp.

One of the panels appeared ghoulish in this light. It

was the one where Merlin was entombed in the cave, trapped there by the evil enchantress, Nimue, who was sometimes called Nineve. The old man seemed stricken and bloodied, but I knew it was a trick of the light. The so-called blood was the rich colors of his coat and the stricken look on his face was actually one of resignation and exhaustion.

I shivered, looking away from the wall hanging to the outside world. What I saw made me stop. The security lights on the deck not only outlined the space, but it also illuminated the slumped figure of a man who leaned precariously against the railing, snow piled around his legs and his arms tucked into his armpits.

"Holy moly," I whispered. It was Dewin, propped against the three-tiered railing, his head lolled forward. He wore the same clothing from the night before—dark pants and a green sweater. Both were damp now and I shivered just to see him. Was he drunk? He seemed calm, almost sleepy, as though it was the most natural thing in the world to be sitting on a deck in a snowdrift.

I cracked open the door to the deck, sliding it through the snow piled against it. "Dewin, get in here," I whispered loudly.

He didn't stir.

"Dewin, come on. You'll get frostbite out there."

Still no movement. I pushed the door open farther and stepped out on the deck. It was a muddled mess of snow and footprints, some leading around the edge to the kitchen, some heading off to the opposite side, where the steps led down to the docks. I didn't pause to examine how many or where they went. It was cold and damp and I was too exposed on that wide expanse of wooden planking.

I reached Dewin and grabbed his arm. His head rolled around like a ball on a string then he squinted at me. "What?" he asked blearily.

"Come on. Get up." I pulled on his arm. It was like hauling on a stack of disjointed firewood—heavy, inert and moving randomly when you least expected it. He pitched forward and put his hands in the snow, almost taking me with him. I think the shock of the cold on his bare hands must have helped wake him because he began to struggle to his feet.

He muttered something I didn't understand. To be honest, I didn't pay much attention. I was too busy try to haul him upright. I got an arm around his waist and he leaned heavily against me, babbling something. Then I heard the word "Arthur."

"What?" I demanded, pulling away to peer at him. Big mistake. He started to topple and I grabbed him, keeping him somewhat mobile. "What about Arthur?" I began a slow walk to the doorway, dragging Dewin with me.

"Damn it. He was supposed to flush them out, not get us killed." Dewin's voice was thick and almost unrecognizable. He wasn't shivering, which I expected, but his body was like a block of ice pressed against my side.

"What?" I shook him a bit, trying to shake the words out of him.

Dewin stumbled and I had a hell of a time keeping him from pitching face forward. "Leroy," he said blurrily. "We were helping him. Damn hot shot FBI agent from D.C." He barked out a laugh that evolved into a cough.

"D.C.? Not Des Moines?" I held on to Dewin as

much for support as to give support.

He peered down at me, his eyes unfocused. "You're so naïve."

I released my hold on his waist and he fell forward, slamming into the French door with his shoulder, bouncing off, then stumbling and banging his head. "Oops." I grabbed his sweater and pulled hard until he was almost vertical. The soft fabric stretched and he teetered. "Sorry."

"Be careful." He sounded peeved, which told me he was shaking off whatever had him in its grip.

"You're a fine one to tell me to be careful. I'm not the one who sat in the snow on the deck half the night. What happened to you?" There was an imprint of his body where he sat, the area clear of snow. "How long were you out here?"

Dewin blinked wearily. "I saw someone out here and I came out before locking the house. That's all I remember." He touched his neck gingerly. "It hurts. I think somebody hit me."

"Let's get inside." I opened the door and propelled him ahead of me. Dewin stumbled on the rug and fell onto the leather couch.

I went behind him to look at his head but he twisted to peer up at me. "I don't remember anything. I came downstairs and walked out on the deck and that's the last I remember." He leaned back cautiously, shivering, tugging his sweater up around his ears and holding it there. "I'm cold."

"Where is everybody? What's going on?" I came around the couch to confront Dewin, staring down at him where he alternately shivered and glared at me.

"I'm cold," he repeated insistently.

"I'm pissed off. Talk." I strode to the fireplace, tossed in some kindling with a wad of newspaper then lit it using a long-handled lighter from the mantel. I spied a blanket lying on the floor near a deep leather club chair against the wall. I grabbed the blanket and tossed it to Dewin. "Here. Cover up. Tell me what's going on. Where's John?" I added logs to the meager blaze.

The birch wood caught fire immediately, sending out welcome light and some warmth. I added an oak log and more birch then turned back to Dewin, who was cuddled into the blanket like a child with his binky.

"John? He was here." Dewin's hands twisted the blanket. "Lying on the sofa." He nodded toward the corner where I found the blanket. "Leroy came in and got him. They're going after Brad and Eve."

"Damn it, why didn't you tell me what was going on?" I fed another log to the fire. I wanted to hit Dewin with it, but instead I tossed it on the flames.

"We were sworn to secrecy." Dewin was starting to sound like himself again, pompous and pissed off and arrogant. "This whole weekend was a setup to get them to expose their hand. The only way to make it work was to use you." His sharp gaze searched my face and I guess he read my surprise there. "You are naïve."

I didn't debate his evaluation of my character because he was probably right. My mind was racing, sifting through everything that happened in the last few days.

Able came to me for the sword. He knew the sword would take me to Northern Minnesota. He knew they were meeting here. He set me up. He admitted as much. "What about his father? Luther Leroy?" I demanded.

"Where's he? Where's Morris? Where is everybody?"

"Morris is a patsy, just like you." Dewin pulled the blanket higher and inched to the end of the couch, nearer the fire where the blaze was now sending out heat. "Luther and I have been in discussions for months about the merger. His son came to him and told him that he suspected both Brad and Eve of black market software racketeering. Luther came to me, we all discussed it and we realized we had to get proof. They covered their tracks too well."

It would be easy to cover their trail, I thought. Neither Brad nor Eve had any direct contact with the software code so if any wrongdoing was discovered, the blame would fall on someone else in their respective companies. The only way to get them was to force them to make a move.

"Leroy used you to set the trap." Dewin stretched out his hands toward the fire, almost falling off the couch to reach the flames. "He knew that Brad set the wiretaps in your store."

"I know about that. Able told me."

"Eve made Brad do it." Dewin rubbed his hands.

"There you go, blaming the woman again."

"This time it's true. She had him under her thumb."

I raised an eyebrow at this blunt dismissal. "She had you under her thumb, too," I pointed out.

He waved a hand. "I was just playing along."

I almost laughed at the idea of Dewin, the undercover operative. "So the merger and everything was a setup?"

"We are interested in a merger. That's all real. But it won't happen until we get to the bottom of whatever it is Eve and Brad are trying to do." Dewin leaned back on the couch again, pulling the blanket tighter. "Brad and Arthur Leroy hate each other. I won't be surprised if Leroy doesn't kill him if he can get his hands on him." He regarded me from the depths of his blanket like some little old woman with her shawl pulled tightly around her. "He's a Special Agent with the FBI. He's not just a consultant."

Simmering anger replaced confusion and worry. "Brad's not the only one who might get killed," I muttered. Damn that Able Leroy. Why did he have to lie to me? I was going to tear a strip of skin off him when I found him. If I found him. "Where are they now?" I demanded. "Where's Luther? Morris? Where's Able?"

"I think Brad and Eve went down to the dock. Arthur Leroy and John Reeve were going to try to cut them off. Luther is in his room." Dewin pressed a hand to his neck again. "I think he and Morris were drugged. They're sleeping like there's no tomorrow."

I whirled and ran for the side door.

"Where are you going? You can't go down there!" Dewin reached for me but missed and fell off the couch onto the braided rug.

"Watch me." I raced out of the room, so angry I could barely see straight. This whole weekend was a setup, was it? Was the seduction also part of Able's plan to catch the crooks? What kind of hot shot FBI agent was he?

Damn it, I trusted him and look where it got me. I reached the exit leading to the outside steps and burst through the door, belatedly realizing that I should probably be quiet and stealthy. I flailed for the door, stopping it from slamming and closed it quietly. Then I crept to the edge of the deck and peered over the side.

The snow-covered steps stretched below me, lit faintly by the lamps along the side and shadowed by the pines bordering them. The snow on the steps was disturbed by several sets of feet or so it appeared. I couldn't see anything at the bottom because the trees hid everything. I thought I saw movement, but it was fifty feet below me and partially hidden by pines.

I glanced behind me but everything was quiet in the house. I inched forward and started down the stairs, going one step at a time and hesitating between each to listen and peer forward. I was so focused on what was in front of me that I didn't pay any attention to what was behind me. So when Dewin grabbed me, I gave a strangled scream in surprise.

"What are you doing?" I gasped, struggling, but he had my biceps in a painfully tight grip. His position on the step behind and above me gave him the advantage because I was slipping on the steps, almost falling while my feet went out from under me.

Dewin pulled me hard against him and leaned toward my ear. "You are so naïve." He pushed me and this time I did fall, stumbling down two steps before I could grab onto the railing to stop my momentum.

"Be careful," I snapped. "I almost took a header."

"Get going." He shoved me again, his hand between my shoulder blades. It was all I could do to keep upright.

"Dewin, quit it."

He stared over my head, ignoring my protests. "It's me. Don't shoot," he called out.

I slipped and slid down the remaining steps. "What's going on?"

Dewin grabbed my arm again when I reached the bottom step and the path to the dock. "What are you doing?" I dug in my feet, trying to stop our forward progress, but the boards were slippery and all I succeeded in doing was make him grip me tighter, dragging me to my feet when I started to fall.

We emerged onto the dock and Dewin dragged me to a stop. Eve Lake stood in front of us in a classic shooting stance, her gun straight out ahead of her, her eyes focused along the sights. It was a Colt or maybe a Luger.

It was big and it was pointed right at me.

"What the hell…" My voice trailed away when I saw what was at her feet. It was a body, a man in jeans and a dark jacket. For one horrified second I thought it was Able then I saw the gruesome remains of the man's face.

Brad Devere lay in a crumpled, bloody heap at her feet.

Eve laughed. "Dewin was right. You are stupid."

Chapter 15

"What did you do?" My attention cycled from Dewin to Eve, who held the large gun without any apparent hesitation. That told me she knew handguns. I chalked up another thing I misread about her. She wasn't some girly girlfriend. This was a woman who was probably as in charge, if not more so, than Dewin.

"Isn't it obvious?" Dewin walked past me and stepped over Brad like he wasn't even there, like his body was just a pile of fishing tackle lying on the snowy dock. He joined Eve near Able's boat. "We're leaving. My plane is waiting for us in one of the northern bays, in Canada. From there we're flying to my island in Micronesia."

"A country which does not have an extradition treaty with the U.S."

I turned in surprise. Able stood in his boat. "You're okay?" I asked stupidly. "What happened? How did you get here?"

Able shifted position and I saw the plastic ties around his wrists. "Sucker that I was I thought I could get the drop on them. I went to the house, grabbed John and we split up. Brad got the drop on me and took my gun. I don't know what happened to John." He looked at Brad's body, shaking his head.

"What?" I couldn't make sense of what anyone was saying. I edged closer to the boat where Able sat, thinking that I might be able to jump in and somehow we could drive our way out of this. Then I saw the cold water sloshing against the gunwale and I changed my mind.

"You got the cop, right?" Eve demanded. Able scowled at her, his eyes narrowing when he focused on the gun. Damn. It was probably his gun.

"That's what delayed me. I have him knocked out and in a closet, but I was just getting ready to leave when I saw Vivian coming. I didn't have time to get out so I pretended to be hurt. I knew she'd come after him." He nodded toward Able then he turned to me. "Get in the boat."

"You don't need her," Able said, getting to his feet. "Leave her out of this." The boat swayed but Able easily kept his feet, moving in time with the waves.

The swaying motion made me think about what Dewin said. "You bought an island? When? How do you buy an island? Aren't islands owned by countries or something?"

"Not all of them." Dewin smiled. "It's easy if you have enough money."

"I thought you were in financial trouble."

"Is that what your brother told you?" Dewin's smile widened to a grin. "Good. I've been planting rumors for months about that. I had to make the merger look feasible. Eve went to work at Scabbard and we found the perfect chance to start selling the code."

"What?" None of this made sense to me. Was I truly this stupid or was it all that complex?

Dewin saw my confusion and explained impatiently. "Eve found Brad Devere and Faye Morgan, two people who were open to our idea. She went to work for Scabbard so she could be closer to the source. During the merger, the code would somehow be pirated."

"But the merger hasn't happened yet. Aren't you jumping the gun?" I glanced at what remained of Brad. What I thought was a dark stocking cap was part of his head, bloodied and matted and maybe his brains. I swallowed hard. "So to speak. Why did you kill him?"

"We didn't need him anymore," Eve said. "He served his purpose. He followed Arthur Leroy, got him and tied him up." She was dressed for the part of undercover spy with her blonde hair in a tight braid, her dark trench coat and pants and—oh, for heaven's sake. Even now she wore high-heeled boots. I would have laughed if I wasn't so scared.

"The merger hasn't happened yet. Why do all this now?"

"They can say they opened their code vault for evaluation," Able said. "And it was pirated and sold." He watched us all with a calm expression that didn't fool me a bit. He couldn't wait to get his hands on Eve or Dewin or both of them.

"We won't get as much as we would if we could have sold both Dewin code and Scabbard code," Dewin said.

"So you had this all planned?" I asked Dewin.

"Of course. I knew who Arthur Leroy was. When Faye started talking to Eve about the merger, I did a background check on her whole company, including her family."

Faye. Holy moly, I forgot all about poor Faye.

"It turned up the fact that her stepfather was Luther Leroy and her stepbrother was Arthur Leroy, a Special

Agent with the FBI in their computer fraud division. Bingo."

Eve's smile appeared forced. "It was me who initiated the background check."

He waved a hand. "Whoever."

Oops. Wrong thing to say. Eve shot him a frosty glare, but Dewin ignored it and continued his saga. "Faye got cold feet when she saw her brother here in town. She threatened to spill." He laughed. "When she saw him in Avalon I thought she'd have a heart attack. It was a simple matter to give her a real one."

Dewin made Faye a martini that night. An apple martini. I swallowed hard.

"Simple?" Eve's voice was shrill. "It was damn tricky. I had to make sure I got the poison to you before you made her drink that night then I had to sneak down here in the middle of the night and get the vial and throw it in the fucking lake. Simple?" She barked out a disparaging laugh. "You're lucky Morris is so stupid. Every night he fell asleep right away and he never questioned why."

"Enough talk," Dewin said. "Get in the boat, Vivian." He gestured impatiently and Eve duplicated the gesture with the gun she held.

I walked out hesitantly onto the snowy, slippery dock. The water was so close and I knew it had to be deep here for the moorings. I went to Able's boat and held onto the deck post.

"Come on," Able said. He tried to raise his arms and only succeeded in bending slightly, grimacing when he remembered they were tied behind his back. I stepped gingerly on the back platform of the boat. It rocked and I fell into Able, who couldn't catch me. We both stumbled, me banging my hip hard against the passenger chair and sprawling on the flooring.

Eve jumped lithely into the boat, making it sway even more. I rolled with the waves, ending near the motor where the covered tarp sat on the floor. "Stay down," she snapped when I started to rise, my hand on the tarp.

I eyed her gun and decided to comply. I moved so I leaned against the back of the boat, my body hiding the bundled sword behind me.

"Get down there with her." Eve gestured with her gun to Able.

He hesitated. "Leave her here. You have me."

"Leave her? Leave Vivian? Are you kidding?" Dewin dragged Brad's body to the far end of the dock, where the water was deepest. Eve alternated watching him and watching us.

Able walked to the side of the boat to watch Dewin. Eve turned slightly to keep him in sight. That was the chance I needed. I leaned back and fumbled with the tarp behind me, inching it off the sword. The hilt of the sword was angled toward the side of the boat, so I had to scoot along the floor to pull it out of the scabbard, creeping one inch at a time.

"She's my insurance policy. I know if I have her, you'll behave." Dewin straightened to regard Able and I froze in place when he looked at me, too. Then he resumed dragging the body. "You're coming with us. I'll leave you on an island and we'll leave Vivian with the boat."

I barely heard what he said. As soon as he bent to drag the corpse, I continued sliding the sword out of the scabbard. I hazarded a glance behind me and saw that about six inches of the blade was free.

Eve turned, gun in hand. "What are you doing?"

I bent my head, twisting it right then left. "I get seasick," I mumbled. "I don't feel good."

She stepped back like I was contagious. "Stay down."

"Oh, I will," I said in what I hoped was an almost-sick-to-my-stomach voice.

A loud splash told me that Dewin had succeeded in dumping the body into the lake. "The blood will tell them right where it is," I said to Able, who came to kneel beside me.

"He's counting on that, probably. When John gets free, he and whoever he calls will spend time dragging for the body. By the time they know who it is Dewin and Eve will be long gone." Able leaned forward, touching his cheek to mine. It was icy cold. "Are you okay?"

"I'm scared," I said in a wavering voice. Eve shot me a disgusted look and went to Dewin, who was casting off our mooring lines. "Get down here," I hissed.

Able frowned, eyebrows drawn together. "What?"

"Get down here." I nodded to the floor next to me. *I have the sword,* I mouthed.

His mouth sagged open. "What?" he breathed.

I nodded frantically, my hair bouncing wildly around my face. I blew a recalcitrant curl out of my eyes then lowered my head when Eve turned my way. I breathed a sigh of relief when she turned away again, probably afraid I'd get sick someplace near her expensive boots.

Able dropped to his knees at the same moment

Dewin jumped into the boat. Able crashed into me and we both tumbled back against the boat's side, landing on top of the sword.

"Watch them," Dewin snapped, sliding into the captain's chair and fiddling with the boat controls. Eve stayed near him, her gun aimed at us but her gaze alternating between us and Dewin.

"How'd he get the key for the boat?" I asked, leaning forward to hide what Able was doing, which was angling his bound wrists toward the blade.

Good God. The blade. He might sever a vein. It took every ounce of self-control for me to look at Eve and maintain eye contact with her while Able did whatever he was doing.

"They don't have keys," Eve said before Able could answer. "There's a starter switch. Don't you know anything?"

"I guess not," I mumbled, remembering I was supposed to be sick and incapacitated. I turned away, keeping my head down so I could watch Able out of the corner of my eye.

The engine coughed to life and Dewin put it in reverse. I held my breath when Able positioned his hands above the blade. "Hold it for me," he breathed.

I leaned against him, trying to look weak and tired. I reached behind me and found the scabbard. I shifted it so the blade was pointing up, not lying flat on its side. "Be careful." I spoke softly but I wasn't worried about being overheard. We were near the engine and it was loud enough to drown out what we said.

Dewin backed out of the mooring spot and the boat idled for a moment while he changed gears. The boat rocked alarmingly at the same moment Able lowered his wrists toward the upright blade. I prayed like I've never prayed before and my prayers were answered two long minutes later when I felt Able's arms pull away from me.

Eve chose that moment to look at us. I leaned hard against Able, pushing him back slightly so his hands were well hidden. "I'm surprised you're going along with this scheme," I said to her. "You seem like a smart woman."

"Smart doesn't get you far and beauty doesn't last forever." Eve's eyes raked over me. "You know."

I laughed. "I've never been beautiful so no—I don't know what you're saying."

Able's head snapped to face me. "You're the most beautiful woman I know. The most beautiful woman I've ever known."

I gaped at him. Seriously, I gaped—my jaw sagged, my eyes widened and I had what I suspect was a stupid look on my face. "What?"

Eve gestured with the gun. "Nobody cares if he thinks you're beautiful. Your time is past. It's my turn to be the lady of the lake, Dewin's lady. "

All my frustration, all my unrequited anger boiled inside me. Only this time I didn't have Dewin to say *Patience.* No Dewin to calm me. Dewin was the cause of this eruption and that just added to my rage. I fumbled behind me for the sword.

Able clasped my wrist. "Patience, Sunshine," he murmured.

I glared at him, so angry I wanted to hit someone. He squeezed my wrist. "Patience," he murmured. It was a promise of future mayhem, not advice to calm down.

I subsided, grudgingly. "Why didn't you kill

Able?" I asked Eve. "You didn't seem to have any problem killing Brad."

"And have the FBI after us?" She shuddered melodramatically. "No, thanks."

I acknowledged that logic with a reluctant nod. "You know, Dewin always did need someone to lead. It's a pity he found someone as immoral as he is."

Dewin glared at me while he edged the boat forward, out of the protected cove. "You don't think I can pull off something like this? You don't think I have the brains to do it?"

"I didn't think you had the balls. And I was right." I looked at Eve. "She has the balls. All you had was the money." As we moved away from the shore, I saw a figure behind us moving down the steps, holding the rail and walking carefully. "Who's that?"

Dewin twisted in his seat. "Damn it, John Reeve shouldn't be following us. I hit him hard enough to knock him into next week. I was sure he couldn't get out of that closet where I tossed him."

Able peered over my shoulder, still pretending to be tied up. "It's my father," he said. "And John. They're heading for the boats."

"What?" Dewin turned on Eve. "Didn't you give him the knock-out stuff?"

"I put it in his glass," Eve protested.

The glass he never sipped from. Luther drank water all evening. Eve handed him an empty glass, he put bourbon in it, but I never saw him sip it. I filed that little nugget of information away in my brain to examine later.

"They won't catch us," Dewin said confidently and the boat surged forward. I gulped, struggling to swallow my several fears of water, guns, and crazy people. Eve laughed and leaned over Dewin, momentarily forgetting us, letting her gun waver.

Gun.

Holy moly. I forgot. I was packing heat. I leaned closer to Able. "I have a gun," I said.

He shook his head, frowning in puzzlement. The damn motor was so loud he couldn't hear me. I nudged him hard in the ribs and nodded down at my side. *Gun,* I mouthed.

His eyes widened then I felt his hand at my waist, sliding ever so slowly around to rest on the butt of my gun. I leaned forward again, pretending to be dizzy and effectively hiding him while he slid the gun out of the holster. "Hold on," he whispered in my ear.

Eve turned and Able lunged to his feet, kicking out and knocking the gun from her hand. Dewin heard the commotion and twisted to look behind him. The boat rocked, swaying from side to side. Eve tumbled back, hitting the passenger chair and landing in the foot well. Able moved forward, gun up. "Stop the boat!" he shouted, the gun aimed at Eve. "Now!"

Dewin pulled the wheel hard to the right and the boat veered. I rolled around on the flooring, cold water soaking my jeans. I clung to the scabbard of the sword, using it as ballast to keep me from moving too far. Eve clung to the metal support of the chair for the same reason, using it to pull herself upright.

Able was flung hard against the left side of the boat, almost toppling over the side when the boat sheered on one side. I held on for dear life, unable to help and hating my fear because it stopped me from doing anything.

"Take the wheel," Dewin shouted.

Eve scrambled to her feet and set her gun on the passenger chair before slipping into the driver's chair when Dewin jumped out. The boat thankfully stopped its crazy seesawing when Eve righted the wheel.

Dewin was across the boat in seconds. He grabbed my right arm, yanking me to my feet. I released the scabbard and the sword fell back into the tarp, once again blending in with its surroundings like some chameleon.

"Drop the gun," Dewin said.

I tried to pull away from him but froze when I felt something metallic and cold against the side of my head. "What are you doing?"

"I'm holding you hostage. He won't do anything while I have you." Dewin glared at Able, who was getting to his feet.

"That's bullshit," I said, slowly pulling my head away from the gun barrel. "He doesn't care about me."

"We'll take you as insurance. We can always put you ashore once we get to Canada." Dewin stared at Able. "Jump."

"You're crazy," I said. "He won't do it."

Dewin shot me a pitying look. "On the contrary, Vivian. *He* loves you. I just pretended to still love you. It was the perfect cover for our relationship." He smiled at Eve, who returned his smile with a smug one of her own.

Oh, how I longed to wipe that smirk off her Barbie doll face. That comment about age still stung.

Able nodded. "He's right. I won't do anything if he has you." He held out my gun and set it on the passenger chair.

Well, shit. This wasn't working out like I thought it would. I struggled in Dewin's grip, but it was tight.

It was tight around my shoulders. My feet were free. I didn't stop to think through the ramifications of what might happen. I kicked out and hit the back of the driver's seat where Eve sat. The boat spun crazily.

Able lunged for Dewin and the two went down in a tangle. Eve twirled the chair and reached for her gun in the passenger chair next to her. I reached behind me and grabbed the sword. It slid cleanly out of the scabbard and I raised it, not even noticing the weight. "Who are you calling washed up, you bitch?"

Eve's eyes got so big I thought they might pop out of her head. She dove out of the way and landed on the floor when I let the sword fall. It slashed into the dashboard and sparks started to sizzle. I raised it again and turned, but as I did, Dewin barreled into me. The impact made me stagger to my right. At the same moment, the boat sheered to the left.

I went overboard, the sword in my hand.

My first impression was darkness. The water was black, the only light coming from the faint running lights of the boat. Then the cold hit me. This lake was cold even in summertime and it was mid-October now. I don't know what the temperature was, but it was bitterly cold. Within a few minutes hypothermia would set in.

I popped to the surface and treaded water, getting my bearings. Able's boat was ahead of me, moving away at a fast speed. I turned. Another boat was coming toward me, but I don't think he could see me. It was so dark and it all happened so fast. If I wasn't careful, he'd run me over. Then the boat turned, heading after Able's boat and I breathed a sigh of relief.

A sigh that turned to a groan when I realized the boat wouldn't come for me. I couldn't see the shore, I had no idea how far I was from the dock and I was cold, frightened and lost.

And I was holding a sword. Holy moly, I still had the sword. I raised it, discovering just how damn heavy the thing was. I thought about letting it go. I thought about letting it sink to the bottom of the lake. But for some reason, I clung to it, refusing to release my grip. This was Able's sword and I wasn't going to lose it.

I fumbled for my belt and my holster. I managed to work the Velcro closure for my gun around the grip of the sword, right below the pommel, securing it tightly. I kept my hand on the pommel then I flipped onto my back and began to kick my way backward toward the spot where the second boat had appeared. The sword trailed underneath me, not pulling me down but not helping, either.

I counted out loud while I kicked. I had to do something to keep scary thoughts at bay. Underneath me was a cold lake and I had no idea what the depth was. Even if I got back to Dewin's house, what would I do? Well, I'd get warm first thing, that's for sure. I'd fix myself a big old liquor drink and I'd get on the phone and I'd call out the Mounted Police and the FBI and the CIA and anybody else I could find.

I kept the boogie man at bay while I considered that idea, visualizing me on the phone to the local authorities. It wasn't until I started to sink that I realized I was tiring. My legs were all tingly and aching and I was having a hard time getting a deep breath because it hurt to inhale. When I paused, my legs started to tighten up. Cramps. Damn.

I resumed kicking, singing in between gasps for breath. *Yellow Submarine.* The rhythm was exactly right for what I was doing. Slow kicks, keeping me upright, barely moving me, but keeping me going. All I could see was the vague glimmer of lights somewhere in the distance. It could have been miles away for all I knew.

I had no choice. I kept kicking but now my muscles began to cramp a lot. I shifted position, twisting onto my side, but that didn't work because my head was underwater too much. I flipped onto my back again and kicked, slower this time. I shifted to singing *Sgt. Pepper's* and when I exhausted that, I went on to *The Long and Winding Road.*

I was on *All Things Must Pass* when I heard the sound of a motor, coming toward me. It was another thirty or forty kicks before I heard someone shouting my name. "Vivian!"

I would have cried with relief if I wasn't so dehydrated and freezing. "Here!" I waved an arm and got a mouthful of lake water for the effort. I bobbed to the surface, kicking frantically. Bright lights were puttering toward me, the beams swinging to and fro. They'll never find me, I thought. I'm going to be right under their noses and they won't even see me. "Here!" I shouted again. "Able!"

The motor was too loud and they were too far away. I floated, praying and waiting for them to get closer. It was another twenty or thirty kicks before I saw the outline of the boat, ghostly in the night. "I'm here. Over here!"

The beams swung in the night, cutting through the

water. I fumbled for the sword, freeing it from the holster. I managed to raise it overhead. The blade caught the light and glimmered.

"There! She's there!" The boat came toward me at a snail's pace while I continued to hold the blade above me, using it as a beacon to guide them. I kicked for all I was worth but I could barely feel my legs anymore. I bobbed up, down and underwater but kept the sword upright all the time. When I surfaced, I saw the boat nearing me.

It wasn't until the boat was within touching distance that I thought to worry if it was Dewin or Able in the boat. Then I reasoned that Dewin sure as shit wouldn't come back to look for me so I had nothing to worry about.

It wasn't Able's fishing boat. This was bigger, a cabin cruiser. "There she is," someone shouted and the beam landed on me, blinding me.

"Drop the sword, Vivian."

I peered upward. Able leaned over the side of the boat and a rope ladder unrolled near him, dangling enticingly nearby.

"Drop it, Vivian. You can't climb the ladder with the sword."

I shook my head stubbornly. "I'm not giving it up." I reached for the bottom rung of the ladder and grabbed for it, but my hands were too cold to grasp. I managed to hook my arm through the rung and I clung to it, bouncing against the side of the boat where it swayed on the waves. The sword was in my right hand and I swear my fingers were frozen around the hilt.

"Drop it, Vivian. It's okay."

I barely heard him. The cramps were returning to

my legs and arms. The muscles were bunching and shortening. The pain was amazing, all over and all encompassing. I hung on to the ladder only because it was too much effort to let go. The sword dragged my right shoulder down and my left arm clung to the ladder, hooked into the rope.

Something splashed nearby. I blinked groggily, trying to see but my eyelashes had little chunks of ice on them and everything was hazy.

"I have it," Able said.

I raised my head. Able bobbed in the water next to me, one arm around me and the ladder, propping me up with his body. In his other hand he had the sword.

"Don't drop it," I whispered. "It's valuable."

He kissed me, his warm lips painful on my cold face. "So are you." He swung away from me, peering upward. "Catch!" He tossed the sword and for one heartbreaking instant I was afraid he missed and it would go overboard after all.

I heard it fall onto the deck with a clang and excited voices above me. Then Luther stepped forward and held the sword above his head. "I have it. Bring her aboard."

Able pried my arm from the rung and positioned my hands on the rope. "I'm holding you. Come on. One step at a time. Come on."

I don't know how long it took. My legs didn't want to bend and my hands were like skeleton fingers, all brittle and hard. We went one step at a time, Able surrounding me with his hands next to mind on the rope, nudging me upward one rung at a time.

When I got close to the top, strong arms grabbed me and pulled me over the railing. I was barely conscious by that time. My cold clothing was pried off and I was bundled into a bathrobe so big I was lost in its folds. Heavy blankets wrapped around me. I was placed in a warm cabin on a soft couch and lukewarm tea was pressed into my hands. Luther was by my side the whole time, urging me to drink. "You're fine, now," he kept repeating, gently rubbing my bare feet which were stripped of socks and shoes. "You're safe now."

I nodded, more to make him feel better than to indicate I believed him. I didn't care if I was safe or not. All I cared about was being warm and not having to swim anymore, not having to worry about a damn lake underneath me.

Of course, a lake was underneath me, but it didn't bother me that much anymore. I didn't have time to consider the thought because Able came in wearing a matching bathrobe with a blanket around his shoulders. "Are you okay?" I asked, struggling to rise from my semi-recumbent slouch.

"I'm fine. I'm more worried about you." He sat down and I leaned against him, happy to have his solid warmth next to me.

"Nothing a nice hot tub soak won't cure," I said.

He kissed my cheek. "I'll join you."

We sat for a moment in silence, Luther watching us from an armchair nearby. Then I stirred myself. "Where's Dewin? What happened?"

"I found John downstairs and we followed," Luther said. "We caught them just as Arthur knocked out Dewin. Eve had a gun but we were able to stop her."

"You didn't drink her drink." I nodded sleepily.

He raised an eyebrow. "Indeed I didn't. I thought she might do something."

I yawned. "She fooled us all, didn't she?" I glared at Able. "You fooled me, too. Why didn't you tell me you were with the FBI? Why didn't you tell me—?"

"I was just a consultant on this case. It involved my family so I couldn't be here in any official capacity." He pulled me against him. "I lied about a lot of things but not about one important thing."

"About what?" I smiled sleepily at Luther when he got to his feet and slipped out of the cabin.

"About how I feel."

I shook my head, yawning. "I can't believe I misread you all this time."

He smiled. "It just proves how trusting you are."

Either that or I'm an idiot, I thought.

"It also proves that our family legend is true." He whispered this into my ear, making me shiver.

"It's just a family legend," I said dismissively.

"It's true," Able said, moving closer to me. "You're Vivian and you gave me the sword."

"I'm not the Lady of the Lake, Arthur. I'm afraid of water, remember?"

"You used to be afraid of the water. You aren't any more, are you?"

I wasn't about to admit that I was cured. "What does it mean—I give you the sword and it changes everything? In what way? Will the world stop spinning on its axis? Will the seasons reverse? Will dogs and cats stop fighting each other? Will—"

Able pulled me to him and his lips came down on mine. I was lost in the depths of his kiss, stunned by the ferocity of it. His body pressed into mine and the hard planes of his chest met the soft pliancy of my breasts.

"I love you." He drew back and stared at me, my

head pinioned by his hands. "It changes everything."

I gazed into his dark eyes and saw only love there.

He was right.

Everything changed.

A word about the author…

J L Wilson is a Midwestern author who writes 'mysteries with a touch of romance…and romance with a touch of gray.'

She can be found out and about on the Interwebs at various spots. For more details, check her Facebook page (https://www.facebook.com/jayeAtplay/) or web site (jayellwilson.com).

~*~

Other J L Wilson titles
available from The Wild Rose Press, Inc.:
Autographs, Abductions, and A-list Authors
Brownies, Bodies, and Breaking the Code
Candy, Corpses, and Classified Ads
Daisies, Deadly Force, and Disastrous Divorce Disputes
Dogged
Ex-Wives, Extortion and Erotic First Editions
Foxgloves, Fancy Fungus, and Fatal Family Feuds
Homicide, Hostages, and Hot Rod Restoration
Human Touch
Leap of Faith
Lilacs, Litigation, and Lethal Love Affairs
Living Proof
Mayhem, Marriage, and Murderous Mystery Manuscripts
PhDs, Pornography and Premeditated Murder
Resorts, Regrets, and Returning to Love
Sun, Surf and Sandy Strangulation

Thank you for purchasing
this publication of The Wild Rose Press, Inc.

If you enjoyed the story, we would appreciate your
letting others know by leaving a review.

For other wonderful stories,
please visit our on-line bookstore at
www.thewildrosepress.com.

For questions or more information
contact us at
info@thewildrosepress.com.

The Wild Rose Press, Inc.
www.thewildrosepress.com

Stay current with The Wild Rose Press, Inc.

Like us on Facebook

https://www.facebook.com/TheWildRosePress

And Follow us on Twitter
https://twitter.com/WildRosePress